Hunted

A Vampwitch Novel

Book One

Kathleen Harryman

Hunted
Copyright © 2021 Kathleen Harryman

Edited by Judith Boling

Cover Design by Kathleen Harryman

Books by Kathleen Harryman

THRILLER
WHEN DARKNESS FALLS
HIDDEN DANGER

ROMANTIC SUSPENSE
THE OTHER SIDE OF THE LOOKING GLASS

HISTORICAL ROMANCE
THE PROMISE

PARANORMAL ROMANTIC-SUSPENSE
VAMPWITCH SERIES:
HUNTED

POETRY
LIFE'S ECHOES

COMING SOON

THRILLER
(The sequel to WHEN DARKNESS FALLS)
DARKNESS RISING

PARANORMAL ROMANTIC-SUSPENSE
ANGELS AT WAR TRILOGY:
THE BLACK FEATHER

Acknowledgments

I once read that writing is a lonesome profession. For me, writing is a wonderful experience. It is a place far from the stresses of life, and the steel chains of conformity and expectations. It is an amazing place, full of surprises, constant chatter, and ideas. A place of wonder where storyteller and reader become one. Hand in hand we take this journey together, outside the cosmos, to a world very different from the one we live in.

An author is not a slave to the story, but a chrysalis. The story is reborn each time a reader picks it up. Without a reader what is a story but an injured bird never to spread its wings and fly to new heights. Thank you for choosing to read Hunted and setting the story free.

For my family, my parents June and Neville Chappell, without whom I would not be the person I am today. You are my blessing, one that I shall always be grateful for. Though dad is no more of this world, he is and always will be part of me.

My sister's Maureen and Julie, sometimes the path beneath our feet crumbles and we slide, but the rock our love is made from keeps us from falling.

To Stephen, my husband, for his patience and support, and to my wonderful children Victoria and Maddison. Let us always treat each day like it is our last. Enjoy each moment and know how special we are.

Since publishing my first novel in 2015, I have forged some remarkable friendships amongst my fellow authors. To them I wish to say thank you for their support and kindness. Sandy, you always bring the sunshine, even when dark clouds threaten. Lisette, you were my first author friend. You continue to be incredible, and amazing in everything you do. Jeff may our minds never stand still, for there is too much brainstorming for us to do for them ever to remain quiet.

Hunted is the first book I ever wrote. It is a shame it has taken me so long to put it into print. I hope it makes you smile.

Dedicated to my girls
Victoria and Maddison

Prologue

"Get back!" A man screams, halting my advance.

I stumble, coming to an abrupt stop in the middle of the living room.

In front of me is a strange-looking chap with pink-candy-floss-hair. Wild eyes dance within their sockets and flames line his palms. On instinct I freeze, my gaze fixing on the fire as it leaves his hands, shooting through the air like a firework. Fear and confusion merge. The erratic beat of my heart sweeps through my body, vibrating in my ears. Sweat trickles down my back as I track the yellow and orange blaze. It lands near Mum's feet. Horrified, I watch the heated ball as it gains momentum, creeping closer to her. Fiery rings hold her in place.

"Get out, Alice!" Tears fall down her cheeks.

I shake my head, even though my brain can't make sense of what is happening, I'm not leaving her to die. Grabbing a blanket off the sofa, I beat at the fire. Smoke fills my lungs and heat bites at the delicate flesh of my trachea.

Candy Man's laughter mixes with the crackling of burning furniture. "Still think you can win, Nathaniel?"

Rings of molten heat circle round Nathaniel's neck and ankles. The flames almost touching his skin. Tears roll down his face. There is a familiarity about him I can't place. Deep inside me, something stirs, answering the silent emotional call from the man bound in fiery chains.

"Alice, do what your mother tells you! *Go.*" I ignore Nathaniel and continue to beat the flames as they grow in momentum.

Heat pushes against the large window; it buckles exploding and spitting out shards of glass. Oxygen fuels the fire and Mum's face disappears, consumed by flames and smoke. Her screams vibrate deep within my soul. I stare at the blanket, recognising how useless my actions are.

"No, Mum." My cries are too late. She's gone.

But I'm not listening to reason. With renewed vigour, I beat at the inferno at my feet.

A woman's cry erupts from my right. A large piece of glass protrudes from her leg. Candy Man's laughter taunts me, and my hands tighten around the blanket. Rage consumes me. I throw down the blanket and run at him. My actions involve no thinking, I just want to pound my fists into his flesh until he stops his insane laughing.

"Stop her!" I don't wait to see who Nathaniel is shouting at as I charge, focused only on the root cause of my pain.

Candy Man's arms fold over his chest, his lips curving into a sneer. "That's it, Alice, come get me!"

One minute my legs are flying in the air, ready to connect with his face, the next I'm yanked back by the hood of my coat - fabric tearing.

"What the hell. Let me go." I beat my fists into the fingers gripping my arms.

Golden-brown eyes meet mine as a low growl falls from his lips. He changes his grip, pressing me against his body, holding me prisoner, pinning my arms at my sides. I open my mouth and scream into his face.

"Ethan, take her out of here." A man similar in looks to Nathaniel, though younger, appears in the doorway.

Before I can register what is about to happen, I'm airborne over Ethan's shoulder. Like a sack of potatoes, he carries me from the room.

"Put me down!" My cries go unheeded.

As the fire magnifies, so does the heat and smoke filling my lungs, making breathing difficult. I don't care. The only thing that matters is Mum, and she's dead. Consumed by the flames sent flying from Candy Man's hands.

Grief hits and my world splinters. My human brain can't rationalise what has happened. Mum's dead and I don't understand how or why.

I have always thought a heart can withstand the pain of death. I am wrong. The heaviness of loss clutching my heart is a weight I have never experienced before. With my head upside down and my eyes staring at the ground, my body convulses in grief. It rips its way through my internal organs until I no longer know how to feel.

Chapter One

From my hiding place behind the Ye Old Deli Shop, I watch the door to Hobson Solicitors open. A man steps out into the frosty night, pulling up the collar of his coat and adjusting the scarf around his neck.

Hobson Solicitors is on the Shambles, which is the oldest street in York. Though Mr Hobson Solicitor can't see them, the narrow street, with its cobbled floor, is littered with ghosts. Some float amongst the few humans wandering the street. Others replay the traumatic moment of their death in a continuous loop.

"You sure that's him?"

Polly leans over me, "yep, that's him alright."

The man doesn't fit my preconceptions of a thief. Money drips off him. From the expensive cut of his trousers to the confident manner in which he strolls down the street.

Polly's vibrant red hair flies about her face. I can taste her excitement as it floods her system. Her pink neon leggings clash with her lime-green coat and vivid orange gloves. Not quite the getup for prowling about undetected. It is, however, conservative for Polly.

HUNTED

No one wears colour like Polly Palmer. She's the vivacious member in the Palmer clan. Her older brother Richard is a lawyer. His jollity left when he hit puberty. Ben is a computer nerd who has a knack for making me feel uneducated. It's not my fault he talks gibberish.

Polly and I have been friends since nursery. Her fashion sense and easy-going nature haven't changed at all.

She's a remarkable lady and friend.

"Look at the brazen bugger, Alice."

Gripped within the soft leather of his gloves is the package containing the stolen antique. The box might appear plain, but what's inside will set you back a small fortune.

"Right, remember the plan, and stick to it." Shadows prevent my stern glare from reaching her.

"I still don't understand why you can't just zap him." My eyes roll at her words.

"Pol, I'm a Vampwitch, not a superhero. I swear you watch too much TV." Polly flashes her teeth at me.

Six weeks ago, I found out I wasn't human, thanks to a fire demon called Aeden. For twenty-five years I have been oblivious of the preternatural DNA within my makeup. It's fair to say I am not dealing well with my newfound knowledge. Deception and lies hurt when uncovered.

Unable to kill me, Aeden, the candy-floss-haired monster, killed my Mum. Grief is a hard emotion. It requires acceptance in order for the person to move on. Time is also a factor, allowing the mind and heart to heal. I am in a place right now which won't grant either. This, I blame on my father, Nathaniel, and take out on my half-brother, Julian, as he is around more than my father.

Throw in the fact I have little control over my new powers, being part vampire, part witch with a dash of fae isn't helping the situation. Like I said, lies and deception hurt.

13

As the first of my kind, no one knows what to expect. I have no desire to wrap my mouth around someone's neck and suck out their blood. A plus for me. The dormant vampire is awake and its effects on me are startling. I now possess enhanced hearing and sight. And speed and strength. There is also a need to feed on violence and strong emotions, or anything else that increases the tempo of the heart.

The witch stuff I remain uneducated about and unstimulated to find out more. I know it involves a lot of studying.

Mum's death has changed me. I no longer dream of finding my dad alive and full of regret. Instead, I harbour feelings of resentment and wish he had stayed dead, rather than undead. I now have more relatives than I can shake a bat at, and all have my *best interest at heart*. It's an appalling way to say, *control you*.

My tears hadn't dried on my face when Nathaniel, Julian, and Mum's sister Dot, informed me of my lack of humanity (supernatural birthright).

As the only daughter of a single parent, with no relatives taking them for trips to the ice-cream van or park, I find my present situation overwhelming and unwelcome.

The time for additional family sailed with Noah and his arc.

What puzzles me is their reaction to my unenthusiastic response and open hostility. They were ill-prepared for my anger when I found out the truth. Their confusion at my emotional discord leaves me baffled. What did they expect?

My attitude isn't helping my relationship with my brother, Julian.

As a master vampire, he's used to obedience and hates the constant challenges I raise. Announcing my supernatural status to my best friend, sent him into a frenzy of frustrated anger. How was I supposed to know that *'not telling anyone'* also included Polly? We share everything.

To maintain family life balance, as we all live at Roseley, Julian and I have reached a mutual understanding by agreeing to disagree.

"Your eyes are sparkling green and gold fire." Polly's words yank me back to the present.

"Sorry, I was thinking."

"You know what I've told you about that. It's dangerous."

"Hm..."

Polly's sense of humour and breezy outlook never alters. Julian will lock us up in separate cages if he finds out we're prowling the streets with a death threat hanging over my head.

Polly nudges me. "It would be good if you could zap him."

"Even Vampwitches have their limitations, Pol."

"It wouldn't happen to Supergirl."

"What about kryptonite?"

"She can still zap."

Mr Hobson Solicitor is inching closer. "Hm... right, time to go."

Polly grabs my arm as I move out from the shadows.

"Be careful, Alice."

I flash her a toothy smile. "I might be no superhero, but I've got some awesome moves."

Running at a speed too quick for human eyes, I make a beeline for the thief. We collide, hitting the rain-soaked floor. The guy groans as I let out a scream of surprise – playing the part of the unsuspecting victim. The solicitor is on top, so there's no argument of whom ran into whom.

"What happened?" His voice is like velvet, a good reassuring quality for a man in his profession.

You walked into me stupid! is what I want to say.

Instead, I let a flicker of a smile cross my lips, my brows furrowing. "I think you tripped us up."

I arch my eyebrows, wondering when he's going to move, so I can get off the damp stones. The hat I'd been wearing is dancing across the cobbles, and I am blinded by a mass of black curls, as the wind plays with my waist-length hair.

A flicker of surprise lights his face. "Sorry, I didn't see you."

"Well, I was there. Large as life." My arms float in the air and I sound grumpy. "If you don't mind moving so I can get up." Dampness is soaking through my coat into my jeans, causing me to shiver.

Vamps are cold-blooded creatures.

As a living vampire, low-body temperature makes your teeth rattle. Winter is a season of dread and rattling bones.

"Oh! Y- yes sorry."

Polly slithers from the shadows in exaggerating moves and exchanges the boxes. She throws me a thumbs up, and a big grin, hopping from foot to foot as she disappears down the street. I resist the impulse to peer at the sky for help.

Mr Hobson Solicitor dangles a hand in front of me. I take it with a slight smile.

"Thanks."

I examine my red duffel coat for dirt, watching him survey the floor. His heartbeat increases its rhythm as he searches for the stolen goods.

Eyes lighting up, he grabs the package.

"Hope it's not broken," I say dusting off my coat.

"What?" Nerves raise his voice an octave.

I point at the parcel. "Whatever's in there."

"Oh." His fingers curl round it. "No… no… I'm sure it is fine."

The Edwardian ten-point-seven carat old mine diamond solitaire ring carries an estimated value of one hundred and eighty thousand pounds.

Fine seems such an under-descriptive word to associate with the expensive sparkling stone.

The term *old mine* refers to gemstones originating from historical/ancient mining sources.

If the word Edwardian doesn't give its age away, old mine will.

I notice he makes no move to question my own well-being. Annoyance clouds my face and I swipe at my coat with more vigour. "I'm OK, too.

His eyes widen. "Yes, um, are you alright, I didn't hurt you, did I?"

"Hm…" I stare at him, so he knows I'm not buying his sudden concern. "I'll live."

My boots hit the stones as I walk away, grumbling to myself about idiots and selfish people.

Chapter Two

The Golden Fleece comes into view as I approach the end of the Shambles. I whistle crossing the road onto Pavement, which is one of the major streets into York city centre.

'Damn, I'm good.' I congratulate myself.

Great-Great Grandma Palmer's Edwardian diamond solitaire ring will soon be back in the not-so-safe hands of her granddaughter, Polly.

A smile curves my lips as I consider the possibility that I just might be a superhero.

Ha!

Heat hits me as I enter the pub, along with the constant drum of conversation. Grateful to be in the warmth, my body sighs.

Built in 1503, The Golden Fleece is one of Britain's most haunted pubs. York boasts more phantoms than many of its counterparts. Therefore, it isn't surprising that this watering hole is their central meeting place.

Living or dead, we are still creatures of habit. The pub possess a mix of resident ghosts, from those who died on its premises over the years, and spectres who use it as a social gathering.

HUNTED

Lady Alice Peckett wanders round the small rooms, supervising the goings-on, and moving furniture as she sees fit. As the wife of John Peckett, Lord Mayor of York during 1701-1702, and owner of the property, Lady Alice takes her role as mistress of the house with utmost seriousness. Death has not prevented her from tending to her duties. My favourite resident is Geoff Monroe, a Canadian airman who fell to his death from the pub's upper floor window in 1945. Despite his premature demise, Geoff is jolly, and his stories entertaining. He waves at me through his gathering flock of ghosts and vampires as I pass. His legendary stories make him popular.

Boots clanging on the old wooden floor I walk over to Polly. I try not to make eye contact with the spirits milling amongst the living. Some acknowledge me with an incline of their heads, others ignore me. They know better than to harass me. Vampires have an affinity with the dead, not surprising given their undead status. That analogy passed onto me via my father, Nathaniel Quinn.

My lips flatline. The thought of my father is enough to dampen my high spirits. Nathaniel and Julian became vampires in the 1700s, just before the Industrial Revolution hit.

Both were forced to become creatures of the night, for sporting reasons, by a master vampire with psychological issues.

Polly sits tucked away in a corner at the back of the pub. Her nerves are on display as she nurses a glass of Coke. The package containing the ring is hidden from sight. As I wave, relief lights up her face.

"What took you so long?" She groans as I reach the table.

"I've only been ten minutes. It's not as if I could cut and run."

"Crikey!" Her voice squeaks in disbelief as she checks her watch. "It feels like hours."

"Hm…" I point at the half-drunk Coke. "You want another one?"

"No, thanks."

As I sit down, her fingers circle through my arm, nodding over at her coat. "Should we open it here? Or wait till we get back to Roseley?"

Her heart rate speeds up. Blood rushes through her veins, triggering my vampire instincts. Swallowing them down, I battle for control, aware I can't afford to vamp out here. The hunter in me sensing its prey.

"Let me get a drink first."

"OK." Polly's voice becomes gloomy as her eagerness dies.

The predator in me evaporates.

"I know you need the visual reassurance of seeing the ring, but it's best it stays hidden until we're back at Roseley."

"You think?"

"Yeah, I do. We don't want to attract any unwanted attention. Ghosts talk just as bad as humans, and it's packed in here tonight."

Polly scans the room. "I don't see any ghosts."

"It's a vampire, werewolf, and a witch thing. OK, it's a supernatural thing." I nudge her arm. "Come on, Pol, it won't be long, and we'll be home. Let's enjoy my freedom before I have to endure a lecture about my safety."

"I guess. Richard and Ben would kill me if they knew I'd lost it."

"You didn't lose it, someone stole it. There's a big difference."

Polly grins. "Too right."

"That's better. No peeking while I'm gone. Promise you'll wait."

"You used to be so trusting. When did you turn into a cynic?"

"Since I lost my flat and was forced to live at Roseley."

"Is Roseley such a terrible place?"

"Humph." Polly giggles at my lack of comment.

Roseley's country Victorian style is breath-taking. Surrounded by woodland and streams, it oozes peace.

Positioned on the outskirts of Poppleton, five miles from the centre of York, and with no immediate neighbours, Roseley remains secluded from wandering travellers.

"Right, I'm going for that drink. Are you sure I can't tempt you?"

"Yeah, too much Coke makes me burp."

I hesitate as a familiar scent drifts over. "What the chuff is he doing here?"

A keen sense of smell is another vampire trait, and the aroma of my earlier mark is assailing my nostrils.

"Who? Where?" Polly's eyes dart around the room.

"Him." I point at our target as he comes into view.

"Oh." The colour drains from her face. "What do you think he wants?"

"How the chuff would I know." My comment earns me a sharp look. "I guess I'd better find out." As I stand, Polly's lime-green coat moves.

"Make sure that stays out of sight." I point at the parcel.

With a gasp, Polly reaches for it. With shaking hands, she wraps the fabric around the package.

"Why don't I get you something a little stronger than Coke?"

Her rapid heartbeat amplifies, banging with vigour against her chest. Blood rushes through her veins and the pulse on her neck throbs.

"OK, get me a shot of vodka." My eyebrows disappear into my hairline. It's stronger than I was thinking, but if it helps to slow down her heart rate, I'll get her a double.

Trisha is attending the bar tonight, which means my lack of purse won't be an issue. Julian can pick up the tab.

Mr Hobson Solicitor's elbow lodges into my side as I enter the crowd at the bar.

"We should stop meeting like this," I say moving away from his elbow.

He looks at me in surprise, and I curse under my breath. I should have stayed in the shadows with Polly.

Shock fades from his features as he pulls himself together. "Let me buy you a drink to say sorry for earlier."

"Sure, I'll have a triple vodka and Coke," I say catching Trisha's eyes.

Trisha nods at me as she takes his order. I offer her a smile, tapping my foot eager to be off and back with Polly. As my vodka hits the wooden countertop, I grab it.

"Thanks," I call.

His eyes stare at my receding back, and I try not to let my tension show. Walking in Geoff's direction, I loop back round to Polly as Mr Hobson Solicitor turns his attention back to the bar.

"Well?" Polly asks as I slide the glass of vodka over to her.

"I don't know why he's here, other than to drink. He seemed surprised to see me, so I thought it best to leave things alone."

Polly chokes on the vodka, and I pat her back. "This a double?"

"Triple, I thought you could do with it."

"You're the one that's going to need it. I predict trouble heading your way… fast." My head snaps up.

Crap.

Julian strides towards us. Anger radiates off him like a snap of electricity.

"Just what the hell do you think you're doing?" His eyes blaze golden-green fire. An air of magnetic danger rolls off him. Under his right arm is a motorcycle helmet. The black-leather Dainese motorcycle suit adds to the threatening display of danger and sexual appeal. I try not to smile. He looks very striking when he's cross.

"I'm having a drink."

My flippancy increases his displeasure.

"You'll get yourself killed."

Vampires like to exaggerate.

Aeden's death threat lingers like a morbid net over me. I refuse to accept the bait and allow Julian's concern and annoyance affect me. Death threats aside, I need my independence and to take back control of my life, otherwise, I might as well be dead.

Aeden, the candy-haired demon who killed Mum, is the leader of MAMS (Magic Against Mixed Species). A radical group of beings who kill half-breeds such as me.

The name is unoriginal and lacks in aggressive strength. As their numbers increase, so does the pile of dead half-breeds.

Their belief that mixed breeding is weakening their world has led to widespread hysteria amongst some preternatural creatures.

I don't share MAMS theory, failing to understand how beings like me are weakening them. We are an unknown element. Our powers are varied and unexplored. Perhaps it is fear of the unfamiliar which rules and governs their actions, not the mixing of species.

Nathaniel and Julian are law enforcers known as Le Sang. Charged with enforcing the laws set by the Keepers (mystical beings who rule over the supernatural world). Because of this, and the fact my grandfather is a Keeper, my death is on MAMS priority list of kills.

My frustration mounts. Though I want to shout my exasperation at Julian, I know that sarcasm and indifference are more irritating to a vampire.

"Julian, you're getting your leather-clad body worked up for nothing. It's not like Aeden is going to show up, and set me on fire, with all these nice humans around to watch as you all like to keep your existence hidden."

Arms folding across my chest, smugness emanates off me. The muscle in his jaw twitches and I know my comment has hit its mark.

"Don't make light of the death threat, Alice. At the moment you're defenceless. You need training. To understand and home in on your vampire skills."

All I hear is blah… blah… blah…. Same old record on play.

Drinkers move like the Red Sea parted for Moses and Nathaniel appears. Fire burns within his sharp green-gold eyes. The colour intensifies as they land on me. Nathaniel strides through the crowd, a hunter in full pursuit of its prey. The soft red leathers of his motorcycle suit hug his body as he walks. At six- five, he's a shade shorter than Julian. They are both over a foot taller than me.

Jack materialises at my side, making me jump. Annoyance prickles my consciousness at his amused smile. Polly remains unaware of the ghost's presence. Jack's shaggy mousey hair falls over his piercing blue eyes, and his square jaw juts out. He reminds me of a hippy-come hit man. Big biceps sit on a lanky frame. Before his sudden death in his mid-thirties, Jack was a warlock. Either he lived life on the edge or was terrible with the magic.

Nathaniel pulls out a chair, and with a grace I can only dream of possessing, lowers himself down, placing his helmet on the table. The threat of violence surrounding him has Polly snuggling closer to me. Nathaniel's silence is worse than Julian's verbal tirade over my lack of safety.

"Well, isn't this peachy! The entire gang is just about here," I say through gritted teeth.

Julian pulls out the other chair and sits down. "What did you expect when you disappeared?"

"I left a note on the fridge. Perhaps you should have read it before sending out a search party?"

The crowd parts and Ethan Jefferies steps forward. Ethan is a werewolf and Alpha of the Yorkshire Pack. Polly's elbow digs into my ribs. I have a thing for Ethan. Who wouldn't? He is gorgeous with a capital G! His short bright copper hair, and large muscular body has my heart working overtime. I shoot her a warning glance, earning me a flash of her teeth. My cheeks redden in response. The deep red t-shirt under Ethan's leather bomber-style jacket clings to his upper torso, outlining the ripple of muscle hidden beneath. A werewolf's natural body temperature runs high so the cold the never bothers them.

"All I need is for Aunt Dot to appear and I'll have a full house."

Incensed by their lack of faith in me, I raise my arms, letting them fall to my knees in a loud slap.

The grumble hasn't time to die on my lips when Aunt Dot pushes her way through the crowd of drinkers, who are ignoring her attempts to push her way through. Her willowy physique makes her appear fragile. Wisps of silver hair fall from the bun sitting on top of her head. Her loose-fitting trousers swing about her thin legs as she walks. The long down coat she is wearing makes her resemble the Michelin Man, better known overseas as Bibendum. Unlike most supernatural creatures, witches feel the cold.

"Did no one read my message?" I say sliding along the bench to make room for her, pushing Polly closer to Nathaniel. Her fingers dig into my arm in fear, unhappy to be any nearer to the angry vampire.

"Oh, we got your note." Jack smiles at me.

"Then I'm baffled! Why the posse?"

"How did you expect us to react?" I shoot Nathaniel what I hope is a lethal glare.

"I left a note." People turn in our direction as my voice carries above the music.

"A note that serves only to highlight your lack of responsibility or awareness to the gravity of your situation. We can't protect you if we don't know where you are."

The need to stick a finger in Nathaniel's eye is strong.

Jack gives a dramatic sigh. "Vampires have a tendency to overreact, Alice."

Ignoring Jack, I pick up Polly's vodka and throw the contents down my throat. It burns like hell, making me cough.

"You ready to go, Pol?" I ask.

Polly scrambles for her coat, hiding the package down the sleeve.

"Your aunt will take you home."

I look at Nathaniel. "Gee thanks, but I'm going to say no. Polly brought her car, I'll go with her."

Aunt Dot's hand rests on my knee. "Alice Mary Quinn, you stop right there." I cringe at the use of my full name. "Remove that tone from your voice. Nathaniel is your father. He worries about you."

Father, my arse. He never bothered with me for twenty-five years of my life. It's too late to worry now.

"Ethan's left work, and Jack's been flying around the place looking for you. At least show them some respect."

Aunt Dot's words should resonate somewhere within my capacity to feel guilt. However, I'm too incensed to acknowledge her concern for my welfare, and the tiredness darkening the skin beneath her eyes. "I left a note. It's what normal people do." Despite my twenty-something-years, I feel twelve.

Jack snorts. "I'd wake up and smell the coffee if I were you, Alice." He spreads out his hands. "Girl, your life is so far removed from normal that it's damn right weird."

"Thanks for the reminder, Jack."

"Is the ghost here?" Polly asks her coat still gripped in her hands

"I'm afraid so."

Ethan steps forward, placing a gentle hand on my shoulders. The heat from his touch sinks through the fabric of my sweater. "If MAMS wasn't out there ready to kill you, your message would have been acceptable. The threat from MAMS is real. Your mixed heritage is enough for them to want you dead, your relationship with Nathaniel and your grandfather's position within the supernatural community provides them with more of an incentive."

"Sorry." It pains me to mutter the word, but this is Ethan.

Ethan's fingers squeeze my shoulder. "Things will get easier. Let's eliminate the threat MAMS poses first."

Julian stands. "Alice, you'll ride back to Roseley with Ethan. Jack and Dot will go with Polly." This time I didn't argue. Not because I agree with Julian's barked orders.

Spite will not force me into missing out on spending time with Ethan, even if it is a car journey.

Chapter Three

"Who the hell are you?" I gawk at the gnome.

His red-pointy hat twitches and his beady dark eyes stare unblinking. In his blue smock and green pants, he doesn't look dangerous, however, I'm not about to underestimate him.

Julian hasn't jumped him, so I assume he's on our team. Otherwise he would be dead.

The little man taps the toe of his brown clog at me. I find the action and his attitude disconcerting. Hands stroking his long white beard, he tilts his head to one side, and I wonder if he's going to answer my rude question.

"That's what happens when you leave notes." Julian emerges from the kitchen waving a hand at the chap who is now wearing a sour expression.

"I don't see the relevance. Lots of people leave messages, and gnomes don't get shipped to their house."

"They're not related to a Keeper." The vampire inclines his head at the gnome. "Your grandfather sent him."

"I can speak for myself." Indignation vibrates in the little man's voice.

Julian grunts, wandering back into the kitchen, leaving me alone with the grumpy chap.

"The Seelie King and Keeper requested my presence here."

My ancestor's title is getting longer. "Isn't that what Julian said?" The gnome blinks, hands on his hips. Regardless of his nonverbal response, he's in no rush to go.

Hanging my coat on the peg, I kick off my boots. "I didn't think gnomes liked humans?"

"I am a house gnome. We don't have a personal dislike of people."

"Right."

"We prefer animals, they're not as cruel."

"*Okey-dokey.*" The gnome's message is received and understood.

On cue, Jeremiah, my Persian cat, waltzes into the hall. His flat face puckers in curiosity at the little chap with the tappy foot and dancing bell.

"Get that away from me!" The gnome cries hopping from foot to foot, pointing a chubby finger at the ginger moggy, whose interest is escalating.

I don't mention that his erratic movements are generating unwanted attention, for fear of the demented man taking out his frustrations on me. It's obvious he doesn't want to be here. A feeling I understand too well. "I thought you liked animals." Confused by his reaction to Jeremiah's presence, I scratch my head.

"Not cats! Gnomes hate them with a passion." Eyes narrowing, he hisses at the cat.

Jeremiah's face puckers up further in response. The gnome isn't helping to lessen the cat's interest.

"Look, buddy, this is *the cat's* home. You don't hurt the cat, not here, ever!" I move between Jeremiah and the bad-tempered man. "Got it, Grumpy?"

The little man's cheeks redden, and his foot increases its tapping.

Jack mists in, signalling Polly and Aunt Dot's return to Roseley. The front door opens, and they walk inside.

"Hey! Where'd the cute guy come from? Wow! he's very realistic." Polly leans in closer.

Jeremiah slinks forward, his tail swishing, his nose almost touching the gnome's smock. A ginger paw swipes at the bell bobbing about his hat.

The chap jumps back, a look of outrage falling across his face. "I am not cute! Stuffed cats are cute."

The gnome pulls out a knife from his belt and I grab Jeremiah.

"Blimey, Alice, he's grumpy!" Polly's lips press together in thought. "That could be his name, Grumpy."

"If it isn't, it should be."

"I'm a gnome! Not a dwarf." He screams his clog hitting the wooden floor.

Jack shakes his head. "I see your manners haven't improved, Arthur."

"There's nothing wrong with my behaviour." The gnome straightens his hat and Jeremiah squirms, desperate to batt the moving bell.

"First, I need to unpack. Then we will talk." I raise my brows at Arthur's demand, not liking the thought of the crabby man staying here.

Roseley is getting overcrowded despite its opulent size.

The house has seven bedrooms. I have Mum's old room, Ethan's is opposite mine, Nathaniel, Julian and Aunt Dot's are on the opposite side. Polly, who moved in three days ago, is in the attic. That leaves two available, and both are near mine.

31

The notion is too creepy and unsettling to contemplate.

"I will stay in the woodlands."

"Isn't that extreme? I'm sure we can find somewhere nicer than the woods?" I nibble my bottom lips in thought. "Don't you live in houses? If you are a house gnome, sleeping in the woods makes no sense."

"There is an old stump where Martin lived before, they killed him." He folds his arms over his chest, trapping his beard and jutting out his jaw. "I trust you have no objection." Arthur turns and marches down the hall, not waiting for a response. His frustration at being ordered here to spy on us is obvious in the resounding thump of his clogs on the floor.

"Oh, dear."

I turn to face Aunt Dot. "Grandfather sent him."

She nods, "yes, he would."

"Out of all the gnomes he could have dispatched, it's typical of him to send over the opinionated twit." Jack grumbles.

"It is Arthur's loyalty, which makes him a desirable choice, not his opinions."

"More like absolute devotion, Dot."

"What happened to Martin?" I interrupt their exchange.

Jack snorts. "He died of old age. Gnomes age faster outside of Faerieland."

"I'm confused. Why does Grumpy think you killed him?" I look at Aunt Dot.

"Arthur has never understood Martin's choice to live outside of Faerieland."

"Well, I agree with Jack. Arthur's too opinionated, and we've enough people like that already." The ghost smiles at me.

It is getting late, and tiredness is making my limbs feel heavy. There's a battle of words brewing with the little man, and my emotional state can't take it.

I yawn. "Look, I'm done in. I'll see you all in the morning."

"I thought Grumpy wanted to talk to you."

"It's eleven o'clock, Pol, and I am tired. Mr Attitude will need to wait."

I can feel Aunt Dot's disapproval as I walk to the stairs.

My continued avoidance of tackling problems and refusing to study witchcraft is spearheading its ugly point towards my arse.

There will come a time when she's going to stop her silent disapproval of my actions and start pressurising me into responsibility.

Today is not that day.

As tired as I am, I'm not sure sleep will happen. Each time I close my eyes, I relive the last moments of Mum's life. Even in slumber, I still see the flames licking their way up her body. There is no moving on. No stopping the torment. The nightmares come each night as Mum's screams ring through my dreams. Like a phantom, I am snared within a loop, forever reliving the events of her death. Doubt has me wondering if she would be alive if I had reacted quicker. Got to the flames before they reached her.

I have woken too many times from the constant nightmare. My breath coming in short uneven bursts, wishing for the pain and memory of that night to go away. I have told no one, not even Polly, about my shame induced nightmares. To give them a voice is to make my guilt-ridden torment real. The fact remains, in loving me, Mum sentenced herself to death.

The bedroom door closes behind me as I prepare to face another sleepless night.

Chapter Four

Bang! Bang! Bang!

Whoever is battering on my bedroom door is getting their hands cut-off. Maybe I should burn them at the stake. Vampires can regenerate.

It's been another restless night. Hope of sleep arrived in the shape of Ethan as the first rays of morning filtered through the gap in the curtains.

My favourite dream is helping the werewolf to strip. I'm good at it. If I had the nerve to suggest it to, Ethan would find out how fabulous I am.

Ethan's semi-naked form is still there in my subconscious. It's too soon to contemplate getting up and risk leaving him in half his clothes. The jeans have to go.

To block out the noise, I wrap a feather pillow around my head. With a sigh, I snuggle deeper into the duvet.

The pounding becomes louder, and Ethan vanishes.

Ah!

Sweeping hair from my eyes, the door opens, which is strange, considering I do not recall uttering the words *come in.* Displeasure increasing, I stretch, pondering having a lock put on the door.

Julian walks in, followed by Arthur, who looks grumpier than yesterday.

"We need to talk," Arthur says.

I glare at the little man. "Good morning to you too, sunshine."

The gnome leaps onto the bed, uninvited, and makes himself comfortable. I resist the urge to extend my foot under the duvet and kick him off the end.

Beside me, Jeremiah's tail swings. After staring at the bell, he decides it's too much effort, and it's not long before he's snoring and I'm now jealous of a cat.

Mornings aren't for me. Six weeks of living in the same house, I feel the vampire should know this. From the look on their faces, I'm in for a lecture. I predict this meeting won't end well.

Julian smiles down at me from his lofty height. Not a good sign. The last time he smiled like that, I lost my flat, from which I've still to collect my belongings.

For someone born in the 1700s, where the average person was five-six, Julian and Nathanial are tall at over six-foot. Given my lack of height, I find it unfair I didn't inherit the tall gene. DNA is laughing at me. It has been for years.

I have Nathaniel's eyes, hair colour and pale skin. Mum was blonde, petite and curvaceous. I am a stick insect; blink and you will miss the inadequate swell of my breasts.

Julian has been chewing off my ear about our father for a while. He's unhappy that I blame him for pretty much everything that's happened to me. I thought we were at an impasse, but he has that expression which dictates otherwise.

Nathaniel's position as a dad is under dispute. I see him as a DNA contributor, not a parent, and myself as a by-product.

Given Nathaniel's undead status, I shouldn't exist.

Why nature needed to get involved in the whole witch/vampire relationship, I do not understand. But here I am, the impossible child.

"This is for you," Julian says handing me a mug and I breathe in the rich aroma of arabica beans.

My nose wrinkles in distaste, as my taste buds remind it, we don't drink coffee; it's too bitter. Julian knows I'm not a coffee drinker. My anger dissolves replaced with apprehension. Is his news so bad I need the caffeine hit? I take it without argument.

The thick, dark, uninviting liquid swirls as I blow at it. I hate black coffee even more than white.

"The Seelie King and Keeper is coming today." Arthur bounces on the bed in excitement.

Sleep-deprived, my tolerance levels are depleting fast. A hyper arse kissing gnome is not what I need.

While my grandfather is the one relative I've not met, his presence is felt. Given the chatty over exuberant chap making me seasick as he continues to bounce on the bed.

Unlike the rest of them, the keeper is excellent at exercising his dominance and enforcing it without needing to visit and stamp his authority over me, though I find being related to a king appealing. More so than a vampire. Not that I see myself as royalty.

My curiosity does not mean I want to meet my grandfather. I find distance is a wonderful feeling.

I hold no hope that his expectations of me differ from everyone else's. So long as he doesn't beat me down with oppression or place me into servitude, we'll get on great.

When gathering information on the fae and their courts, I used Google. Where else would I go? According to the electronic oracle, Seelie's are a blend of spring and summer. Much like the seasons, each court is different, and so are the fae living there.

Spring fae are calm, happy, and mischievous, whereas those in the summer court are polite, well mannered, cruel, secretive and underhanded.

The Unseelie reign during Winter and Autumn.

While the Seelie are The Golden Ones, the Unseelie are The Unblessed.

I'm not sure how helpful this information is. Time no doubt will enlighten me.

My imagination doesn't stretch to calling the Seelie King grandpa or gramps. Nor can I see myself bowing and calling him my liege. So what do I call him?

"Does he have a shorter title?"

Arthur looks horrified. "He is a King and, Keeper not a pet!"

"I wasn't thinking of calling him Fluffy."

"You can call him Alston," Julian says stopping our bickering.

"It means noble-stone," the gnome clarifies.

I do not question how a stone can be majestic.

"What about Aunt Dot?"

A puzzled expression crosses both their faces.

"The whole granny having an affair and producing Mum?" I remind them.

Arthur stops his insane jumping and frowns at me. "Being impregnated by such a being is a privilege."

I shake my head at the gnome, this is one delusional chap. "Uh-uh, now back to reality…"

"It was years ago. Why would it be an issue?" I stare at Julian.

Vampires are unobservant creatures.

Aunt Dot's mouth pulls at the corners whenever some-one mentions the king. While she tries to hide her discord, it is still there. I'm perceptive to the emotions of others, so the small tell is easy for me to spot.

Time doesn't always heal.

Children see their parents as super-beings that don't make mistakes. An affair which results in breaking up a home isn't something a kid gets over, even as an adult.

Grandpa up and left when granny's pregnancy became known. No one has heard from him since. I know from rum-blings the preternatural community blames his actions on the fact he is human.

Given their oblivion to Aunt Dot's discontent towards the king, I change the subject. "How many Keepers are there?"

Arthur waves his arms in the air. "The girl is more ig-norant than rumour predicted."

"They talk about me in Faerie?" Why am I surprised?

"Whisperings of your stupidity are rife."

"Inexperience is different to being stupid. Poor deci-sion-making is at fault, not me. I blame your precious king."

"How dare you! The Seelie King…"

"Enough, Arthur!" Julian's anger nibbles at my skin.

The gnome's cheeks puff out. "We do not have time for this…"

I point at Arthur. "You heard what the vampire said, shut it shorty!"

"I do not take orders from dim-witted creatures." Ar-thur folds his arms jutting out his jaw.

"Letting you stay here was dumb. Not knowing about my heritage isn't. It's like the song about a hole in the bucket. Well, there is a hole in my knowledge, and no one's doing a damn thing about it. The blame for the hole, short stuff, isn't mine."

"Talk to your father, he will enlighten you," Arthur says.

I snort at him. "Right, because it's not like I don't keep asking, and Nathaniel's such a fantastic father. I didn't know he was walking the earth until Mum died and I find out there's a bunch of supernatural crazies lining up to kill me."

The gnome sighs. "All I hear are excuses."

I'll give him excuses when my fist connects with his jaw.

"Arthur!" Julian roars.

I look down at the cooling liquid. "And the reason for the coffee becomes clear."

"Alice," Julian says.

"Don't," I warn him.

Julian ignores me. "Arthur's right, Nathaniel is your father. You must stop being angry at him, it weakens us all."

"You're like a praying mantis seeking an opportunity to pounce," I grumble. "I thought we had a silent understanding to not talk about this."

How do I explain part of my anger at Nathaniel isn't about him being a non-existent father, it's about guilt?

When Mum died Nathaniel was incapable of moving. I can still see the madness shining in his eyes, as he fought against the fiery chains. I'd frozen to the spot, watching the horror unfold. My attempt at beating down the flames was unproductive and cost Mum her life. Each time I look at Nathaniel, I taste my shame. It's easier to concentrate on Nathaniel's shortcomings as a father, than to face my disgrace.

"DNA doesn't make him a father in the true meaning of the word. He left us. It was his decision."

Agitated, my brother glares down at me.

"I don't know him, Julian, so how can I call him, dad?"

"If you don't open your heart to him, you'll never discover how."

"Perhaps, but it won't change the fact he left."

"I have explained this, he had no choice. He never wanted to leave you or Sophie. A sire can trigger a vampire's magic, it's how we control our fledglings. The threat from MAMS and others like them are real."

Julian's right, I've heard all this before.

"You're wrong. Nathaniel sacrificed his happiness to keep you safe." Julian's words make me snigger. "That's what fathers do."

The gnome's clogs hit the floor. "You need to stop this at once! The Seelie King..." I tune him out.

"You're having a laugh. Nathaniel gave up nothing for me. Not his lavish lifestyle or job."

"Your narrow mindset is stilting your growth. You can never move on as you are." Julian's eyes are like sparks of green fire.

The predator is awake and wanting to kill.

"I know you mean well, I do, but we will never agree on this subject. It's impossible for me to open myself up to more disappointment and pain. Nathaniel is undead, not beneath the ground rotting. He's had twenty-five years to be a dad to me."

"I did not come here to discuss..." The bedroom door slams behind Arthur.

"No one blames you for feeling let down He's your father, Alice, even if you choose not to accept it. Nothing will change that."

I look at Julian. "You're wrong, it changes everything."

"The only thing he's guilty of is protecting you."

I'm not prepared to acknowledge that. My brother is fortunate, he grew up with both a mother and a father. Me, my dad watched from the side-lines.

I can't be ok with that.

"He never meant to hurt you. You're a miracle, Alice. A living vampire. Never in history has a vampire outside of their first flush of turning, been able to have a child. A human child with vampire abilities. The witch's DNA is what ties you to this world and prevents you from becoming a full vampire. Don't hate him for protecting something so extraordinary."

My fingers fiddle with the duvet. "I never wanted to be special, Julian. I just wanted a dad." My voice is small, holding childish longing I thought I'd long grown out of.

"Have it your way." Julian moves away from the bed.

"If you want to collect your things from the flat, you need to move. Alston is due at two. Don't keep him waiting." The bedroom door closes on his words.

Chapter Five

Walking over to the sink, I dump my breakfast pots, aware time is against me.

I'm not inclined to change my plans and rearrange going to the flat with Jack, which increases the possibility I'll be late for Alston's imminent arrival.

This provides the gnome the opportunity to highlight my tardiness to the Seelie... blar... blar... blar, with gnome-ish relish.

It is but a tangled web of nemeses where some will win, and others lose. The large invisible L on my forehead names me the loser.

My back stiffens as the soft musky smell of sandalwood drifts into the kitchen announcing Nathaniel's presence.

"You're not due until two," I snap as the grandfather clock in the hall chimes eleven.

Sometimes mechanical instruments are a blessing.

Turning to face Nathaniel, I lean against the sink, folding my arms over my chest, I stick out my chin announcing my displeasure. My body language verifies my feelings of hostility for my father.

Nathaniel's graceful swagger and high cheekbones help to fuel my annoyance. It is unfair for this man to possess these traits. His relaxed manner at my growing irritation keeps any other emotions from forming. He unzips the black motorbike suit revealing a deep red t-shirt and strides into the kitchen like a panther.

Father and son never speak about the past. It is Jack who has enriched my knowledge of the circumstances around their transition from human to vampire. Marion Petty, a master vampire with psychological issues, turned Nathaniel as he reached his fifty-fifth year. Julian was next.

Forcing them to watch, Marion ordered her fledglings to burn down their home, while she fed on their family. Tearing into the delicate flesh of Nathaniel's wife and ten-year-old daughter.

The transition from human to vampire isn't a pleasant process. Riddled with pain and fever, the internal organs shutdown as the body convulses fighting off the attack from the vampirism virus. Death is never pretty. The transformation from human to undead less so.

Marion's sole purpose for transforming Nathaniel and Julian from human to monster was so she could continue to abuse them. A vampire's body isn't as fragile as mortals are, and Marion has a thing for torture. Human or supernatural, our requirement to utilise anger, to shut away our pain is paramount for our defences to remain intact. It is this anger that allowed Nathaniel and Julian to survive the Marion Petty years.

The stubborn and unreasonable actions I use against Nathaniel reflect my need to protect my mind from the constant itch of insanity. Inner voices are not fun. They twist opinions and are not the voice of our conscience everyone views them to be.

My animosity bounces off Nathaniel like an arrow trying to penetrate steel. "There's been a change of plan. Alston is here."

"Here! Bloody hell, what is wrong with you people?" I throw my hands in the air. "Do you enjoy messing up every plan I make?"

Hands on hips, I toss my hair over my shoulder. "He'll just have to wait."

"You can go later."

Nathaniel's casual dismissal of my plans make me want to scream, however impaling him with a stake would work better. I turn, my fingers gripping at the Belfast sink. Part of me considers ripping it off and throwing it at him. That would work to remove some of my aggression.

Instead, I brood. Gazing through the window at the well-tended lawn I allow a string of curses to scream through my head. I try to convince myself that my lack of knowledge doesn't make me a doormat.

The air shifts around me as Nathaniel moves.

"Don't." It's the only warning he's going to get.

He stops.

Because I am feeling suicidal today, I open the link our DNA has forged. Arthur's words echo in my head *"Talk to your father, he will enlighten you."* The talking bit isn't easy, so I close my eyes and concentrate on my passage into Nathaniel's mind.

My action catch him by surprise, giving me the advantage I need to dig deeper, before he can shut down.

I swerve past the happy bubble of joy which bursts from him at finding out Mum is pregnant and wander further. Despair threatens to suffocate as I hit the emotional pain of removing himself from our lives. How deep this goes I don't know, skirting around it, I acknowledge I'm not ready to know. Instead, I continue my journey.

A thirst hits me. This isn't the normal *I need a drink* thirst. It demands quenching. Heats my blood as it washes through my veins, devouring the reasonable mind. Nothing matters but quelling the hunger. Repulsion cries, but I can't fight it, and I realise this is the moment Nathaniel woke from his fever as a fledgling vampire.

There is no stopping this voyage, my demon is awake and drives us deeper.

My world has changed, and I want to know more. What does undead mean? This is my chance to find out.

Colour and sound burst around me, leaving me in awe. Nothing is the same, not even the air that tickles my skin. It is then I realise I have yet to a draw breath. The requirement for oxygen is in the past. My lungs no longer rise and fall.

A bird beats its wings high above my head, and a caterpillar crawls along a leaf, teeth tearing, biting, and gnawing. The noise is like a drum… bang… bang, beating against my eardrum.

Movement is fast, almost a blur. It feels awkward, unnatural and frustrating. Human speed is sluggish, I see that now. Mind and body can no longer connect. Each fighting against the other, as I gain control over command and motion.

Hunger creates a fever, burning through my insides. I need to kill, to survive. This is the only emotion I feel, and it is paramount to anything else. It pulsates through my body, calling to the madness inside me. A deer strolls through the meadow. In a flash, I move my arms, encircle its neck sinking my teeth into its flesh. The metallic taste of blood fills my mouth. From the blood I ingest oxygen and my heart beats wanting more. My teeth tear at the deer's flesh. There is no blood left, but the hunger remains.

No longer do I fight against my reflexes. As one, I move through the woods. All my senses are alert, and it isn't long before I once again sink my teeth into tissue and my mouth fills with my victim's blood. I feel no pleasure, just the simple base need to devour. There is no control and no one there to help me, so I give into the monster, letting it dictate my next actions.

Nathaniel slams the link shut, and my connection with his demon is severed.

I open my eyes to find Nathaniel cradling me in his arms. For once, I feel the comfort of a father and see his concern staring back at me. Tears fall down my cheeks as he pulls me to him. I let him hold me as my body shakes. It is my first taste of blood addiction.

"Sorry." His forehead touches mine and my senses return.

How easy it would be to lean into him. To breathe in the scent of sandalwood and make believe that everything is going to be OK. But I refuse to give in. To become snared within the warmth and love he offers. My heart has yet to heal from losing Mum. I'm not prepared to open myself up to the possibility of love, for my heart to crumble with the loss of another parent.

"I'm fine." My hands push at his chest and his arms drop to his side.

Cold air brushes my skin and I remind myself to love is to feel pain.

The blood bond between us is growing, I can feel it pounding inside me. Stupid… stupid… stupid… In opening our connection, I have further tied us together. If I wanted to scream before, now I just want to run, bury my head in my pillow and cry.

Nathaniel sighs, something he does when I'm around. He moves to the other side of the centre island, a safe distance away, and I watch him shut off his emotions.

"Alston is waiting." Nathaniel's voice is distant, vacant of emotion.

Disappointment hits me in the gut. Wasn't this what I wanted? That is an interesting question, because I'm no longer sure. I curse my stupidity. If Julian knew how I was feeling, he would do cartwheels.

I need time to rebuild my defences before I meet the king. "The fae call me ignorant. They're right, I know nothing of my heritage or Alston, other than he's a king and keeper."

Nathaniel blinks at me, another habit he reserves for me.

"I'm unprepared as it is, don't make it worse."

He nods. "The Council which govern our laws are answerable to three Keepers. As part of Le Sang Julian, Ethan and your aunt and me operate outside of the Council's rule, accountable only to the Keepers. It is our duty to ensure the preternatural world remains hidden from mortals and we remain at peace."

"A group of assassins killing half-breeds doesn't resemble peace."

Nathaniel sighs "I meant a war of dominance. We control the numbers of each specie. Births and deaths are registered to maintain a balance. Aeden's killing frenzy is not an act of war."

"What about unexpected pregnancies?"

Nathaniel lifts an eyebrow. "We offset minor additions by reducing future numbers."

"So when Mum had me, you got one less vampire?"
He nods.

"It's time. You have procrastinated long enough."

I want to argue with him, but he's walking out of the kitchen, leaving me to tag behind him like a lost puppy.

Chapter Six

A wall of heat hits me as I enter the living room. Despite the warmth coming from the log burner, an unnatural chill hangs in the air.

Unaffected by the contradicting climates, Nathaniel strides forward, stopping at the large sash window.

The low winter sun bounces off him, dispelling any belief that vampires go poof in sunlight.

Three oversized sofas create a U-shape around the Inglenook fireplace. Aunt Dot faces the burner, while Julian and Ethan sit opposite the stranger in the room.

The living room is light, the space substantial despite the sizable furniture. Today, however, it appears to have shrunk in on itself, as expectations and dissension gathers.

Arthur rests on the hearth at his king's feet, eyes wide in adoration. His lips twist with envy as he stares at the scruffy Yorkshire Terrier on Alston's knee.

The Seelie King is a slim man with mousey brown hair. On his left cheek is a large mole. Ancient eyes stare from a young man's face.

Dressed in brown-cotton trousers and a plaid shirt, the king resembles a 1970s American country boy. I make a mental note that fashion isn't his strong suit.

HUNTED

When someone says king it conjures up certain images. I am English after all, and while our monarchy is human there is a regalness about them. The man in front of me doesn't match my preconceived ideas, and his chosen visual representation shatter my illusions.

It is obvious why Alston chose this image through glamour. A golden god he isn't, but John-Boy Walton.

The persona of John-Boy Walton, although non-threatening, it is an optical illusion. Glamour can hide a multitude of things — it cannot conceal the threat of menace and the requirement for obedience the creature in front of me commands. He is a ruler without compassion. I would do well to remember this, however my mouth often engages before thought processing has commenced.

Emotions are my downfall.

My dysfunctional-control-freakish family wait for me to take a seat. It's a tough decision as all options have their drawbacks. If I sit with Ethan, I am within my brother's grasp. Alston isn't even an option, so it will be Aunt Dot who gets my company.

The king presents me with a pleasant smile which intensifies the spike in my nerves. "Alice."

I sit at my aunt's side and acknowledge him with a small incline of my head. My cautiousness is out of character and I notice Julian arch an eyebrow at me.

"It is good to meet you, though the circumstances are regrettable," Alston says.

I want to shove his stupid *regrettable circumstances* back down his throat. The difficulties of my circumstances are his doing. It was Alston that banned my father from my life and cultivated my ignorance. Nathaniel is at fault for following orders.

"While your mother's death is upsetting, other issues require immediate attention."

My eyebrows raise in silent question.

"Aeden, dear." Aunt Dot whispers in my ear.

Why the fire demon should require my immediate attention is interesting as it is perplexing. Unless the king is looking for advice on how best to kill Aeden, I'm not following what this has to do with me. I have specific ideas and several ways in which death can be administered to the demon and I am open to discussing these at length. Call it sixth sense, but I'm sure Alston is not wanting my input on killing the demon.

"I'm confused, isn't that the Council or Le Sang's job?"

Arthur jumps to his feet. "You should not speak to The Seelie King and Keeper unless asked."

I lean forward eyes narrowing. "And since when do you speak for The Seelie King and Keeper?"

"Arthur, sit." Lips set in a straight line, the gnome does as his master bids.

"To a simple mind, it is for the Council to deal with such matters, and for Le Sang to ensure their actions are swift. However, support for the fire demon is increasing, and it seems they have infiltrated the Council. You are intelligent enough to work out the danger this poses."

Short stuff sniggers and my cheeks redden at the snub.

"Nathaniel will investigate the Council and find who leaked your information to MAMS. Whatever punishment your father inflicts under our laws will fit the crime." Alston's words offer no comfort.

Punishment is a strange concept that doesn't reach the soul and allow it to heal. The word and its meaning sound lenient. Given what MAMS took from me, I prefer a word which incorporates a lot of pain to its definition.

Torture equals suffering, and I find I prefer that word. To make Aeden pay is to feel vengeance, and I have a lot of retribution that needs dishing out.

"Nathaniel's investigation needs executing without MAMS finding out what is happening, and therefore a distraction is essential to allow for this to occur."

"Huh?" My mind is busy exercising its will of revenge in the form of a daydream. I am undecided which action would cause the most pain. Does Nathaniel dice up the fire demon and his associates into tiny pieces, or burn off their flesh? This brings its own conundrum. Can fire demons burn? It is at this point in my decision making that Alston's words penetrate my thoughts.

"What kind of distraction?"

Anger shimmers in the keeper's brown eyes, causing an involuntary shiver down my spine.

The word *distraction* makes me uneasy. Whatever the plan, I'm sure I won't like it.

One logical option for a diversion I can think of is to use someone as bait. Someone that MAMS wants dead. That's when it hits. Alston smiles as I catch up with his plan.

"You are quite the catch and therefore you're the best asset we have against MAMS."

Ethan places a hand on Julian's arm. It's ironic that brother and sister can find a subject they agree on, to discover it is the one thing neither can fight.

"I am aware of the unpopularity of my decision." Alston's tone is dismissive.

In my naivety, I thought I had a choice to act as bait or not. Ridiculous, if I think about it.

The king's mouth is moving even though I'm no longer listening. "Well?" He says, an expectant look on his face.

I could grunt at him highlighting my lack of intellect, but I choose an honest approach. "You lost my attention at bait."

"Insolent fool!" The gnome jumps to his feet.

"Sit." Arthur inches closer to Alston, his bottom almost touching the king's shoe.

If the little man would move closer, it could be my foot connecting with his posterior.

"Tell me about your ability to see a person's aura," Alston asks.

I'm not sure what game is being played, or what the king hopes to gain. Uncomfortable with the situation, knowing somehow, I'll screw up, I cogitate what to say.

Unblinking, the king strokes the Yorkshire Terrier lazing on his knee, as he waits for my response. While the king appears relaxed, there is an undercurrent of energy radiating off him which says otherwise.

An aura is the electromagnetic field which surrounds the body, known as the Auric Egg.

I have never given my ability to see auras any thought, as it isn't uncommon for humans to see the colours emanating from a person's aura. My talent also extends to seeing intentions through auras. This is rare, but it happens.

Since my last boyfriend's affair, I have closed myself off to auras. It is hard suspecting your boyfriend is cheating on you without seeing it within his aura. Tony and Tania's affair was an emotional pain I never wanted to experience again.

Alston leans forward. "Tell me, Alice, what do you see when you look at me?"

The eagerness in his voice makes me hesitate. This is a creature with a lot of power. Do I lie if I see something, I know will upset him? If I lie, there's a good chance he knows I'm lying. I swallow.

My brain is in shambles. It grasps at any unintelligent bit of information it can. "Ur... John-Boy Walton."

Jack giggles from the corner where he perches on the sideboard. Colour stains Arthur's cheeks, and he's looking less grumpy as he tries not to laugh. Tears roll down his face.

"Sorry, I didn't mean... well, I did... but... I... I think I'll shut up." What is it they say about holes? Throwing my spade away, I seal my lips together.

Aunt Dot places a hand on my arm. "It's OK dear."

It wasn't alright, but I don't comment.

The king waits for my answer without amusement.

On a deep breath, I stare at the colours swirling around him, within which is his true essence. There are many shades to a person's aura, which change as we grow. Some become tainted with darkness, while others keep their light.

Alston's colours are green, clear red, yellow and orange. These waves of colours speak to me.

Green tells of the king's growth and balance and the love he holds for his people. This creature is a teacher of change. The clearness of the red denotes his power and energy and his naturally competitive nature.

Yellow and orange show his intelligence. The perfectionist within him has a temper, demanding he and those around him achieve more. There is little tolerance towards errors. Removing his emotions, he will strike out. Decisions and judgments passed without empathy. Yet, he has a patience few possess. He will spend his time teaching and nurturing those close to him, making them strong and confident in self-belief.

I blink away the king's aura. "You are kind, but ruthless."

"And Aeden."

The thought of sticking a plastic daffodil in my eye appeals more than recalling the fire demon's aura, but there is no refusing the Seelie King. Not if I value all my body parts. Despair and guilt claw along my skin. This time I refuse to hear its call and concentrate only on Aeden. My voice cracks as I speak. "Black surrounds him. He pulls energy from others, transforming and using it against them. Muddy green stains the black as his jealousy eats at his soul. But it's his fear that rules him. Dark grey and blue puncture his aura..." I pause as I realise the person responsible for his fear. "He's afraid of me... why?"

Alston's pleasure bursts from him. "Have you looked at your own aura, Alice?"

My eyes widen in horror. "Why would I do that? Do I look suicidal?" It's bad enough seeing other people's auras without looking at my own.

"You should. Your aura is violet. It is the most intuitive of colours within the aura spectrum. It signifies magic, visionary and physic power. Rainbow stripes fall from your body. You are new life. This is your first incarnation on earth. The mixing of species has made you powerful, more powerful than Aeden. He knows it and fears it."

I stare at Alston, my mouth dropping open.

"Imagine how Aeden feels. A crossbreed with more power than he could ever hope to steal," Alstone says.

Silence falls. No one moves, and only those who have to breathe do so with regret.

"Aeden is my son." The Seelie Kings stares at me waiting for a reaction.

My mouth falls open. "Bloody hell."

The air in the room becomes oppressive. Time has frozen. Magic buzzes around the place, nibbling at my skin. No one moves as Alston's control slips. So much rage and sadness fill his essence in a mix of conflicting emotions. And all I want is the fire demon's death.

"He is my son... *my Son*! And yet, he needs to steal power from others, like a parasite."

I try to keep my face neutral. The best defence I have is keeping my lips locked together.

Without a sound, Jack jumps off the sideboard. Nathaniel moves away from the window, stepping closer to the sofa. A thread of violence hovers.

"I thought Aeden was a fire demon," I ask. None of this made sense.

Alston wasn't a demon despite the wildness shining in his eyes.

"He's just not a very good one," Jack mumbles beneath his breath as he stands next to Nathaniel.

There is a feeling that they are barricading me in within their protection, should the monster strike.

A sharp laugh falls from the kings lips. "That is the paradox, Alice. The leader of MAMs is a half-breed."

I see nothing funny in the situation.

The king shakes and his control snaps back in place. "Aeden blames his lack of power on his breeding."

I can understand the fire demon's assumptions. His father is a keeper, a being, so magical he along with three others cradle the supernatural world within his hands. All that power and you inherit none of it.

My abilities remain unexplored. I am aware I hold it back, scared to embrace the predator that is my vampire and identify with the witch whose magic tickles my skin. As for my fae heritage, it is a conversation we all wish not to embark on.

While I can understand the fire demon's anger at his lack of magic power, I cannot comprehend his motives for killing innocents.

"I appreciate Aeden is my son, and no one wants to upset me," Alston says.

The king makes a valid point. Given his status and power, there won't be many queuing up for the job of demon killer.

"However, he has sealed his own fate and is answerable for his crimes. No one is above the laws we have set. Should you have no choice, do not be afraid to harm him, Alice. Aeden may be of my blood, and in being so of yours, but the anger and hate that festers inside him have rotted his soul. Nothing can change his destiny."

The room remains quiet as we all absorb Alston's words. Life for me is getting interesting. I am about to leave the safety of Roseley and vampire protection and make myself available for capture and sudden death. I suppose life is a tenuous thread.

"It is time to accept your powers, Alice, and let fate have its way."

"Are you sure using Alice as bait will create the diversion you want," Jack asks. "She's unseasoned, knows nothing about our world, or its power. I'm not sure she'll survive long enough for you to accomplish your goal."

I nod my head in agreement with Jack. Revenge isn't worth dying for, nor is it a good enough reason to allow someone to use me. "Jack is right. I won't do it."

Alston's eyes blaze at my defiance.

"If you're as powerful as you say, you get rid of your son," I tell the king.

Arthur mindful of the dangerous mix of emotions coming off his king stays quiet and settles for waving his fists in my direction.

Alston's hand hovers along the dog's back. "Life is never that simple, Alice. You think everyone has lied to you, and you feel let down and hurt. Your anger burns, and you refuse to let others love you or to allow yourself to love them. The power to change your feelings rests inside you, and yet you prefer to cling to your anger. If you have the power to love, why not use it?" Though Alston has a point I refuse to acknowledge it.

"I am a Keeper, entrusted to ensure the survival of all preternatural beings. If I operate outside of my law, I become no better than Aeden and those associated with him. Little more than a killer. How do I then maintain control of the supernatural world?"

Alston's hand lowers onto the dog's back. "I have not made this decision without consideration. However, I have no choice but to use those I trust, knowing what it is I am asking of them."

Warmth stains my cheeks.

"You're not on your own, Alice, we will train you and make you strong," Julian says. The tenderness in his voice makes me want to cry.

I can't afford to show my weakness to the creature in front of me. "Fine, you win, I'll do as instructed."

"There are no winners, Alice," Alston says.

"Perhaps, but for the record, never mess with my head again. You can't play with people's lives without consequence. You won't be losing a son, but a grandchild too. I'll not become your toy." Nathaniel's hand rest on my shoulder, sadness leaks from him.

Alston shakes his head. "No one is playing with any-one."

I stand up and face Nathaniel and Julian. "Give me time, start trusting me and treating my feelings with respect, and I'll be capable of love. Don't think you can walk into my life and own me."

"Alice."

"Don't, Julian. It's best we clear the air. I care about you all, but that's all it is. With luck, we might have time to build on it. Now, if you will excuse me, I have a flat to vacate to-day." I turn to face the king. "I trust I've your consent to leave?"

"Go."

Julian's voice stops me as I reach the door. "Let me know when you're ready and Jack will go with you as ar-ranged."

"I won't forget, after all, you wouldn't want me wan-dering the streets with a death threat over my head. Not until I've played my role in the king's plan."

I walk out of the room closing the door behind me and let my tears fall where no one can see them.

Chapter Seven

I poke my head round the kitchen door to find Aunt Dot on tea duty again. This time she's loaded the tray with chocolate cookies. My tummy growls.

As she passes, I snag a biscuit.

Her brow creases in concern as I stand munching in my coat and boots ready to collect my things. It's taken me two hours to get my invisible body armour in place. If I'd paid for it, I would ask for my money back. The design is flawed and not fit for purpose. However, it is the best defence I have.

"Be careful, dear."

I nod at Aunt Dot, slapping my hands together, crumbs dropping to the floor.

"I'll let Jack know you're ready to leave."

"OK, I'll wait outside, I could do with the fresh air."

A laboured sigh escapes her lips as she wanders down the hall into the living room. Alston has left, and they are busy planning how best to train me. They aren't interested in my opinion, so I don't provide one.

I feel suffocated and tired of the constant ping-ponging of emotions. The front door closes behind me and I breathe in the cool evening air, closing my eyes and enjoying the peace. Life is hard, uncompromising and rigid. There's nothing flexible about it. It's either dealing you a stack of bent cards or straightening down the edges. For every good time, there's a bad one waiting.

As the cold nibbles at my flesh, I walk over to the car. My Mini sits next to Julian's BMW. The SUV looks down on the rusted paintwork on my 1980 Mini Cooper in disdain.

Ah… how times have changed for this understated little car.

The door squeaks as it opens, and I settle myself into the front seat, patting the steering wheel as the engine grumbles to life. It's good to know not everything has changed.

"You're funny. You know that, right?" The sound of Jack's voice makes me jump.

"Chuffing-hell, Jack! You trying to give me a heart attack?"

His laughter fills the car and the richness of his low rumble washes over me.

"So where are we going," Jack asks.

"Home." Blimey, that sounds good.

"I was thinking more about the location, but home will do."

"Right… Garforth, it's on the outskirts of Leeds, so it won't take long to get there."

"Sounds fun."

"We're not going on a day trip. We're collecting my stuff."

"Where's your sense of adventure, Alice?"

"It went up in smoke."

Gravel crunches under the car's tyres as I press down on the accelerator and we make our way along the drive. In silence, I drive onto the A64, before veering onto the M1.

The rolling of the Mini's tyres on tarmac releases the tension. Music blares from the radio and I join in with Queen's *I Want To Break Free*. Jack adds his tuneless voice to mine, and we blend inharmonious rapture.

"What Alston said about using you as bait, we're not dropping you, Alice, we will protect you," Jack announces as the song fades and the adverts take over.

"Sure."

"No one is happy with the king using you as bait. As Le Sang, they have a duty to the Keepers."

"And what about Nathaniel's duty as a father?"

Jack shrugs. "I've never been responsible enough to want kids, so that's a tough one to answer."

The adverts finish and some guy I've never heard of and hope never to listen to again starts singing about love.

"So how come it's different for you? How come you get a choice?"

Jack smiles. "Death, it releases a lot of chains that living binds us to."

"You're giving me a headache."

"Ghosts live outside of the Keeper's control. We are an irritation to them and the supernatural world. In their eyes, by refusing to move on we leave a stain upon the world."

"That's harsh."

"True, but then I once shared their point of view. That changed when I died." He snorts. "As a ghost, our power diminishes, and so does our usefulness. It sucks, but it's the way it is."

The singer with the unknown name has finished, replaced with Elton John, who is *Still Standing.* Jack sings along, signalling an end to our conversation.

Turning off the M1, we make our approach onto the A642, which takes us into Garforth. A smile falls on my lips as the building where I live (I mean lived) comes into view.

The old three-storey family terrace house is now three flats. My flat is in the attic. Though it's the smallest of the three it has a spacious sense to it, due to it being set over two floors.

I swing my bag across my body and climb out of the car. Keys jingling in my hand, I walk the short distance to the front door. My steps falter as I notice Tom Watson's motorbike at the side of the house.

Jack shimmers into the hall as I close the door behind me.

"What time is it?" I whisper.

"Why? You got somewhere else you want to go?"

"No, I was just curious."

Jack looks disgruntled. "I'm a ghost, not a walking, talking clock."

"Right, sorry, I just thought with you being one, with the spirit world, time would be something you'd feel."

He sends me an exasperated stare.

If Tom-the-letch is around, I need to be hitting the stairs double-quick. That guy can hear a feather fall a mile away.

My boot hovers over the bottom step when the door to Tom's flat bursts open. His long blonde hair is wet, and rivulets of water trickle down his hairy chest over his tattoo.

I gulp as I notice the only item, he's wearing is a towel. It is wrapped loosely around his hips. In silence I beg the towel not to fall.

Ever since moving into the attic flat, Tom has pestered me to go out with him. He sees my refusals as a game of hard to get. I'm not playing with Tom, we aren't compatible. He's arrogant, picks his nose and is obnoxious. Even if he was good-looking, his personality would dim any interest.

Egotistical, self-absorbed, leeches are born for bachelorhood. No one else can appreciate their varied talents like they do.

"I think your lucks in, Alice." Jack nods at Tom as he raises a thick arm against the door frame of his flat, making himself available, but not inviting.

His ample belly wobbles as he moves his feet to support his pose. Inside, I cringe. The yellow-and red-inked snake threads its way across his back and around his shoulder, before plunging and twisting downward to his navel. As his belly dances, so does the snake. I feel ill.

Tom leers at me. "Hi Alice, long time no see." He winks.

"Yeah, I'm living at my aunt's at the moment."

With a twist of his head, droplets of water fly from Tom's long locks. Brock O'Hurn, model, actor and trainer would make the action look sexy; Tom just makes me want to vomit.

"I heard about your Mum, that's got to be tough for you. You know old relatives don't get us young folk. Come on in, let me give you some Tommy love."

"Tommy love!?!" Jack laughs, tears rolling down his face as he puckers up. "Go on Alice, how can you resist?"

Tom isn't psychic and remains unaware of the ghost's presence.

He's lucky.

"I'm sorry, I can't. My aunt's expecting me back and I need to get my stuff."

"OK, I get it, you haven't got time for Tommy's love at the moment, but I bet you've got time for a Tommy hug."

Tom steps forward, arms outstretched. His towel comes undone and falls to the floor.

"Your towel!" I shriek.

Tom smiles like a very *proud* peacock and continues strutting forward, closing the gap.

He winks and I know I won't like what's he's about to say. "You know Alice, you don't have to look. Come here and have a feel."

Jack sniggers. "I didn't think they made them that small. I wouldn't bother, you won't feel a thing."

My boots hit the stairs. "I can't…"

Hands gripping the bannister, I race upstairs, heart hammering in my chest.

"Later, then," Tom calls undeterred.

There will be no later, not even in Tom's dreams.

I step inside my flat, slamming the door and sliding the bolts across for extra security.

"The dude's delusional." Jack's voice makes me jump.

"Chuffing-hell, will you stop doing that!"

"Doing what?"

"Yeah, right, like you don't know."

Laughter fills the flat as he looks round the open-plan space. From where I stand, I survey my home, The kitchenette and lounge are small but serviceable. The mismatching furniture worn, but comfortable.

A spiral staircase hugs the back wall, leading to the bedroom and bathroom. There is no comparing this to the grandeur of Roseley, but for all its cramped style I've been happy here.

"Best get this over with," I say, a sigh on my lips.

There is no point in prolonging the agony over losing my flat.

Heading to the staircase, I make my way into the bedroom, grabbing a suitcase from under the bed. I try not to think how sad all this is, instead I dump the contents of my wardrobe and drawers inside the case.

It doesn't take long before I've stripped the room of my belongings.

Jack sits in the middle of the bed staring at the bulging case. "You going to get it closed?"

"You have such little faith, Jack."

I flip the lid and crawl on top, bringing the sides together as I pull on the zip. By the time I've finished, I'm a little sweaty, but the case is closed, and my point is made.

Triumphant I look up to find Jack has disappeared, and my moment of glory goes unnoticed.

Voices sound downstairs, and I peer over the bannister. Jack stands in the living room, arms outstretched, jaw tense as a white veil of light springs from his hands.

A dark shadow leaks from under the door, gaining solidity as it enters. My feet clatter against the metal steps as I approach Jack.

"Stay behind me I'm going to close the protection circle," Jack says.

"What is it?"

"A shadow demon."

The demon grows, towering over us. From its dense black form, red eyes shine. Tentacles strike at the shield of protection coming from Jack's hands. I watch Jack stumble as the demon tries battering its way inside.

"How long can you hold it off," I ask Jack, as he wavers and his spiritual light dims.

"Long enough for Julian to get here. Open the link and tell him we're under attack."

Without hesitation, the link snaps open, and I feel Julian's presence. His eyes lock onto the creature before us through my own. Like a train travelling at hyper-speed, he heads towards us.

The demon tears a hole through Jack's protection, and it cries in victory.

"What can I do to help?"

Jack doesn't respond.

The tentacles move closer to us, the rip in the veil increasing. Panicked, I reach out to Jack and step inside his body. He jumps as our essence merge.

A flame of white fire bursts from our joined hands, and we push the demon back. The creature screams in frustration, its high-pitched screech filling my ears, as our protective shield snaps back into place. I can sense Jack's exhaustion, and his fear, he knows he's fading.

The amount of energy he's expelling is costings him his very existence. The only thing I can do is pour more of my energy into him, counteracting the effects of what he's using. If I don't do something, he'll die his ultimate death.

Wooden fragments of the flat door fly at us and Julian stands in the opening. Coils of amber rope swing around him. The demon shrieks as the razored coil lashes out at him, and it shrinks back into the shadows. Julian twists the rope, and the noose wraps around the demon's neck. In one swift pull and the coil slices through the demon. It wails as it disappears.

Our protective shield drops and Julian rushes forward as Jack vanishes from the room.

"Jack! Where'd he go?"

"Don't worry, he'll be fine."

I gaze at the vacant spot where Jack was. "You think?"

Julian nods. "He's been through worse."

"I hope you're right."

It's then that it hits me, I care for these people. Like it or not, they are my family.

"Let's get you back to Roseley," Julian says, carrying my suitcase downstairs. I walk behind him, still shaken by the shadow demon's sudden attack.

Tom's door flies open, and he walks out in a pair of jeans, his torso bare. Julian's heated gaze lands on him and he slithers back into the safety of his flat.

"A friend of yours?"

"No, just a concerned neighbour." I gaze over the concrete drive expecting to see Julian's motorbike or SUV, but only the Mini inhabits the space.

"How did you… did you fly or something?"

Julian raises an eyebrow and my mouth snaps shut.

Chapter Eight

Light spills from the kitchen at Roseley, illuminating the space in front of us as I bring the Mini to a stop, pulling on the handbrake. Julian sits next to me, his knees resting on his chin, and his head sticking to the fabric roof. If he's found the journey uncomfortable, he hasn't said.

The car isn't made for tall people.

Lost in thought, worried about Jack and shaken from the shadow demon's attack, I step from the car.

Julian pulls the lever and his seat slides forward. He grabs the case off the back seat, bumping his head on the way out. His dislike for the car is clear from the look he sends it.

The Mini's compact design makes travelling light essential.

"I can take it," I say.

Julian ignores me.

It's a desolate sight to see my whole life fit into one case.

Self-doubt rears its head. Lost in grief and unable to cope, I've allowed my misery to dictate my actions. Had I been receptive to the changes in my life, I would know and understand how my witch's magic works. I could have helped Jack. Instead, my inexperience almost killed him.

Why do I keep making these mistakes?

Annoyed at my weakness I walk over to the front door grinding the heels of my boots into the tiny stones. Julian stays back, allowing me space.

In the woods, a wolf howls.

Earlier I had listed Tom's bad points.

- Egotistical.
- Obnoxious

To name a few.

But what about my own?

The wolf calls again, I shake my head.

How can someone as gorgeous as Ethan find anything attractive about the pitiful creature I have become? In my head, everything makes sense. The conversation balances in my favour and I sound intelligent and constructive and the person I am talking to is receptive and understanding.

When I open my mouth in reality, I come across as un-intelligent and narrow-minded. What is attractive about that?

"Alice." Julian calls, but I'm too lost in self-pity to hear him.

As the wolf howls again, my speed increases.

"Alice!"

"What?" I spin, throwing my arms in the air before continuing towards the house.

A scream falls from my lips as I collide with an unseen, solid object. "*OW!* What the heck is going on?"

It's as if someone has placed an invisible wall around Roseley. I bounce off the concealed barrier falling to the floor. Stones dig into my palms as dampness sinks into my clothes and skin.

The door opens and Aunt Dot appears her mouth hanging open.

"Oh, dear."

Julian's fingers grip my arm as he hauls me onto my feet.

"Your aunt has placed a protective barrier around the property." He nods at the crystal in her hand.

"Sorry dear, if you give me a moment, I'll reset it so the spell will allow you to enter."

"Humph," is my only comment.

Arthur pokes his head through the door, laughter dancing in his eyes.

"Don't you say a thing," I warn him.

Temptation's too strong for the gnome. "As part witch, you should have been able to sense the protection barrier."

It takes just one sentence to make my flaws visible for all to see.

Aunt Dot signals for me to enter and I walk past the little man without a word.

"Your silence speaks for itself."

I kick off my boots and walk upstairs. A low growl rattles from my throat. One day, I promise, I am going to introduce the little man to my boot.

"Julian?" Aunt Dot's voice drifts up.

I slam the bedroom door and let my tears fall. God, I'm so sick of crying!

My body hits the bed and I punch the pillow, I hate, hate, hate everything my life entails. The gnome is right to call me ignorant. While I blame my lack of knowledge on Nathaniel, my lack of interest, self-loathing and anger has been the primary reason for not trying to understand my heritage.

A tentative knot sounds and I raise my head, swiping at the tears, and running my jumper sleeve under my nose. "What?"

The door opens, and Aunt Dot's head appears. "I've brought you a drink, dear."

I push myself up and hug my pillow as she walks into the room.

"It's not been the best of days today, has it?" She sets the mug on the night-table.

"Jack almost died," I say as tears threatening to spill.

Her hand touches my arm. "You're not alone, dear. I know these last few weeks haven't been easy for you, but we love you, even if you feel we don't."

I pick at an invisible feather.

"We won't let anything happen to you, dear."

I think back to the shadow demon. "What about everyone else? Mum died trying to save me, and Jack almost faded away today trying to protect me. I don't want to lose anyone else or be responsible for their death."

"I know dear, but you must understand, our lives would still be in danger. While MAMS is operating, we will continue to fight them, and in doing so our lives are at risk." Her nose wrinkles as I slide my sleeve under my nose, wiping away the snot.

"We signed on to protect all supernatural species when we became part of Le Sang, dear."

Julian appears in the doorway with my case.

"Thanks." My eyes track him as he places it near the wardrobe and hovers.

Aunt Dot pats my leg. "I'll leave you two to chat. Drink your tea while it's warm dear, it will help to calm you."

As the door closes, Julian perches on the end of the bed.

"I thought you'd like to know Jack's fine."

"Did you see him? Was he here?" I ask.

"No."

"Then how do you know he's fine?"

Julian isn't used to the constant questions I produce, and frustration rolls off him through our link.

"I can't help it if you're not being clear," I say.

"I sent word to Geoff Monroe."

"You could have just said that."

"I didn't think you would quiz me on it." Julian stands up. "Unpack and later we'll go through your training schedule. I can't change the king's decision, but I can make sure you're prepared."

As the door closes, I reach for my tea.

The shadow demon's appearance has highlighted how unready I am. If the plan is to work, I need to sort myself out. It wasn't just my life on the line; it was Julian, Nathaniel, Aunt Dot's, Ethan's and Jack's.

A Google search won't prepare me for the fight ahead. I need physical and magical backup. It's about time I discovered how powerful I am.

There is a sense of starting a new job and I'm aware I don't have the right qualifications, and everyone is talking in a language I don't understand.

But that's about to change. There's no point in spending the rest of the day feeling sorry for myself, it's time to unpack and embrace my new life.

My old life is over, and there's no going back.

****

It doesn't take long to unpack my old life. At a loss what to do next and not wanting to face Aunt Dot and Julian, I leave the confines of my bedroom and sneak into the orangery. I tell myself change is a gradual process.

Shadows creep into the room as night falls.

One of the best things about vampirism is night vision. No longer do I fumble about in the dark. Though there are still the obvious difference between day and night, I am no longer blinded by a blanket of black.

I walk into the room and with my back against the wall, I sink to the floor, eyes resting on the garden. It's strange how alive everything is within the darkness. A hedgehog wanders in search of bugs, and an owl hoots from the woods.

The underfloor heating warms my bum as I contemplate my fears. That's what has drawn me here. I'm scared of failing and frightened of what I might become. There is no getting away from the monster inside me and its insatiable appetite for blood and pain, mixed within my human soul. Vampires are lucky, if their emotions become too much, they can switch them off. A soul doesn't allow for such luxuries. At some point it forces us to care.

The smell of moss and earth tickles my nose, and my heart responds to the smell of wolf.

"Are we saving money, or are you trying to combat global warming?" Ethan asks.

"Neither I'm hiding from Julian and Aunt Dot."

Ethan moves into the room, sitting next to me. "Why are we hiding?"

A smile tugs at the corner of my lips. "I'm taking time off from being unreasonable, and I'm not ready to declare it."

"Ah, right, got you."

I turn my head as I look over at him. "So why are you hiding?"

"I've had to be sensible all day, and I don't want anyone knowing I'm taking time off from reasonable, to be unreasonable."

"It sounds like you've had an awful day."

"Patients aren't always the nicest of people." He sighs. "Their high expectations from the medical world turn them grouchy."

I snort. "That's the problem when you're a doctor, sick people expect you to make them better."

"Consultant, there's a difference," Ethan corrects me.

I shrug. "If you say so, though, in theory, doctor or consultant, your job is to make people better. By definition, they are the same thing."

"Your viewpoint is very simplistic."

"I know, that's why I'm good at being unreasonable, I never over-think something." Ethan laughs.

The sound of the front door opening and closing filters through the hall into the orangery, carrying the odour of sandalwood.

"It sounds like you've one less person to be reasonable too."

"I guess I can stop hiding now, Aunt Dot is too nice to be unreasonable with. Which let me tell you is annoying."

"Darn the woman." I laugh at Ethan as my stomach growls.

"It sounds like Julian left in the nick of time. Come on, I'll make you a snack, I could do with something to eat myself."

Ethan stands up, offering me his hand. His fingers wrapping around mine and I try not to think about what else I'd like them to do.

The kitchen is void of life as we enter, and like thieves, we raid the fridge.

"OK, what do you fancy?"

I look over Ethan's shoulder. "How about a bacon butty?"

"Sounds good to me, here start buttering the bread, and I'll get the bacon on."

"How many slices do you want?"

"We'll start with the brown loaf and take it from there."

We both have amazing appetites.

I count the slices. "That's six butties each, is there enough bacon?"

"Plenty."

"Enough for the white loaf?"

"You that hungry?"

"Hey, wolves aren't the only ones with a good appetite, us Vampwitch's need our sustenance too."

Hands on hips, Ethan looks at the bread piling up. "You think you can take on a wolf?"

I smile at him. "Bring it on."

He grabs a pack of sausages and eggs.

"Just so you know, I haven't eaten since breakfast, and a lot's happened since then," I warn him.

Ethan throws the sausages into the frying pan. "Just so you know, I've come back from a run."

That will explain the shorts and clinging t-shirt. Not that I'm complaining.

By the time the food hits the table, I'm salivating worse than a dog. With hungry eyes, we admire our feast.

"Let the Vampwitch win," I say grabbing a butty.

Teeth sinking into the bread, I swallow it before the contents hit the side of my mouth. My tase buds explode with flavour and my stomach groans in pleasure.

With no evidence of slowing down, Ethan watches his wolf dancing close to the surface. In no time the food has gone, our hunger reducing to a dull ache.

"Something smells divine," Polly calls, walking through the front door.

Ethan and I sit back, patting our stomachs as she steps into the room. "I was going to ask if there was anything left."

"You know that old saying Pol, never come between a Vampwitch, or wolf and their food."

She shakes her head. "Nope, I can't say I've heard of that one."

"That's a shame, it's relevant here." I turn to Ethan. "What's for pudding."

A smile lights his face. "Your aunt's made a chocolate cake."

My chair legs scrape against the floor. "I'll get the forks if you grab the cake."

Polly's eyes travel over the kitchen. "How much did you guys eat?"

"I've a good excuse, I skipped lunch."

"And I went for a run."

Ethan returns with the chocolate cake. Polly runs for a knife and a plate. "I'm so having a slice of that."

"Hey, don't take it all," I shout at her as she cuts off a good-sized slice.

"It's tiny."

"Tiny would be a crumb."

She waves a fork at me. "I'd stop worrying what's on my plate and start taking notice at what the wolf is doing."

Ethan looks up, his fork loaded with cake.

"What?" His lips lock round the cake.

"That was sneaky, "I say grabbing my fork.

"I know." He looks smug.

A buzzing noise alerts us that someone's at the barrier.

"You going to get that?" Polly asks.

"Nope." I sink my fork into the cake.

"What about you?"

Ethan shakes his head. "They can wait."

Footsteps sound in the hall. "I'll get it, dear."

I point my empty fork in the general direction of the front door. "See, Aunt Dot's got it."

Heels click on the wooden floor, and our heads turn in union as a woman appears in the doorway.

Her lips twist in annoyance at us. "Ethan, you're not dressed."

"Yes, he is." Polly and I say together.

Ethan places his fork down. "It's all yours."

I stare at the plate. "There isn't anything left."

"I know, that's why it's yours."

The woman taps her foot, leaning against the door frame.

Ethan smiles. "I'd best get changed."

His hand brushes my shoulder as he walks out of the room.

Polly sits back in her chair, taking her cake with her. "So who are you?"

The woman bares her teeth, eyes locking onto me. "I'm Lucy, Ethan's mate."

That would explain the smell of perfumed wolf and the hostility hanging in the air.

While it's depressing to find Ethan has a mate, I'm not sure how matey they are. Six weeks of living here and I've never met or heard anyone speak about her. That doesn't sound like a harmonious relationship to me.

Potential threat averted I downgrade her to wanna-be mate.

"I'm Alice, Julian's sister, and that," I point at Polly, "is Polly, Julian's sister's best friend."

"Hi." Polly bares her teeth at Lucy.

A buzz of magic stings the air as Lucy takes a step into the kitchen. The woman has possessive issues.

"Lucy, dear." Aunt Dot calls. "Why don't you wait for Ethan in the living room."

The wolf hesitates, before turning and walking out of the room.

"What do you think that was about?" Polly asks.

I shrug. "Beats me."

Chapter Nine

After five hours of tossing and turning, I give up on sleep. Throwing on my running gear, I wander into the kitchen, trainers in hand. Aunt Dot has a thing about shoes being worn in the house, and while she can't see me, I abide to her strict rules.

Westminster chimes sound from the grandfather clock, announcing the ridiculous time I'm up. Despondent, I shake my head.

Darkness adds to my misery, coating the house in eery silence. Roseley is a hub of noise and activity, where people congregate, plan and cogitate the dangers of life and their next strategy. At this hellish hour it is still and silent, yet to wake from slumber.

Tiredness makes my limbs heavy, but my head is having none of it. Its constant churning preventing any chance of sleep.

Today I start my witch studies and my nerves have been jingling all night. Uncertainty is a hideous and demanding master, and I name it the source of my sleep deprivation.

The large patio doors have turned into mirrors. I squint at the dishevelled person staring back at me. She is a pathetic creature. Dark circles sit under my eyes, obscured for a moment as I raise the mug of camomile tea to my lips. It's strange to look at the woman before me, and feel her sadness and apprehension, viewing her in the third person.

What advice would I give her? Stay calm and focused? Tell her she can do this? I'm not so sure she can. The enormity of what lays ahead of her, of me, prevents me from believing success can ever be ours. There's so much I don't know. How, in a few short days, can I be ready to face Aeden and MAMS?

Vampire abilities are easier to adjust to than a witch's magic. They are a physical power. Speed, sound, smell. A witch relies on spells and knowledge and understanding herbs and their properties. It is laborious and boring and will emphasise my lack of skill and finesse. Something I am already aware of and doesn't need further stressing.

The mug hits the granite worksurface with more force than intended. I need to run, to hear my trainers beat a path upon the earth, and for my heart to beat a fast and steady rhythm within my chest. To feel alive.

I make my way into the orangery, ignoring the tiredness clinging to my legs and arms. It's difficult preparing yourself to die. No matter what everyone keeps saying, that's what I am about to do.

A sigh escapes as I warm up. Arms above my head, I stretch, coming into a half-plank position. Hands falling to the ground, I kick back my right leg and lower down until the muscle pulls. I count to fifteen and transfer legs. My body wakes up as I go through my warm-up routine. Air fills my lungs and I breathe deep, breathing in positive energy, blowing out negative as my yoga teacher taught me.

Oblivion calls and my feet dance as I throw open the orangery doors. The soft tread of rabbits thumping across the field is like an earthquake banging against my eardrums.

Dampness pours into my lungs, engulfing me in its scent. A smile lights my face and I leap towards the trees.

Amber eyes stare at me as I reach the woods.

"You want to play wolf?" I shout.

Fur flies at me. Large paws landing by my feet, the wolf twists his body about my legs. A cool nose presses against my hips as he tips back his head and howls, revealing razor-sharp teeth. I think he's smiling.

"Ethan?"

His head bobs.

My fingers brush against his thick pelt. "Let's play."

Feet thundering across the grass, Ethan at my heels, we hit the woods. Branches snare my clothes, slowing me down. The wolf races ahead. A soft rumble echoes from him and I'm aware he's laughing at me.

I jump over a fallen tree into a small clearing, gaining speed.

"Bet you thought you had me there, wolf," I shout, catching him up.

He diverts around a tree and I'm in front. "Is that all you've got?"

Teeth glistening in the moonlight, he snarls at me. It's my turn to laugh. I grab a low branch, using it to catapult myself forward. Paws beating on the earth, the wolf's feet kicks up moss and dead leaves, as he runs.

For the first time since forever, I am free from the constant doubt that sits on my shoulder, nagging at me. There is nothing but the sensation of enjoyment and being one with moment and time. Air burns my lungs and my unbound hair flies around me. The wolf is gaining ground and I take a sharp turn over the small humpback bridge. Ethan's wolf clears the water, his tongue hanging out from his jaw. We dash through the next cluster of trees as we double back, making our way towards Roseley.

The house comes into view and I command my legs to go faster, stretching them out and increasing my stride. Together we hit the patio, trainers and paws striking the concrete slabs as one. Our warm breath billows around us and we come to a stop.

I drop to my knees and throw my arms around the wolf at my side. If Ethan was in human form, I would never act this way.

But this is his wolf, not the man.

"Thanks, wolf." His tongue comes out, licking at my cheek, making me laugh.

"If you're lucky, I might even see about getting some sausages under the grill for when you get back," I tell him.

The wolf lets out a howl.

"Yeah, I know ketchup, not brown sauce."

I watch him disappear back into the woods in search of a rabbit. Hoofing off my trainers, my heart's rapid beat slows to a steadier rhythm. Warmth from the underfloor heating soaks into my damp feet as I make my way towards the stairs.

Aunt Dot's voice echoes from the kitchen, and I turn, poking my head round the door frame.

"Morning."

She turns at the sound of my voice, a smile on her lips. "Hello dear."

It's time for my witch studies to start.

"I went for a run with Ethan. It won't take me long to get showered and changed."

"Not to worry, dear."

On impulse, I walk over hugging her. "Thanks."

My actions surprise her, and her eyes sparkle with tears as she wraps her arms around me, holding me tight

"I'll get your breakfast started while you freshen up."

"Can we have sausages? I kind of promised Ethan."

She shakes her head at me, a smile still on her lips.

"You two are going to eat me out of house and home."

I laugh at her as I make my way upstairs to change.

Chapter Ten

Aunt Dot places the sausages on the table as I walk back into the kitchen. Ethan is already pulling out a chair and I jog over before he eats the lot.

His short auburn hair is wet, and the white shirt he's wearing complements his tanned skin. He smells as yummy as the food does.

"Blimey, you were fast." He smiles at my comment.

"You said sausages."

I nod, grabbing three of the succulent beasts and lining them up on a slice of bread.

Polly walks into the kitchen, yawning and stretching out her arms. "I think I need to find a rich man, so I don't have to work for a living. Monday's are depressing."

I bat Ethan's hands away as his fork reaches for the last sausage. "That's mine, you've had twelve."

He stares. "I can't believe you've counted."

"Like you weren't." I snort, sticking my fork into the sausage.

"Here you go." Aunt Dot places another pile in front of us. "I'll go get the Book of Shadows while you finish, and we can start your studies."

"Hey," I shout as Ethan places four sausages onto one slice of bread, loading it down with ketchup. "You had a rabbit, I didn't."

Ethan smiles. "I had two, but I also ran further than you, so the rabbits don't count."

Polly sets her bowl of cereal down and looks at us. "I can't believe how much you two can eat." Her spoon hovers near her mouth. "I wouldn't like to date either of you, the bill would be astronomical."

"Werewolves have a high metabolic rate."

"So do Vampwitches." I pull at the loose waistband of my joggers. "Look, despite the quantity of food I'm eating, I'm still losing weight."

Ethan points his sandwich at me. "You need to eat more."

"I would if you'd let me." My fork becomes a weapon as I stab at his hand. "Off, that's mine."

Polly's spoon clatters against her bowl. "If she eats anymore, Dot will need shares in a meat farm."

"She's jealous because I can eat what I like," I say smiling.

"You've got me there."

Jack mists into the room.

"Well, duty calls," Ethan says leaving the table.

"I'd best go too." Polly picks up her bowl and places it into the dishwasher.

I look across at Jack. "You still know how to clear a room, I see."

"It's one of my better skills."

He jumps up, sitting on the table. His form is solid again. Though it's a relief to see him, I don't tell him, as he'll milk it for a week.

"If Aunt Dot catches you sitting on the table, you'll be in trouble, you know how she is about eating areas."

"In reality, I'm not sitting on it. You know that don't you?"

"You try telling her that."

Aunt Dot walks into the room carrying a large thick leather-bound book. Jack jumps down as she enters, walking over to her.

"Shall we get started?" Aunt Dot asks.

Curious, I gravitate towards the book as she places it on the middle island.

Several symbols scatter along it. In the centre a dragon sits, poised for attack. Above the dragon is a pentagram. My fingers trace the design, caressing each dip and mark within the fabric.

"It's beautiful." Mesmerised, my eyes remain glued to the book.

"This is our family's Book of Shadows. Each generation of witches adds to it, writing spells and providing information about different species." Aunt Dot lays a hand on the book. "It dates back to the eighteenth century when Alison Preston, a descendent of Jennet Preston, breathed life into it. They burnt our original book after the Pendle Witch trials in 1612."

I hadn't realised the book was that old.

"Your ancestor, Jennet Preston, lived in Gisburn. They held her trial at York Assizes, where they found guilty of murdering Thomas Lister of Westby Hall by witchcraft. On the 29th of July 1612, they hung her on the Knavesmire. After the death of her mother, and scared they would hang her for witchcraft, Aida, burnt their Book of Shadows."

"Did she kill Thomas Lister?"

"No." Aunt Dot removes her hand from the book.

"The burning of the book set the magic free. It stayed waiting for a new home. This book holds that magic. Only a witch of Preston line can use and recall it. Our Book of Shadows is the keeper of our spells. It is a living entity, no one has the power to destroy it."

Her eyes meet mine. "Magic doesn't come without consequence. It is important you learn the three categories and understand their effect. White magic causes no harm and gets its power from nature. Black magic requires a blood sacrifice to make it work."

Jack leans forward. "The practitioner of black magic doesn't have to undertake the kill, as the candles used to create lesser dark spells contain human blood within the wax. It gives it spells substance and power, but limits consequence."

"Thank you, Jack." Aunt Dot says. " Grey magic is the hardest to determine, it has the potential to cause harm and can turn to black magic if not used for the right purpose. If you intend to use grey magic, you need to undertake a divination with Tarot cards, so you understand the outcome."

"OK..." I'm learning there is more to witchcraft than throwing a few herbs into a bowl and doing a bit of chanting.

"The practitioner must accept responsibility for their actions to restore cosmic balance." On that note, Aunt Dot clasps her hands together. "It's time to get started."

My reservations towards magic have amplified.

"First thing you will need to learn is how to set a circle. Circles protect us from outside forces and influences. They also prevent anyone outside of the circle from entering." At Aunt Dot's words, my thoughts drift back to the shadow demon.

"You make a circle using salt or magnetic chalk. As you become more practiced, you will also be able to set a circle using a trigger word. However, for stronger spells use magnetic chalk or salt as it doesn't drain your energy levels."

Aunt Dot passes me a small piece of magnetic chalk from her trouser pocket. "Here, dear."

I pluck the chalk from her hand, unsure where to start.

"First draw a pentagram, your circle will then touch each of the five points, sealing it shut. Make sure it is large enough to incorporate the three of us, dear."

I'm no artist, and the pentagram looks a little one-sided. Before I connect the last point of the it together, Jack and Aunt Dot move into the circle. There is a shimmer of light as I join the line to the last point of the pentagram, and I sit back in awe of my talent. Aunt Dot raises her hand, her fingers trailing along the circle. The barrier remains intact.

"To dissolve the circle, you will need to break the connection to the pentagram." She places a hand on my arm. "Not now, Alice."

"Why don't you come and join me on the floor." Jack pats the space at his side. "It's time, Dot."

"Yes, yes, I know." She sounds weary.

"It's time for what?" I ask.

Aunt Dot takes my hands in hers. A sense of impending doom falls over me.

"Given the king's plan, there isn't time to teach you everything you need to know about witchcraft. It has taken me years to control my power and learn the spells I've cast."

Jack looks at me. "We're going to import your aunt's knowledge into you."

"You're going to what?"

"There's no need for hysterics, I thought you'd be pleased. At least this way there's no studying involved." I think Jack's gone mad.

"We've no other choice, dear. You need to learn how to fight and tap into your vampire abilities. They are the priority. A witch's magic is powerful, but it's not physical like a vampire's. We need to make sure you're ready. Alston has allowed us two weeks to train you."

Jack huffs. "Vampire's see witchcraft as the lesser magic."

I tuck my hair behind my ears. "I don't think you can blame the vamps, Jack."

He smiles at me. "Who says I can't?"

"While I can pass on my knowledge, it can't compensate for your lack of experience. All we can hope is that it will be enough," Aunt Dot says.

My feeling of impending doom returns.

From a black bag, she takes out five white candles. "Place these at each point of the pentagram within the circle. Start here." She points to my right. "The top point of the pentagram is for the Spirit and should always be the last candle placed. The other elements need awakening first — water, fire, earth and air."

I take the candle and lighter and crawl over to each point of the wonky pentagram.

Aunt Dot continues to speak as I light the candles. "Each candle contains angelic root and assists in the growth of new ideas and creative energy. It will strengthen the spell."

A tight smile pulls across my lips as I sit down next to her.

Aunt Dot snips off a lock of her hair, before passing the scissors to me. I paid a fortune to get my hair cut, to lessen the frizz. Despite the cost and promises made by the hairdresser, it didn't work. However, I'm still loath to hack at it.

"Alice?" I take the scissors.

Aunt Dot ties our strands together, laying them on three oak twigs, wrapped in twine on the floor in front of us.

"Lift your hands so that your palms are facing upwards, dear."

Aunt Dot nods and Jack hovers his hands above ours. Static electricity nibbles at my skin as the flow of our energies merge.

The energy builds in intensity, responding to Aunt Dot's chant.

Elements of knowledge rise and impart the gift I offer
I call to the Seven Stars from the Seven Heavens
To grant upon this witch
My knowledge clear, true and bright
What is weak within her, now make mighty
Strengthen her with wisdom, with the gift I give
As I will it, mote it be.

The hair on the floor bursts into flames and I'm hit with a jumble of words. Voices spin through my brain, and my head feels as though it's going to explode. As panic falls so too does darkness. I'm aware only of the scream of pain that leaves my lips as I pass out.

****

A strange sensation pricks at my skin. "I've had a poke around and she's fine Dot, no damage done."

"Get out!" I scratch at my skin, throwing my arms about as I try to push Jack's essence out of me.

"It's OK dear, I asked Jack to make sure you were alright."

My insides are like jelly, quivering from the alien force that has invaded it.

The ghost sits at my side, and I flinch. "Yeah....... well.... I'm fine."

I shiver at the thought of Jack poking around my head while I was unconscious.

Aunt Dot breaks the circle. "Come sit down at the table, dear, and I'll make you a cup of camomile tea."

My head is thumping and the last thing I want to do is sit at the table and drink camomile tea. Fingers pressing against my temple, I scrape back a chair, aware once again that as choices go, mine are at subzero.

The kettle boils and she places a bunch of herbs in front of me. A soft whisper echoes in my head. The first herb is broom, used in wind spells, and divination. Next is cinnamon, which is great for mental focus. If you lose something or someone, cinnamon along with celery in a charm will help you find it — *holy shit* the spell worked!

My mouth drops open and Jack laughs at me.

"Here you go." A smile plays at the corners of Aunt Dot's lips.

"Alice." I turn at the sound of Julian's voice. "It's time"

Jack smirks. "Go on, it's off to work with you, Vampwitch."

"Hi-bloody-ho." A sigh escapes my parted lips as I leave the kitchen. My camomile tea remaining untouched.

I am not a fighter. While it looks super cool in the movies, it's not me until now. Shoulders squared back I ready myself for a thrashing.

Julian meets me at the stairs and together we make our way down into the basement, ready to start my vampire fighting lesson.

As my foot hits the concrete, Julian stands arms crossed in the middle of the room. He either thinks I am easy prey, or he's not bothered about getting his suit dirty.

"Do you know anything about fighting stances?"

"Warrior two pose." I wiggle my eyebrows at him as I strike the pose.

Julian cocks a brow at me in response but doesn't smile.

"I also know how to run if that helps?"

The look on his face tells me he's not impressed.

"Jasper," Julian calls.

A vampire with chestnut hair and a wiry frame steps from the shadows. "Alice meet your sparring partner."

I look from Julian to Jasper — *oh shit.*

Chapter Eleven

Jasper's fingers dig into my arm and my feet leave the floor. Like a bobbin he spins me round, playing with me. There's a sharp stab of pain followed by a popping noise as he pulls on my arm and flings me forward. Airborne, I fly, the wall is getting closer and I'm in no position to change my course. Bang! I hit the wall.

Pain shoots through my entire body, radiating from my shoulder and head. Vision impaired, the ringing inside my brain increases. My arm hangs at my side, redundant and incapable of use. A shift in the air tells me there's no time to dwell on the pain.

Fabric rustles a breath away from where I'm sprawled. I push myself into a crouch position and prepare to strike.

Over the last three days, I have learnt how to tap into and restrain the vampire in me. My control over it is flaky, overridden with the need to destroy. DNA programming demands I kill without thought or mercy. It's hard facing this unknown part of me. I've never considered myself to be a violent person. But this new me wants to hurt someone to such a degree that death is its only goal. The intense pleasure of it soothes my inner self, scaring me. Full vampires contain the power to switch off their killer instinct, allowing them control over it. As a living product, I don't possess this ability.

There are two elements to fighting. The main one isn't to remain alive, but to prevent my killer from having full rein. Once unleashed I cannot imprison it. If I'm conscious of my potential to kill, I'm also aware of my mental welfare. My guilt over Mum's death already haunts me. Should I give in to my vampire, shame will devour my soul until I am a crazed mindless zombie or the only part of me left is the vampire.

I hold my breath, remaining still within the flickering lit room. The light effect Julian is using prevents vampires from utilising their enhanced vision, forcing us to use our other senses. Jasper moves and I strike, pushing through my legs and springing into the air, flipping my body round, legs outstretched in front. A cry of surprise and pain fills the room as my foot connects with Jasper's back. Feet hitting the ground, I roll as he stamps his foot a whisper away from where I lay. At the same moment Jasper's foot hits the concrete, I twist and kick out. The tip of my boot connects with Jasper's chin and he falls back. A thrill runs through me and I kick again, striking his kneecap with enough force to shatter it. Bone splinters and he crumbles to the floor.

My vampire is dancing in joy, but there's no time to celebrate my victory, and I jump onto my feet as Jasper thunders into me. Together we crash to the floor. I land on my injured arm. Pain clouds my head as I fight to remain conscious. The weight of Jaspers body pins me down.

"Ah!" I scream in frustration.

The light stops flickering and Jasper climbs off me, a smug smile tugging at his lips. I have lost another battle.

Jasper limps as he moves, favouring his right leg. Some of my irritation evaporates as I notice his discomfort. It's the first time I've caused the vampire any significant damage.

I grab my brother's outstretched hand and he pulls me to my feet.

"You're getting better."

A puff of air leaves my lungs. Better isn't good enough.

"Yeah, but I still lost." The pain in my arm is intensifying as my adrenalin levels drop.

"Your technique is improving." Julian encourages me.

Jasper limps over. "You took out my kneecap. Excellent job."

Vampires are strange creatures.

"Thanks," I accept the compliment and his boyish face lights up.

Jasper became a vampire in his mid-twenties. His undead age is a hundred-and-fifty. He is as translucent as a pane of glass. Even after a hundred-and-fifty years, he still enjoys the social aspect of college life. When you can make those around you forget, reliving your college days becomes easy. Vamps leave no digital footprint, which adds to the ease of reliving the best moments of your life (Jasper's words).

My breath hisses through my teeth as Julian lays a hand on my throbbing shoulder. Concern shines in his eyes.

"I think it's dislocated," I tell him.

Julian looks at the arm hanging at my side. "Let's get Ethan to look at it."

Over the last three days, I have had two broken legs, on separate days, four broken ribs, on the same day and a knife stuck in my stomach. The knife hurt more when Jasper pulled it out, then when he shoved it in.

In retaliation to the embedment of the knife, I squeezed Jasper's eyes out from their sockets, which he regenerated.

As a half-vampire, I have limited healing capacity. The miracle cure comes courtesy of Julian's blood. My fear of becoming a blood addict is growing. When he first stuck his dripping wrist under my nose and commanded me to drink, I wanted to throw up. Now, my lips smack and saliva fills my mouth. It's horrifying to think how bad things have become.

Vampire blood speeds up the recovery process in readiness for me to take another beating, I mean self-defence lesson.

Without Julian's blood, I would have died from the stomach injury.

On this occasion, however, there is no need for a blood transfusion, and I follow my brother upstairs. Ethan meets us as we step into the hall. His lips set into a thin line as he notices my arm.

"Sorry, but we need to get going, sir," Jasper says from behind.

"Don't worry, I'll take care of her, you go." Ethan wraps a gentle arm around my shoulders. "Come on, Trouble."

"I'll get Dot to bring you some painkillers." Julian throws the car keys to Jasper. "I'll meet you outside."

"Yes, sir."

Ethan steers me into the living room. "This is going to hurt."

"Yep, I thought it would."

The words haven't left my lips before Ethan grabs my arm and shoves it back into the socket.

Pain explodes, and I pass out.

Chapter Twelve

On today's menu of everything witchy, is pulling power from a ley line. This is my third and last lesson in the art of witchcraft, after Aunt Dot requested, bargained and bribed her way to gain an extra day.

Even with her knowledge, I still need to learn how to put it into practice. It seems an arse-over-tit way of doing things. I know what I'm doing and don't at the same time. Life is often said to be confusing. You need to live in my world to understand the true meaning of the phrase.

The lesson in charm making was a breeze and spell-casting effortless. However, this coming lesson I know from my newfound knowledge won't be as easy.

Ley line magic is a blending of energies. Get the balance wrong and like any electric current it will send out a shockwave with enough potential to kill.

Julian meets me at the top of the stairs. "I was on my way to get you."

He ruffles my hair as we make our way into the kitchen.

The dynamics of our relationship are changing. There is no surfacing resentment, instead, my chest explodes with a sense of belonging at the casual affection he shows me. I wonder if this is what he'd been like with the sister he lost so many centuries ago. We might not always agree with each other's methods. But as siblings, we are flourishing, even if things can get strained with emotional conflict.

We are both stubborn. And learning to embrace compromise is difficult.

My treacherous heart gives a skip at the sight of Ethan, who is polishing off a plate of eggs, bacon and sausages.

"Morning sleepy." His smile makes my pulse race.

"I can't believe I slept for so long." Nine a.m. is the middle of the day at Roseley.

"It's Dot's special tea, works like a charm." Ethan chuckles at his reference to witchcraft.

I arch a questioning brow at her. "Sorry dear, after dislocating your shoulder, I thought it best you had a good night's sleep, to give your body time to heal."

Before I respond Arthur walks in. "At last," he says jumping onto the stool next to the Aga. "Well come on, you've kept me waiting long enough."

I point at the bad-tempered gnome. "Huh?"

My language skills often amaze me.

"Arthur's going to assist with today's lesson, dear, along with Jack."

I want to ask why, but I'm not prepared to make Grumpy, grumpier. "Right, I'll get something to eat and then we can start."

"There's no rush, dear."

"Take your time, I've only been waiting three hours, what's another three."

I roll my eyes at Arthur's comment.

"You're being facetious. It won't take me three hours to eat breakfast."

Arthur folds his arms over his vast stomach. "Humph, I've seen what you can eat."

I take no notice. The gnome will always need to vent out his opinions

"If I have to wait, I might as well have some elder-flower water… warmed it's cold out there." He sends me an expectant look.

"Don't look at me, I'm not your molly-maid, besides I don't want to keep you waiting." I pull out a chair next to Ethan, as Aunt Dot cooks my breakfast.

"You know where everything is Arthur." The gnome huffs at Julian as he jumps from the stool.

"This wouldn't happen in Faerieland. They look after gnomes there."

"Doesn't the word gnome come the from nineteenth century fairy tales?" I enquire, snagging a sausage off Ethan's plate. "They use it in their stories to reference little people like brownies, or leprechauns."

Arthur's face reddens, angry at the downgrade in his status to the same as brownies and leprechauns.

"Alice." Aunt Dot shouts at me and I drop the half-eaten sausage on the table.

"What?"

She shakes her head at me. "Never take food off a wolf."

Everyone is watching Ethan.

I look at the sausage. "Oh, do you want it back?" I hand him the half-eaten stick. "I've only had a big bite." My lips twitch.

Arthur walks over, pulling out a chair and placing his glass on the table. A low growl omits from Ethan.

"She took the sausage not me." The gnome takes his drink backing away.

Amber sparks light Ethan's eyes. The wolf coming to the surface. I place a hand over Ethan's and his eyes meet mine.

"Sorry, wolf, I didn't mean any disrespect."

The room is quiet, everyone is waiting for a storm to hit, and no one's sure how to break the growing pressure.

"We've shared before and I didn't think," I say trying to explain my lack of thought and calm the wolf.

Ethan shrugs and the wolf recedes. The tension in the room relaxes. "Not to worry." His fingers graze mine as he pushes the sausage in my hand towards my lips.

Arthur huffs.

"I think you're the one he's mad at for sitting too close to him, not me." Meat swirls round my mouth.

Aunt Dot places a plate of food in front of me, and I pick up a sausage. "Here, have one of mine," I say handing the sausage to Ethan.

"I don't believe it." Arthur throws his hands in the air.

"Ok, what did I do now?"

"Nothing, Alice, don't worry," Ethan says as he pulls his chair back, accepting the offered food.

"It's getting late, we'd best go." Ethan nods at Julian.

I watch the two men leave, tucking into my breakfast, aware something significant has happened, but not understanding what.

"Well, that was interesting," Jack says from my right, making me jump.

"I thought we agreed you wouldn't do that anymore."

"Do what?" False innocence rolls off him.

Arthur coughs. "I've better things to do with my time than wait around here."

"OK, OK." I scoop up the last of my breakfast. "You know, if you were less grumpy, and more easy-going, no one would call you Grumpy."

"And if you were respectful, and did more studying, the wolf wouldn't have surfaced."

"The wolf was mad at you, not me."

"That's the interesting part." Jack leans against the wall, head cocked to the side. "Ethan's wolf has accepted you."

"That has to be a good thing," I say as my heart does a happy dance.

"Hm…" Jack doesn't sound convinced.

"What am I missing?"

Aunt Dot collects my plate. "Nothing dear, come on let's start your lesson, Arthur's right it's getting late."

****

"Ouch!… I thought you were supposed to make this easier." My hands clutch at my head.

"If you'd listened, you would find it simpler." Arthur's voice sears its way into my brain, amplifying the pain.

"I listened, and it still went wrong."

Hands on his hips, the gnome bangs his foot against the wooden floor. "Let's test your knowledge before we try again."

"Why?"

"Because you failed."

"No, you didn't follow me as instructed." I rub at my temple.

"I told you not to touch that line."

"Well, I didn't hear you, because of the constant buzzing in my head."

"Arthur! Alice! This isn't helping." Aunt Dot's voice slices through the air, and I clamp my mouth shut, nursing my aching head.

Arthur folds his arms over his smock. "What's a ley line?"

The bell on his hat dances and a soft ringing sneaks its way into my hurting brain. I want to pull the bell off and dump it somewhere muddy, and smelly, and a million miles away from Roseley and me. Instead, I huff.

"Ley lines are energy lines that run underground in a straight-line network. Witch's use them to cast spells rather than herbs." I hold my hand up as Arthur opens his mouth. "You asked shorty and I've not finished."

The gnome's foot taps faster.

"Ley lines offer an invaluable source of energy, which is why spiritual leaders use them to build their places of worship. Some supernatural beings use the lines for travel." Smug, I smile at Arthur. "See, I was listening."

"If you were listening, you wouldn't have jumped that line."

"You never told me not to jump lines."

"How am I supposed to know you'd do something that stupid!"

My hands fly in the air. "Oh, I don't know, because this is all new to me, and unless I'm told I don't know. You're the one who tells me how ignorant I am. Given your insight into my stupidness, I blame you."

"Arthur."

"See you're upsetting Aunt Dot." I point at the gnome.

"Alice." Aunt Dot's shouts at me.

"What did I do?"

Aunt Dot looks at the two of us. "This isn't helping."

"Dot's right, you're even starting to give me a headache, and since I'm a ghost, I'd say that was impossible."

"Fine." Arthur grinds out the word, ensuring that everyone understands how not *fine* is *fine*.

Aunt Dot's penetrating gaze swings in both our directions. "Unless you trust each other, this won't work."

"We could use a gargoyle."

Arthur puffs out his chest at Jack's suggestion "Gnomes make better ley line travellers than gargoyles. Gargoyles sleep too much."

"I bet they're not as grumpy as gnomes."

My comment earns me a warning look from Aunt Dot.

"Jack, this time you will travel with Alice. Alice, no jumping lines. Arthur, be nice."

Arthur's requirement was going to be harder to achieve than mine and Jack's.

"Alice, close your eyes, and this time I want you to feel the energy of the line you're going to use. Do not get distracted by the other lines."

"OK," I mutter, doing as Aunt Dot instructed. The line buzz's inside me once more, and I track its energy running through Roseley.

"Good, Jack, pour your essence into Alice." I brace myself for Jack's entry, trying not to squirm.

"Arthur, connect your hand with Alice."

As our fingers touch the energy shifts and we enter the line, drawing upon its magical power. Beneath me a red ley line calls, singing out its own tune. I try to ignore it, but its song is bewitching.

Each ley line has its own tune. It is that tune a traveller uses to identify the right path. An experienced traveller can leap from line to line until they reach their chosen destination.

There is something about this line that calls to me. I look at Arthur as he continues to pull me along. He doesn't see it, which adds to my curiosity. My fingers reach out for it, trying to get a flavour of its energy. As my fingertips touch it, the red line snaps, and I am catapulted inside the line.

"Alice! No!" Jack's voice buzz's around me, but it's too late.

Pain explodes throughout every molecule of my body, and the vampire in me wakes. My barriers are down, and I can't control the hunger that rises to the surface. The vampire's thirst centres on the red line. I draw more of its energy inside me. Incapable of screaming, my body jerks, as wave after wave of line energy zings and snaps at my body.

"Arthur! Get her out!" Jack's voice floats from another dimension. "Arthur! Now!"

"I'm trying, but she's absorbing too much energy, I can't move her."

"You get her out of here, or I'll make sure that Alston hears what's happened here."

At Jack's threat, the gnome pulls harder. "I don't see why you're blaming me, it's the stupid ignorant…"

"Not now, Arthur. You should have been aware of that line's presence. You didn't focus and missed it. This is your fault. Now get her out."

We hit the line at Roseley, and the searing pain ebbs. My body pulsates with residual energy and sweat breaks out coating my skin. The gnome slides his fingers from mine as we reach the kitchen floor.

"What happened?" Aunt Dot's lays a cool hand against my skin.

Anger vibrates off Jack. "That idiot wasn't watching her, that's what happened."

"I did as asked."

"No, you didn't, all you did was drag her through that line like you were walking a puppy. If you'd told us about the bloodline, we could have protected her." Their voices bang against my fried brain.

"Your king sent you to watch over her, not get her killed," Jack says, his frustration at Arthur increasing.

"The Seelie King and Keeper sent me to observe."

"Shall I ask him?" Arthur sucks in a deep breath at Jack's threat.

"Jack, I need you to explain what happened, so I can protect her." Aunt Dot's voice sounds miles away.

Jack is pacing round the kitchen, his shoes hitting the surface with a bang. I shouldn't be able to hear his feet as he inhabits the ghost plane.

"Why can I hear Jack?" No one responds to my question.

The constant banging of his feet is hurting my head. "Jack, stop. You're making too much noise."

Jack stops his pacing. "Dot?"

Fingers touch my neck. "We're losing her. Jack, can you see her?"

"I'm looking Dot, give me a minute."

"We might not have a minute." Panic vibrates in Aunt Dot's voice.

"I've got her."

"She's with you!" Arthur sounds shocked at Jack's announcement.

"What did you expect, you stupid gnome."

"Arthur, grab the book. In the back you'll find a charm I'll need it to hold her down." Things are bad if the gnome is doing as Aunt Dot asks without argument.

The floor beneath me disappears, and I'm suspended, held in place by nothing but air.

"We're losing her, Dot, she's getting clearer here."

"Hold her, Jack. Arthur, get Julian and Ethan, we may need the wolf."

There's a popping sound as Arthur enters the ley line.

"Why is Arthur jumping a line?" A strange warmth touches my chest, spreading over me as Aunt Dot activates the charm. "Ouch… that hurts."

"Just relax, dear, it will help keep you here while we wait for Julian and Ethan to arrive."

"Where am I if I'm not with you?"

"It doesn't matter dear, just relax, Jack's with you."

My eyelids unglue. "What the hell."

Fear creeps in as I stare at the twisting band of lights gathering around me. Below me there is nothing. No earth, no sun, just the swirling colours within the blackness.

"Alice," Jack calls my name as his arms wrap around me.

All I keep thinking is I shouldn't be able to feel those arms, but I can.

His grip tightens, pressing me hard against his chest. "Don't touch the light, Alice, stay with me."

"What's happening, Jack?" His body shakes in fear.

"You've left us, and we need to bring your soul back down to your body."

"Y-y-you mean I'm dead."

"The witch within you is, but your vampire remains."

"That doesn't sound good."

"No, it doesn't." His lungs inflate and deflate, and I can hear the low rumble of his voice echoing from his chest as he talks.

"Why do you need Julian and Ethan?"

"Julian will control the vampire should it wake before we return your soul."

"And Ethan?"

Jack sighs. "We need his wolf to ground you. Wolves are of the earth, and you have connected. I'm hoping he will return your soul to your body."

"That's sort of sweet, I like Ethan's wolf, he's fun."

Jack's breath tickles my skin.

"You're not happy about the wolf thing, are you?"

"I think you need to rest."

"You mean, I'm asking too many questions."

A small smile tugs at Jack's lips. "That too."

We drift into silence as Jack holds me, his body rocking me in a slow, comforting rhythm. The pretty coloured lights continue to swirl, and I don't mention them again.

They are singing to me, each one calling my name. My fingers long to touch them. Given my previous experience in touching pretty colours that sing, I keep my fingers wrapped around the fabric of Jack's t-shirt.

"Ethan's here," I say.

Jack looks down at me.

"You can feel his spirit at Roseley?" His brows fold in on each other. "The connection is stronger than I thought."

"No, he's here." I point at the swirling colours as the wolf steps forward.

"Bloody hell!"

"What's wrong now?" I ask Jack.

"Nothing it took me by surprise."

The wolf's paws beat against the darkness, and the colourful waves pull away from him. His tail swings around him and his ears twitch. As I reach out for the wolf, the coloured lights descend on me. Ethan jumps, teeth bared, as he roars. The ribbons of colour shrink back. A warm pink tongue darts out, licking at my flesh, amber eyes hold my gaze.

"Hello, you." I lean over and wrap my arms around the wolf, breathing in his essence.

Jack's arms fall away as the wolf's nose nudges me to my feet. On shaking legs, I stand before the creature at my side, my hand grabbing at his thick pelt.

"You need to go with the wolf, I can't come with you," Jack says as he stands. "Take care of her."

A growl rumbles like thunder from Ethan's wolf, and without thinking I climb up on his back, laying my head against his fur and wrapping my arms around his neck. Snuggling into the wolf, a smile dances across my lips.

"Thank you for coming." I lay a small kiss on his fur as we move across the darkness.

The colours stop calling my name, their song dying with each step the wolf takes. Darkness gives way to a bright light. My eyelids snap closed against its glare. Our essences mingle, and without conscious thought, I pour my soul's energy into the wolf that carries me from the plane of the dead, back to the living.

The bond we share strengthens and I take comfort from it.

Chapter Thirteen

Eyes snapping open, I find Julian perching on the edge of my bed. Nathaniel stands next to him and at my feet lays the wolf. The spot where Jeremiah sleeps is empty.

I frown, and the wolf raises his head, amber eyes meeting mine.

"How long was I out for?"

"Four days." Julian places a hand over mine.

The wolf comes to my side and I wrap my arm around him, sitting up. Four days. Blimey, that's worrying.

Nathaniel inclines his head at the wolf. "He hasn't left your side since he brought you back."

"God help him, but I think he likes me." I snuggle deeper into his fur.

"See what I mean." Jack mists into view. "He isn't a puppy Alice."

I cup the wolf's face. "It's not nice to lick your lips at the word puppy, you'll get into serious trouble eating cute puppies."

The wolf blinks.

"You need to do something about this." Jack tells Nathaniel and Julian.

It seems I've woken up in the middle of a conversation, to find I'm the primary subject.

Whatever the problem is, Jack's agitation is clear.

"What have I done wrong now?" The ghost's pacing is making me dizzy.

Nathaniel shoots the marching spook a heated glare. "Ignore him, you're awake, that's all that matters."

Jack's brows disappear into his shaggy hair. "Yeah, right."

Baring his teeth, a rumble emits from the wolf's throat.

"I don't think he likes you, Jack," I say

"I'm sure he doesn't. But he still needs to sort himself out."

"OK, you're giving me a headache, stop walking and tell me what's going on?"

"It's nothing, Alice. Jack is being his normal irritating self," Julian reassures me.

Jack opens his mouth, but the look on Nathaniel's face makes his jaw snap shut.

"Let's give you a chance to dress while we let your aunt and Polly know you're awake," Nathaniel says walking to the door.

Julian pats my hand as he stands. "At least the gnome can stop fretting. He's more irksome than normal."

I have a hard time convincing myself that the grumpy gnome cares.

His concern is more about his own arse than anyone else's welfare. Old grandad, the Seelie King blar... blar... blar... will call for shorty's neck on a block, if the gnome's actions interfere with his plans.

My near-death experience wasn't the gnome's fault. "Arthur isn't to blame. He told me not to touch the line."

Nathaniel shakes his head. "Arthur allowed his prejudice to cloud his judgement. The red ley line is a bloodline. It's a siren of death to a vampire. If he'd told Dot, she could have protected you. He didn't, and you almost died."

"We'll let you get dressed." Julian stands, following Nathaniel out the door.

Jack looks annoyed as he mists out.

"Well, what do you think of that?" Amber eyes meet mine.

"You want to eat Arthur, don't you?" The wolf licks his lips. "He's going to be tough you know and pulverising him won't tenderise the gnome and make him more palatable."

The wolf blinks.

"It's not about that, is it?" His ears twitch.

I ruffle his coat as I swing my feet from the duvet. The wolf flops on the bed as I make my way into the bathroom.

****

I enter the kitchen, and the wolf leaves my side, deeming me in safe hands. Aunt Dot turns, beaming at me. Before she can throw her arms round me, I pull out a chair and sit next to Jack.

"What are you looking for?"

"Hm…"

I tap the Book of Shadows. "What are you looking for?"

"Jack's looking for a trigger word spell to protect you, dear." Aunt Dot places a cup of camomile tea in front of me.

"Huh?"

"We use them to form a protection circle rather than magnetic chalk." Jack chunters, his eyes glued to the pages.

"I know that, but why do you have to look it up if you already know how to do it?"

Aunt Dot lays a hand on my shoulder. "We want to adapt the trigger word, so the circle remains up when you travel through the ley lines. It saves having to use a charm each time."

I look at Jack. "Can you do that?"

His hands hit the table. Even though they make no sound, the gesture highlights his irritation at my constant questioning.

"That's what I'm trying to find out."

"You're getting as grumpy as Arthur." I point out.

"Humph…"

The smell of cooking meat fills the air and my tummy rumbles, reminding me I haven't eaten in four days.

Arthur's clogs announce his arrival.

Is that relief I see etched on his face - I wonder?

"It's good you're awake." The gnome's eyes stare at the floor.

I refrain from commenting. The large plate of sausage sandwiches helping to refocus my attention.

Aunt Dot slides out a chair as she looks where Jack is pointing.

"Time is ticking. The Seelie King…"

"Don't push it, Arthur." He scowls at my interruption. "I'm well aware of the time loss and what's required of me, I don't need the constant reminder."

"It was motivation."

I snort at the gnome. "Incentive doesn't start with The Seelie King… blar… blar."

There is a lot of whispering between Jack and Aunt Dot. Pages turn and Jack points at something.

"See Dot, I knew there was a way." A smile spreads over his lips.

"Well done, Jack." Aunt Dot sits back in her chair.

"Are you going to tell us, or just sit there basking in your own glory?" I ask.

"Alice!" My cheeks warm at my aunt's warning over my rudeness.

"Ghosts always have a point to prove." Arthur motions at the sun. "That'll be going down by the time you tell us."

It's unfair that Arthur's rudeness only earns him a sharp look from Aunt Dot.

Jack's lips slide into a self-conceited smile as he stares at the gnome. "Careful Arthur, I wouldn't want you getting ahead of yourself, one day you might lose it to your precious king. I wonder which spike it will adorn."

Arthur's hands fly to his neck, and he strokes his beard.

The smile never leaves Jack's lips as he turns his attention back to the book, tapping a finger against the page.

"Right, I think we're ready to begin." His eyes cut my way. "Alice, I need you to think up a trigger word. It must be something you relate to on a personal level. If you have a strong connection to it, no one can use it against you."

Everyone is staring at me, and pressure is mounting. Under normal circumstances, people have the comfort of time to cogitate such matters. Me, I get seconds. "Rodin."

The gnome's fist hits the table. "What kind of magical word is that?"

"No one said it had to be magical," I snap at Arthur.

"Don't worry dear it will do, the principal thing is that you have some intimate connection to the word."

"Rodin was the name of our black Labrador when I was growing up." My explanation doesn't help to wipe the look of horror from the little man's face.

Jack leans over. "Then Rodin's a good word."

Arthur huffs but remains silent.

Aunt Dot stands. "I'll just get the things we need."

"We're going to take the basic power word shield spell and give it more oomph." Jack explains as Aunt Dot races round the kitchen picking up herbs and candles.

Given that I have my aunt's knowledge, I know that a power word's function is to absorb harmful magic by creating an impenetrable shield.

"OK dear, I've got everything."

I look at the clutter on the table. Despite the many herbs and candles, my eyes linger on the scissors.

"You need my hair, don't you?"

"Just a strand or two, dear."

I grab the scissors and snip off a chunk. There is no point in arguing, it's best to get it over with than prolong the agony. She takes the offered strands and starts winding them round the oak twigs, before crushing them into the waiting herbs.

"Take the candle, Alice, and light it." Catching me looking for the matches, she shakes her head. "Use the Latin for lighten. You're a witch, using magic needs to become second nature."

Arthur sniggers and my cheeks warm, but being the professional newbie witch I am, I ignore the gnome.

Magic pulses through my veins.

"Alleviate."

A flame flickers to life and I turn, grinning at Arthur.

Aunt Dot hands me a small piece of paper. "Now repeat the spell I've written for you. When you've finished, you need to burn your hair within the candle's flame."

I take the paper, my eyes running over the words as I rehearse them in my head. The last thing I want is to get something wrong and compromise the spell.

Arthur would spend the rest of my life recalling my ineptitude.

Protect me from the call of those that wish me harm,
Keep me safe from their song,
Away from their harm, anger, and violence,
I call upon the Elements to stand guard over me,
Place me in your care and wrap me in your shield,
As I travel through the magic,
Far beneath the earth,
Never let their joyful whispers reach my ears,
As I will it, mote it be.

I place the hair mixture over the flame and a burst of light shoots upwards.

Dust settles over me before sinking beneath my skin. I watch the magic evaporate from sight, pulsating inside me.

"You know what would be good, don't you?" I say, tucking a lock of hair behind my ear.

A smile twitches at the corners of Jack's lips. "Go on, tell us."

"If we could spell away Aeden's hate of crossbreeds. It would save us a lot of time and effort."

Jack nods his head. "True, but some battles you have to fight the old-fashioned way. It makes you a better witch."

"Party pooper."

Jack laughs at me as Arthur slithers off his chair and leaves the kitchen.

Chapter Fourteen

Jasper's lesson in Krav Maga was interesting.

More fascinating was the fact I survived it.

Krav Maga is a military self-defence fighting systems developed for Israel Defence and Security Forces and works by using a combination of techniques.

The merging of aikido, boxing, wrestling, judo and karate uses real-world situations with extreme efficiency.

I'm informed by Jasper that Krav Maga's simple and practical techniques make it easy to pick up. By the time we finish, it is obvious I have a skill for turning the uncomplicated, complex. The vampire at my side is perspiring with frustration, and I'm just sweating like a pig.

"You'll get it."

His reassurance isn't convincing.

We move the training mats against the wall, and I make a silent promise to get up earlier tomorrow and practise on my own for a bit.

Julian and Ethan haven't returned, and Polly is out with the girls from work. I'm not sure where Aunt Dot has got to, and the gnome is entertaining himself in the stump. Even Jack has disappeared.

After consuming three meat feast pizzas and a stick of garlic bread, followed by a box of chocolates, I'm ready to call it a night. The clock dings out ten chimes as I drag my weary body upstairs.

Jeremiah sprawls across the bed, in his normal uncompromising pose. He blinks at me as I walk into the bathroom and turn on the shower. When I return the only movement, he's made is to uncurl his tail. I draw back the duvet and crawl into bed. The cat hisses digging his claws into the fabric as I shove him over. Our normal night-time battle finished, we both get comfortable and fall to sleep.

****

Morning comes too soon, and I can no longer ignore the pressure coming from my bladder. I emerge from the bathroom to find Jeremiah pawing at the door.

Roseley remains as quiet and uncluttered with bodies as it had last night. The cockerel has yet to crow and only the nocturnal creatures are awake. When you live in a house of predawn risers it brings a whole new meaning to getting up early.

After grabbing a snack, I make my way into the basement to practice Krav Maga. There are over two-hundred self-defences and combat techniques. Jasper's lesson yesterday covered thirty-one of the best fighting stances.

Since starting, I've landed on my bottom over forty times and have now decided that fate is telling me to practice the ground defensive position. Why fight it?

My stomach rumbles as I enter the kitchen, washed and changed I feel better about today's accomplishments. Krav Maga may still baffle me, however, I have worked through one of Jasper's routines without my arse meeting the PU leather matting.

Aunt Dot has been busy since I last visited, and a fresh-baked fruit loaf waits for my consumption. Loaded with butter and cheese and carved into eight thick slices, I sit down at the table. Polly is right about the food bill and it's nice not to worry about it. At least living at Roseley has one perk to it.

The Book of Shadows sits on the kitchen table. Curiosity draws me to it. Careful not to get grease on the book, I wipe my hands on my jeans before running my fingers over the dark green leather. The five-pointed star of the pentagram symbolising the four elements points upwards, drawing energy into it. My hands hover above and magic hums, absorbing beneath my skin.

Within the book's binding is an ornate scrying mirror.

Symbols for communication, divination and solution run along the heavy metal frame and sunlight bounces off the obsidian glass. The mirror throbs with energy.

"I don't suppose you've seen Julian?"

"Ah…" The mirror clatters onto the table at the unfamiliar voice.

"Did I make you jump?" The voice sings out in soft feminine tones.

A beautiful vampire leans against the kitchen door, a smile playing across her red lips. She pushes away from the wooden frame, throwing back her long blonde hair. It's so straight you could use it as a ruler. I would kill for hair like that. Not in the literal sense. On second thought, having hair that has a tendency to frizz at will, perhaps it wouldn't take much to persuade me.

Violet eyes blink at me as I continue to stare.

"No… I mean yes. And no, I don't know where Julian is." I stutter.

"Never mind, I came to see you." The graceful predator walks forward.

The vampire's soft flushed skin confirms she's eaten.
That said, we all like to take part in snacks.

I'm aware the vamp will have noticed the increase of
my heart rate. "Why would you want to see me?"

The vampire smiles, flashing her teeth. She's now toying with me. A multitude of questions run through my head.
How did she get past the crystals? Where's Aunt Dot? Has
she eaten her? What about Julian? The house is silent; too silent. What I should think is *run*.

Before conscious thought can intercede the witch in me
takes action. "Rodin"

My protection circle snaps into place and the vampire
stops. A puzzled look falls across her perfect features. Hand
on hip, she cocks her head.

"OK, I've gone about this wrong." Her brows meet.
"I'm Emily Harris."

"And?"

From her expressions there is an expectation that the
name means something to me. Adrenalin is flooding my system, and the brain is too busy working out its next move to
consider the relevance of Emily Harris.

"I'm Julian's girlfriend. You know, the tall brooding
chap, who's your brother?"

"Oh…" I nod my head, remembering why the name
sounds familiar.

Emily looks surprised when I don't lower my circle.
Never meeting Julian's girlfriend, there is nothing to confirm
she is *that* Emily. This could be one of Julian's sneaky tests.
One I'm not falling for.

"Not to be rude. But why should I believe you?" It isn't difficult to sound brave within a protection circle.

Jack mists into view, his translucent body solidifying.

"Are you two going to fight?" He sounds excited at the prospect. "Hang on, let me get a better view. I don't want to miss anything."

"You're so funny my sides are splitting." Emily tosses back her mane, shooting Jack a murderous glare. "I'd never put on a show for you."

Eyes darting between them, I lower my circle.

"You wouldn't know fun if it hit you, Em." Jack snarls.

"Don't beat yourself up about it, Jack. It's just a shame that when you died, you didn't stay dead. At least you could have let me celebrate, before you came back to haunt this world."

"Great, you two are arguing again. How many centuries are going to pass before you learn to get on?" Arthur strides into the kitchen, pulling out a chair he rests his hands on his protruding stomach.

"This has nothing to do with you," Emily hisses.

"You'd know all about grudges, Arthur. The name Martin ring any bells?" The little man's face turns red at Jack's words.

"Nice one." Emily acknowledges.

Jack grins. "Thanks."

The sudden change in their attitudes is startling.

"Jack, Emily, it's good to see you two getting on," Julian says as he walks into the cluttered kitchen.

The ghost shrugs. "I wouldn't go that far, more enemy of my enemy."

Julian nods in the gnome's direction. "The enemy being Arthur, I take it."

"I am not the enemy."

"U-huh." Emily and Jack say.

The gnome huffs at them.

"Julian?" Aunt Dot calls walking into the kitchen. A lump of crystal in her hand. "Ah, there you are."

The kitchen is overcrowded and Jeremiah, not being a cat to miss an opportunity for food, pads into the room a loud *meow*, emanating from his mouth.

"I think the pooch needs feeding," Jack observes as Jeremiah looks at his captivated audience.

"He's a cat, not a dog." I correct Jack as Jeremiah makes a dash for the food I've put down.

Aunt Dot picks up The Book of Shadows. "We'll go to the conservatory."

"I like it here."

"No one was asking you, Arthur." The gnome remains where he is ignoring Jack.

"There's no need to move on our account, I'm taking Alice out for lunch," Emily announces.

It sounds sublime, time away from Roseley, studies, grumpy gnomes, and there's food.

"You are?" My excitement bubbles.

"Take her to The Blood and Bone, you'll be safe there," Julian says pulling out a chair. "If you and Arthur can get along long enough, Jack, we will make a start."

Aunt Dot sets the book back down on the table.

Curious, I look at the foursome. "What are you up to?"

"It's nothing dear." Aunt Dot removes the scrying mirror from the book.

"And it's going to take four of you to do nothing?"

"We can't sit around and wait for you. All you do is sleep." Arthur's cutting remark sets my teeth on edge.

"Don't you start on me, you grumpy little turnip. I've been working hard. And besides, it's not all my fault I almost died."

Arthur's ears redden. "I told you not to touch it."

"And it was your job to watch me! Besides, Nathaniel said it was your fault."

"Since when did you side with Nathaniel?"

"Since now."

Julian slams his hands down on the table, and I jump. "Alice, go with Emily. Arthur, shut up."

"Fine by me." I turn to leave. "Come on, Emily."

Chapter Fifteen

The cool autumn wind whips at my hair and clothes as I step out the front door. Arms circling around my waist, preventing the wind from sapping my heat, I peek through wayward strands.

Emily prowls over to me, her eyes checking for danger. "Come on, we'll take my car."

Lights flash on the silver Jaguar sports car. I grunt at the brand-new Jag, wondering why these people can't have a crappy car.

Without a word, I climb inside, sinking into the leather seat. There's a sense that my backside is too close to the surface of the road. The elongated nose of the vehicle is begging to be broken. I am an uncomplicated girl with no liking for cars that roar across the tarmac.

Emily beams at my side. "Beautiful isn't she. Julian got her for my birthday. I've always been a car junkie, and speed is one of my demons. This baby can do two hundred and fifty miles an hour."

When it was my birthday Mum paid for a new haircut, and we went out for lunch.

"If you like speed and flash, why not a Ferrari?" It's the only car I can think of that's not just fast but says *'I've got too much money.'*

Emily's nose wrinkles and I'm staggered by her reaction. Who would have thought owning a Ferrari could bring forth such repulsion?

"Too flashy, they're cheap too." My eyes bulge at her definition of cheap. "If I wanted to make a statement, I'd have asked for a Bugatti Veyron. That baby purrs like a kitten and bolts like a cheetah."

Her lips twist. "I can't afford the attention, and Julian would go nuts if I ended up behind bars again. The Jag's the safe choice, but she's a good solid car."

Emily isn't kidding when she says she's a speed demon. Before I can think better of my decision to let her drive, the car screeches off the drive. Despite having at least three low gears, the Jaguar goes straight from zero to a hundred. Gravel flies, and she doesn't stop as we hit the junction. A car horn sounds as we leap into its path, flying off at warp speed and kicking up dust as we disappear from view.

"Don't worry. If they've time to sound the horn, they've time to stop." Not sharing her optimism, I sink my nails into the leather seat.

Scenery blurs at an alarming rate, and I'm feeling carsick. Emily laughs at me but doesn't ease off the accelerator. The smell of burning rubber hangs in the air. I only hope that wherever The Blood and Bone is, it isn't too far.

If I wasn't putting all my effort into keeping the fruit loaf down, I would scream in her ear Georgia Brown style. The singer has an eight octave, G10 range. In fact, the vocal note is so high that it's not classed as a musical note but a frequency. Think of a kettle whistling.

Vampires have very sensitive hearing and I know for a fact they all hate her range. I played it on YouTube to get back at Julian, and it got his attention.

The Jag screeches to a stop and I open my eyes to find a sheep staring at me, paralysed in place. It should be grateful it isn't sitting in the passenger seat.

"That was fun." Emily turns, taking in my skin's green tinge. "Sorry, did I go too fast?"

I blink at her, stunned. *Did she go too fast?* "No, I always feel as if my gut has left my body and is hitching a ride back to me."

Emily blinks at my sarcasm. "Your funny."

"So I've been told." Not that I'm feeling funny, just relieved.

"Come on, I'm starving, and Henry is the best chef ever to grace our tiny planet."

I open the door and fall onto the concrete. Pleasure floods my system and I now know why the Pope kisses the ground when he gets off a plane.

Emily's heels hit the concrete, unconcerned, she throws back her blonde hair and inhales. "You'll love it at The Blood and Bone, the food is amazing. Henry studied under the careful guidance of Procopio Cutò."

"Never heard of him," I mutter, climbing to my feet, and dusting off my jeans.

"Before your time. Procopio Cutò was an Italian chef from Sicily and founded Café Procope in 1686. So you know, Café Procope is the oldest surviving café in Paris."

"I've never been to Paris either."

"Poor Henry, he has a heathen in his midst."

"Just because I've never been to Paris or heard of what's his name… Cut-Toe, doesn't make me uncivilised."

"You try telling Henry that. And it's Cutò."

"Whatever." Emily throws me one of her gorgeous smiles and I'm betting dead and alive she's popular with the men.

After the car ride from hell, I'm aware I should dislike her, but I don't. She has a warmth about her despite her predatory nature, proving the soul doesn't die when human life ends.

"Come on, time for Henry to meet you." She throws an arm over my shoulders, steering me towards the sixteenth century pub.

The delicate scent of food engulfs me in its sweet scent. My stomach answers its call regardless of its earlier turmoil.

I'm pleased to announce that the bloody skeletal mouth in which sits a large dripping bone where shadows with long claws hang back waiting, doesn't put me off. The pub sign commands your attention, leaving you wondering at the food served. But my appetite is growing, and while gruesome and explicit, it does little to calm the rumbling in my stomach.

A quick look at the number of diners tells me we are going to be lucky to get a table. My first stop, however, is to remove the pressure from my bladder.

"Won't be a sec, I just need to use the bathroom." I leave Emily to get a table and follow the signs directing me to the 'Ladies'.

A silhouette of a woman sitting on a throne, wearing a crown signals I've reached my destination. Emily is leaning against the far wall as I walk out of the cubicle, making me jump. "Blimey! Have you ever thought of wearing a bell?" I wave a hand at her puzzled expression. "Never mind."

"Our tables ready."

I'm unsure if she's afraid I'll bolt, or despite Julian's re-assurance that The Blood and Bone is safe, something awful will occur if I'm left alone for too long.

Emily threads her arm through mine and leads me to the back of the dining room. Separated from the other diners is a large table set for two. I'm not sure how Emily has wangled it, but I'm grateful.

"Wow, this is great." The heat from the fire warms my skin as I slide into a chair. "You did well to snag this table."

I take a second to appreciate my surroundings. The interior oozes with the authenticity of its heritage. As Henry was alive in the sixteenth century, this shouldn't surprise me, but it does.

Solid, heavy wooden furniture scatter across the vast floor, and tapestries hang from the walls. I'm surprised to see the soft buzz of auras coming off the shadows. It's as if the property is alive.

"Henry always keeps this table empty for visiting guests and speaking of the devil..." She winks.

Henry's smile is infectious as he weaves his rounded belly between the diners, stopping to smile and say a few words as he moves on. His skin carries the pink glow of a vampire well fed. The double-breasted whites stretch over his protruding stomach and his toque Blanche sits to attention upon his head.

I take an instant liking to the merry master chef and my lips twitch into a smile as he stops at our table.

"At last. It is good of you to come. I feared I might not have time to meet you. Well, not until we've sorted out the whole messy affair with MAMS." He raises his hands in wonder. "Why do they fight, why do they not enjoy the simple pleasures life has to offer? Excellent food, like life is for savouring."

His chubby fingers grip the chair as he leans closer. "You have made our houses complete. It is a shame it is under such terrible circumstances."

"Huh? What do you mean made them complete?" I ask, the skin along my brow wrinkling.

Emily sends Henry a cool look, which does nothing to remove the grin from the chefs face. Her hands run along the wooden table, as she contemplates whether she's going to enlighten me.

"News of your existence has spread, raising concern over your safety and not just from MAMS. Other vampire houses want to turn you into a full vampire to boost their house's power. We're a shallow bunch sometimes, and jealousy is rife. With Nathaniel and Julian combining their lines, they have intensified their power. Through your bonds, they hope you will receive the power from both bloodlines. It is a shrewd move. Sharing power is very rare amongst vampires."

Henry remains silent as Emily explains vampire politics. "Nathaniel and Julian are different from other master vampires, as the bond they shared in life also ties them in death. You are their central bond. Their connection to you has reinforced their link, elevating their power, and standing within the vampire community. This power also allows vampires such as Henry to join their line, even though they didn't sire him. You can imagine how the other masters feel about this. The old ones are getting twitchy."

"My apologies, I thought you knew. They keep me in the kitchen because I have a rather big mouth."

"Don't worry about it." I raise my hand, batting away his concerns. "I've been so busy catching up with things, that no one's had time to go through the fundamentals with me."

It's a lie, but I won't take my annoyance out on Henry. I'll save it until I get back to Roseley for Julian and Nathaniel.

"So what's the chef's choice today?" I ask, changing the subject.

The smile returns to Henry's face. "Take the lamb it's intense flavour will make your tase buds dance." He pats the side of his nose. "This tells me a thousand things, more than my tase buds ever could have."

"Then the lamb it is."

"Good… good. Let me get a glass of Cabernet Sauvignon for you. It's rich velvet taste will enhance the flavour of the lamb. And for you, Emily, I have a warm glass of AB negative."

"Yum… my mouth is watering already, Henry." She smacks her lips together and I try not to gag at the thought of her indulging in a pint of blood while I sip at my red wine.

"I shall send Anna over with your drinks while I prepare your meal."

Within moments of Henry's departure, a tall skinny woman marches over to our table. The sour look on her face gives me the impression she'd rather chew on my heart then serve our drinks.

Large goblets hit the table and the contents threaten to spill over the top. On instinct, I shrink back into the chair to protect my cream jumper.

"Here." The word is ground out as Anna stares at me. Hate radiates from her muddy eyes.

Emily grabs her glass, raising it to her lips. "Anna, you're staring."

"It's the smell coming off her." I refrain from sniffing my armpits.

"Play nice Anna, you know how Henry feels about you killing the diners."

"Show her off while you can. The protection this place offers is temporary." Anna's voice drops like acid rain.

Unconcerned Emily laughs. "Come on, Anna, even you must see the irony in this situation." Emily spreads out her hands. "So very close, and yet you can't hurt one hair on her head."

I smooth down my hair, my hands falling to my neck as Anna stares at it. Anna's fingers curl round the tray and I wonder if she's thinking of using it to remove my head.

Emily smiles. "It's a good job Aeden isn't here. He'd combust on the spot…" Her smile broadens. "Hm… maybe it's a shame he's not here. It would save us the trouble of killing him."

I grab my wine and take a good slurp, wishing Emily would stop poking at Anna.

"I'm surprised you can stand the smell. You half-breed's stink." Anna points a finger at me, not that I require the clarification.

"Tut-tut Anna, your evil side is showing, now run along before you put Alice off her lamb." Emily ushers her from the table. "Oh, when you bring the food, make sure a smile graces those ruby lips of yours. You're turning the blood sour."

The pen in Anna's hand snaps. "When the half-breed's dead, you won't be able to stop me from smiling."

In a whirl of anger, she stomps away from our table.

"Hey! Not so fast. I'll have a refill." Emily calls after her.

Anna's footsteps falter, but she doesn't stop.

Emily leans in. "Do you think she heard me?"

"I think the whole pub heard you."

"Good. Well, that was fun, wasn't it?"

"I guess that depends on your definition of the word."

Emily's delicate shoulders lift. "She's been asking for it for a while. I don't know why Henry puts up with her."

I'm confused why Anna is still walking this earth. "What I don't get, is that you know she's part of MAMS and you've done nothing about it. This might be me being selfish, but why the heck is she roaming free? It's obvious she's your key in. You could use her to get to Aeden, rather than the half-breed as bait. That's me, just so you know."

"If it was that simple, I'd be glad to take her out myself. Politics and war are a delicate balance, Alice. We're not barbarians."

"Politics won't save my life. And if you keep winding her up, she'll kill me before I get to eat the lamb and Henry's gone to a lot of trouble."

My fingers grip at the goblet. "If Anna has her way, I'll never get to find out how good Cut-Toe's training was."

"It's Cutò."

"Yeah, him too."

Emily leans back, draining her glass. "You worry too much, you're safe here, no one's going to kill you."

"That's easy for you to say."

"No, it's a fact. Henry had The Blood and Bone built on an old druid burial site in the late 1600s. Whether he knew about the graveyard, I'm not sure. The spirits weren't best pleased about the pub's location at first, but once Henry has his mind set on something, it's hard to change it. He's very stubborn. So he gave the spirits a way out of their loneliness, to walk on the surface of the earth once more. Look around you, see all the shadows floating about. Far too many for them to be natural, don't you think?"

This would explain the extra auras.

I look at the shadows, noticing the layer of darkness that coats them. Even in death they can't get away from the forces of their evil deeds. Dark magic always leaves a stain.

Some of the shadows sit at tables, others hover like hungry hawks ready to pounce. It appears The Blood and Bone is a gathering place for seedy spirits.

"Had Anna tried to, or even killed you, not that I would have let her, the spirits would have taken her down to their grave to feast on her." I swallow.

Emily laughs. "It sounds dramatic, doesn't it? They're harmless so long as you don't kill someone. Besides, you can't blame them for wanting a little company."

A shiver runs down my spine.

"You're worrying again, Alice. Forget about them and enjoy your lamb when it comes. The Blood and Bone is neutral ground."

Chapter Sixteen

The lamb is gorgeous. My lips smack and my tase buds tingle in delight. The portion size was more than adequate, even for me. I used up a lot of nervous energy on the way here, increasing my appetite.

Content, I sit back and contemplate dessert, my teeth nibbling at my lips. Dessert is proving a hard choice, and I'm wondering if it would be greedy to ask for a slice of everything.

"What do you think of Henry's cooking?" Emily's comment breaks through my thoughts.

"Bliss."

"See, what did I tell you?"

I'm not about to argue. "The only problem I have now is pudding, they all sound gorgeous."

Emily raises a hand, and a man walks over, a cheery smile lingers on his lips. It's nice that not everyone thinks I smell or wants to kill me.

"Ready for dessert?" The man asks.

"I can't decide what to have they all sound delicious."

"How about a taster board of them all?" I like this man, he makes sense.

"That would be fantastic, but not too small a piece. Oh, and would it be OK to have some of those chocolate truffles I saw someone get with a coffee, but I'll have a tea with mine." I turn to Emily. "Do I sound gluttonous?"

"You sound like Henry's dream guest."

The stylus pen taps on the screen as the man sends my request to the kitchen before turning to Emily. "Can I get you anything?"

"Nothing for me, thanks. Julian would kill me if I'm caught blood drunk behind the wheel." The man nods and walks away.

"I didn't know you could get drunk on blood."

"Too much in one go gives a vampire the jitters. That's why newbie vamps lose control, their thirst for blood is insatiable, making them OD. It's hard to bring them down from it. It can take months. Mentors help them through the transition."

After experiencing Nathaniel's thirst for blood when he'd turned, I appreciate how overwhelming it could be.

Emily is an enigma and not the girlfriend I would have associated with my brother. She seems too carefree for him.

"How did you and Julian meet?" I ask, finishing off my wine.

"Jack introduced us."

"So you knew he was a warlock?"

"No, but when you meet someone at nursery, it's a case of, *get off, that's my toy, or I'm gonna stab you with this plastic knife*, then anything else. We grew up together, got into mischief together, and terrorised the neighbourhood, together." A smile touches her lips at the memory.

"When I found out Jack was a warlock, I was so angry. We were more like brother and sister than friends. I felt he'd betrayed me. Worse, was the knowledge that he didn't trust me enough to confide in. I thought we told each other everything."

Emily shakes her head. "Funny how it still hurts today." I don't interrupt, fearing I'd say the wrong thing.

"Julian had been visiting for a while. His sudden appearance didn't make much sense. Jack said he was a colleague from work. I can always tell when he's lying. Besides, Julian didn't look the *buddy* type. When Julian and I started dating, Jack went ballistic, and the truth came out. Furious, I got in Julian's Maserati and lost control of it, ending up nose first in a ditch."

"Bloody hell."

Emily smiles. "You would think after that I'd slow down. But speed and I have always had an unhealthy relationship. When they found me, I was bleeding out. The impact sent me straight through the windscreen, I was dying. I remember Jack shouting and screaming at Julian to do something. I was floating in and out of consciousness, so I can't recall what changed Julian's mind. Believe it or not, I used to be a vegetarian. Got to see the irony in me becoming a vampire."

"Do you think you and Jack will ever be friends?"

"That's a hard one. We were never friends, to begin with, we were family. I still love him, and I know he feels the same about me. The bickering is a way for us to communicate without giving away how we feel. We've been like this for a hundred years. It works well for us. Keeps the distance between how we feel and stops it emerging. Despite the time lapse, we aren't ready to deal with our emotions head-on."

"It seems a shame."

Emily shrugs. "We all have our own way of dealing with things."

My dessert arrives along with my tea and truffles. Mouth-watering, I lose myself to the yumminess of the sweet delicacy placed in front of me. The moans of pleasure emitting from me make Emily laugh.

Henry comes waddling over as I place the last truffle in my mouth. My jeans contain a high stretch, allowing my stomach to expand.

"The pleasure on your face is like a thousand thank you's. It is good to cook for someone who appreciates my efforts."

"I didn't know food could taste that good."

"You're too kind." Henry beams.

A commotion comes from the kitchen. "I think you're wanted Henry." Emily says.

"Tsk… they behave like children. Demons, they are a temperamental lot but make good chef's." He throws the tea towel he's holding over his shoulder as he turns to leave. "I shall bid you a safe journey. With this one you will need it." He points a chubby finger at Emily.

"It's not speed that kills, it's the driver. And driving I do very well."

Henry chuckles as he walks away.

"I think I'd best make a pit stop before I get back in the car, so my bladder doesn't feel the need to empty on the leather seating in fear."

Emily frowns. "You're overreacting."

"Keep telling yourself that. Being mortal has its downside."

As I get up to leave, I'm struck by a sober thought. "How many cars have you crashed since turning? On second thought, best you don't answer that."

Emily's laugh follows me into the Ladies.

I walk out of the cubicle and collide with Anna. "Crikey, I wish people would let me pee in peace."

"What's wrong half-breed, no big evil vampire around to protect you." Anna's voice is like venom as she circles round me.

"Excuse me." I'm not sure what her problem is other than hating me.

Our shoulders collide as I walk to the sink and wash my hands.

"What's wrong? Nothing to say now you're on your own?"

"I had nothing to say the first time."

Anna's lips draw into a thin line. "We're going to kill you. Do you want to know my personal favourite way of killing you?"

"I like surprises too much, don't spoil it."

It's like I haven't spoken.

"I want to cut you into tiny pieces. Starting with pulling out your fingernails, then cutting off your fingers five millimetres at a time."

Anna has put a lot of thought into my death.

"I don't mind waiting when you lose consciousness from the pain. Wouldn't want you to miss what I'm going to chop off next. By the time I've finished, you'll be pleading for me to end your putrid existence."

"It's good to know you've given it a lot of thought. We all need something to fantasise about," I say.

At the moment, she's all talk. According to Emily, while I'm at The Blood and Bone, there isn't anything she can do to me. And I'm not about to let her scare me. Well, maybe a bit.

Her fingers dig into my hair, tightening their hold. A black shadow drifts in, floating about us in a frenzy of excitement.

"Let go, Anna. This isn't the place for you to be playing big bad... whatever you are."

"What are you planning on doing about it?" Her breath tickles my neck.

"Me? Nothing, but you're gathering a crowd."

She pauses, her fingers releasing their grip as she notices the shadows congregating around us.

Colour drains from her face. "You're not worth it."

Disappointment radiates from the shadows.

"You should tell that to Aeden."

The door slams behind her, and I massage my head as Emily walks in, crossing her arms.

"Well?"

"What?" I throw my hands in the air. "You started it at the table, it's not my fault she came back for more."

"Hm... maybe you're right, but it was fun, wasn't it?"

"You've a strange sense of fun, Emily."

"It's not that strange when you're as old as me. Come on, we'd best get you back before Julian worries about you." Emily hands me my coat. "He's got this crazy notion about my driving; I don't know where he gets these ideas from."

"I can enlighten you."

Emily sends me a smile. "No, ignorance is bliss."

"You want to tell Arthur that?"

The temperature outside has fallen, and rain is falling. The roads are going to be slippery. I look at the Jag. Even the sheep have gone seeking shelter.

"I've never driven a sports car. It might be fun."

Emily shakes her head. "You've had too much wine."

"Just a glass and the food will have absorbed some of it, plus my metabolic rate is so fast the alcohol soon leaves my system."

"Nice try. Come on, get in the car. I promise to go slower."

Defeated, I lower myself into the passenger seat.

Emily hits the accelerator, and we fly onto the road. My stomach lurches, and I close my eyes, wanting this to be over.

A car beeps and I refuse to unglue my eyelids and see the horror unfold. I'm unsure of Emily's definition of *slower*. The dictionary defines slow as moving at a low speed. Over a hundred does not meet the dictionary's criteria of *slow*.

Chapter Seventeen

By the time we arrive at Roseley, I'm doubtful there's any rubber left on the Jag's tyres.

Gravel shoots up, peppering the paintwork as we skid to a sudden stop and I promise myself that once my legs have stopped shaking, I'm jumping out and singing *hallelujah*.

Emily turns in the driver's seat, a frown marring her beautiful face. "I didn't go over a hundred and ten."

She must have missed the various speed signs that didn't exceed sixty. When we'd cut through the village, I remember seeing the number thirty displayed within the ring of red.

Before I can mention this, the front door opens, and Arthur walks out.

I groan. "Why did we get lumbered with Grumpy? There have to be nicer gnomes in Faerieland."

Emily shakes her head. "None that kisses arse like he does."

"I blame it on the amount of practice he gets."

"No," Emily corrects me, "he's a natural arse kisser."

Arthur comes to a stop a few feet from the car, placing his hands on his hips. My brain is already working out what I've done wrong.

"Aeden has taken Dot." He shouts.

"Shit!" I open the car door and run towards Roseley.
The front door bangs against the wall as I enter.

"Julian."

My first stop is the kitchen which is empty.

"Julian!"

Heart hammering I run into the living room.

Julian looks up from where he and Ethan are talking as I enter, Emily at my back. "Where has he taken her?" I demand.

"Arthur." Julian roars.

"There's no need to shout. My hearing is fine." The little man complains as he pushes past us.

"There's every reason. I told you not to say anything."

"She was going to find out at some point."

"There was no need to broadcast it."

Arthur sits in front of the log burner. "It's not a secret. Aeden knows he's got Dot."

Ethan steps forward. "Yes, but until you announced it, they didn't know we'd found out. Now, they're expecting our retaliation."

Arthur huffs at Ethan, dismissing his concerns.

"How did he get her?" I ask.

"She went to pick up some supplies." Julian waves his hand at the sofa. "Sit down, Alice, there isn't anything we can do right now. Nathaniel will be here soon, and we'll see what the chatter is in Faerieland."

In silence Emily walks over to Julian, placing a hand on his knee. The tension in the room is building. Sitting, I stare at my brother. "But Aeden could do anything to her."

Ethan lays a comforting hand on my shoulder. "At the moment, she's too useful to him."

"I'll contact Henry in a minute and find out if Anna has mentioned anything. The decision to take Dot felt spur of the moment, so she might be of no help to us," Julian says.

Jumping off the sofa I glare at Julian. "You can't trust her. She's part of MAMS."

He sends me an icy stare. "I'm well aware of Anna's divided loyalties."

"I don't get it. Aunt Dot is who knows where, and I don't even want to think what Aeden is doing to her, while Anna's walking round free as a bird."

"Anna is far from *free*. She is of great use to us."

"What use can she be to you?" Julian isn't used to justifying himself.

His annoyance thrums through our bond as his face remains unaffected.

"Anna's been with Henry for over two hundred years. During that time she has shared his blood. The blood keeps her young and alive, but it also allows us power over her. She doesn't know it, but Henry is hypnotising her for information."

My mouth falls open. "Oh…"

"Anna is a sorceress. A practitioner of the dark arts. She's not immortal. The blood she takes from Henry stops her body from crumbling to dust. Julian and Nathaniel have the power to take back the life force she digests." Ethan reaches for my hand, pulling me to his side. "Anna has forgotten this. She will die, Alice, but for now, we need the secrets she holds."

Ethan's eyes shine with the amber fire of his wolf, and I can feel its presence humming through our joined hands.

"Anna has signed her own death warrant, she's just too dumb to realise it." Emily says.

145

"As a master vampire, life and death are a delicate balance. While I cannot afford to show leniency, I must still abide by the politics that govern us. Not to indulge in the political games is to demonstrate weakness. Anna will die for her treachery. It is a simple matter of when," Julian's words do little to remove my concern.

The delicate scent of lilies and wolf fills the air and I turn to see Lucy leaning against the door frame ready to steak her claim on Ethan. While her posture appears casual her eyes shine with jealousy. I turn my head, dismissing her. Ethan is mine.

Never would I verbalise this. However, the emotion is there, and I know it's mutual between me and the wolf. As for the man, it's hard to say. Neither of us can deny the connection we feel for each other, but is it just chemistry toying with us? I wish I knew.

Hunger burns in Lucy's eyes, sighting her prey, she strides into the room. Her lips roll back as she snarls at me. My fingers entwine round Ethan's and I stare back at her, not prepared to back down.

"*Mine!*" The word echoes round my head.

"Lupin," Julian warns.

Ethan remains still at my side, his wolf waiting for Lucy to make her move.

Rage burns from her, as she prepares to attack me. Ethan's hand slips from mine.

The lupine screams as Ethan strikes, and his wolf roars. She hits the ground, whimpering at his feet, her eyelashes concealing her gaze.

"You forget your place." The growl of Ethan's wolf echoes in his voice.

Lucy crawls forward, her fingers pawing the rug.

"Leave!" The wolf dismisses her.

Lucy scurries to her feet, teeth flashing in my direction.

The wolf's power crashes down on the lupine. There is no snapping of electrically charged energy that vampires possess. Instead, a wolf's power rises from the earth. Strong. Resilient. It is more direct and throws itself at Lucy like a net.

A vampire power will nibble at all in the room, whereas a wolf's is singular in destination, touching those it needs to.

Lucy cringes, falling to the floor, her body shaking as she presses herself against the unrelenting surface. When Ethan speaks it is the wolf that talks. It's deep voice rumbling from his throat.

"Report to Ben, he will be expecting you. Now leave my sight."

Her head remains on the floor as the shaking in her limbs increases.

"No! P- please," Lucy begs.

"Do not make this worse."

I'm understanding the harshness of the supernatural world. It is a world of dominance, ruled with fear. Of survival. A weak leader cannot care for their flock, and lenience is a luxury.

Lucy never returns to her feet. She crawls from the room. Her tears hit the floor in a loud plop. Humans are the only ones who cannot hear tears fall. They are lucky.

Ethan pulls the mobile from his trouser pocket. "You have a new arrival. She is not to change this moon."

The hunter within Emily watches the lupine slither from the room. "Lucy's had this coming for a while."

"What will happen to her?" I ask.

"Ben will place her within the circle of The Morrigan," Ethan says sitting down next to me. "The Morrigan is the

147

shape-shifting Celtic Goddess of War, Fate and Death. You will know her as the patroness of magic, prophecy, witches, priestesses and revenge. At the next full moon, The Morrigan will prevent Lucy from answering Lycaon's call. While some see the mythological king of Arcadia as the god of wolves, he is just one element of our heritage, given to us when Zeus turned Lycaon into a wolf, because of his trickery. It is Lycaon's actions that bind us to the full moon."

Arthur opens his mouth, but Ethan ignores him.

"The Morrigan is a shifter of many forms and is the veritable goddess of were-animals."

"You've wasted enough time!"

"Shut up, Arthur." Julian snaps.

The gnome huffs, arms folding over his chest, jaw set at a stubborn angle. Before he can retaliate, the crunch of gravel echoes through the room.

Upon soundless footsteps, Emily sits next to me. Ethan stands, walking to the door. There is a pulse of power as he steps through the threshold into the hall, changing from man to wolf.

Only the Alpha has the power to change without the clicking and snapping of bones.

Their actions confirm something bad is heading our way.

In slow motion, Julian stands. "Set a circle, Alice. Emily, keep her safe."

Emily grips my arm as I go to follow Julian. "Set the circle, Alice."

"Rodin." Colour flickers over us as the protection circle snaps into place.

A feeling of impotence falls over me and my guilt rises. Memories of Mum fill my head.

A ball of fire hits the window, making me jump. The crystals respond to the attack and golden light bursts over Roseley. Rebounding off the crystal's protection, the flames fall to the ground.

In quick succession, magic hits the defensive shield of the crystals, and they hiss out their displeasure. I'm not sure how much fire they can take before they fall.

"Keep the circle in place, if Aeden and his men get through, Julian needs to know your protected," Emily says at my side.

My hands shake in fear and frustration. Arthur pales within the light of the fire. The confident, outspoken gnome is replaced by one riddled with terror.

Aeden's laughter fills the room as another fire ball hits the house. Cold sweat sits on my skin and I am transported back to the night Mum died. Images flash before me as I relive the horror of watching her die.

Emily's fingers dig into my flesh as she tries to pull me out of the memory.

"Come on Alice, come out to play, "Aeden sings.

My protection circle wavers.

"Don't Alice, he's trying to get a reaction out of you. At the moment the crystals are holding, but we can't be sure what else he has planned."

"I can't just sit here. Julian and Ethan are out there. I've got to do something."

How can I make her understand? I can't do nothing again and let Aeden kill another member of my family?

"You're doing more than sitting here, you're letting Ethan and Julian do their job."

"No, I'm not. I'm sat here like a lemon... I've lost Mum, I'm not prepared to lose Julian and Ethan."

Life is repeating itself, and again I'm taking no action to protect those I love.

In a burst of light, Jack appears. "You OK?"

Aeden's laugh cuts through the room. "Here Alice, come get your present."

I lower my circle and run for the door.

"Shit…" Emily charges towards me like a hurricane.

I hit the front door, flinging it open to see Aeden disappear in a flash of flames. On the ground is a white box.

"No!" I scream at the vacant spot, my boots clattering against the pebbles.

Emily's fingers close round my arm as I run. The cold hits me then Emily. The force of our colliding bodies sends us skidding over the gravel. We lose our balance as we slide, and I'm trapped beneath Emily's body as she pins me to the floor. Tiny stones dig into my back.

In one gigantic leap, Ethan is at my side.

Julian's boot comes into view as he walks over to us and the wolf nudges Emily, signalling she can get off me.

It's good to get my face out of the gravel and I take a lungful of clean air.

"I told you to wait inside."

There is nothing I can say to Julian, that will redeem me, so I remain silent.

We stand looking down at the box. With the danger gone, the gnome strides from the house to join us.

Arthur's clog taps against the box. "What's inside?"

"I don't know, but it smells of blood." My eyes don't leave the box as I speak.

"Do you want me to look?" Jack asks as we gather round the box.

"Be my guest." Julian stands back as Jack walks forward and buries his head inside.

In quick movements, he rocks back, flickering from view for a heartbeat. Whatever is in the container, it can't be good.

"Take it inside. Alston is going to want to know about this." Jack isn't looking so good.

"What is it?"

"Not now, Alice, inside." Julian picks up the box and walks to the front door.

Emily's hand presses into the middle of my back and the wolf nudges my leg, leaving me little choice but to follow them.

The night has gone still.

Not even the natural sounds of nature echo within its darkness.

Chapter Eighteen

The metallic smell of blood coats the air as we stand staring at the white box on the kitchen table. Inside is Aunt Dot's left hand.

Julian and Ethan are in the living room, bringing Nathaniel up to speed.

Things are turning bad — quick.

Despite their reassurances that Aunt Dot is alive, I'm no longer convinced.

Emily and Jack stand next to me. The gnome has retreated to his stump to regain control over his emotions. His agitated state was affecting us, and we needed a break from the constant dribble pouring from his mouth.

My fingers wind round my hair. "I can't remember is Aunt Dot left or right-handed?"

"She's right-handed," Jack says, scratching at his jaw.

"That's good, she can still write when we find her."

Emily looks up at me but doesn't comment.

The sound of clogs echo and I prepare myself for one of Arthur's cutting remarks.

"If you're not careful, the next delivery will be her head." The gnome says as he approaches the table.

My lungs deflate and air gushes from them.

Alston made my role clear and even though it pains me to side with Arthur, he's right. I have dallied for too long.

"Dot's not dead." Julian's voice silences the gnome.

"We don't know that. There's every chance Arthur's right." My hair knots round my fingers as my worry grows.

"The gnome needs to learn to keep his mouth shut," Emily snaps.

Jack joins forces with Emily against their chosen enemy. "Em's right. His lips need sealing shut."

"Sticking his lips together won't solve the problem, and it won't change anything. Time's ticking, and it's all my fault," I say, eyes glued to the box.

"Enough." Nathaniel's voice booms behind me. "Anymore, Arthur, and I'll have you removed."

The gnome's face reddens.

The wolf nudges my leg, and my hand trails along his jaw.

"So what now?" I ask, aware there isn't time for indulging in self-pity.

"First, we ensure our perimeters are safe. Ethan, Emily you go check." Nathaniel barks out the orders. "Arthur, you come with me, the less contact you have with everybody the better. Julian, go to The Blood and Bone and talk to Henry. We need as much information as we can get from Anna. I don't care how it's done."

Within seconds, the kitchen empties.

"What do you want me to do?" I ask Nathaniel as he walks out the kitchen.

"Nothing."

Running after him I grab his arm. "What do you mean nothing… I can't just sit around here and wait!"

"Yes, you can. Aeden is expecting us to retaliate. Let's keep him waiting."

"But…"

"No, if we react too quickly, we lose any advantage we have. If MAMS gets hold of you, Dot's as good as dead."

The front door closes behind Nathaniel and Arthur.

Frustration growing, I walk back into the empty kitchen, my eyes catching the white box. I don't care what Nathaniel says, I'm not prepared to sit back and do nothing.

The box can't stay where it is, the heat will affect it. As they put dead bodies, in fridges, that's where it goes. Hm… the sausages don't look that appetising anymore.

"Why are you putting Dot's hand in the fridge?"

I close the door and face Jack. "To preserve it, in case Ethan can sew it back on."

"Right." If he thinks I'm being irrational, he doesn't say.

I walk over to The Book of Shadows. "How about trying a tracker spell?"

Jack shakes his head. "I've tried. They must have locked the place down there's no sensing her."

The ghost wanders over to me. "Ghosts are excellent trackers. It's the reason the Keepers tolerate us. We investigate, record events and locate those like Aeden who kill. Right now he's hiding behind MAMS, but we'll get him."

"There has to be a spell we can try." My fingers tap against the granite surface as I stand by the centre island.

"Aren't you supposed to be doing nothing?"

"Humph… No one said I couldn't do a bit of reading."

Jack's brain is whirring, weighing up the pros and cons of allowing me to look in the book.

I fold my arms over my chest. "Well?"

He walks over to the table where the Book of Shadows sits. "OK, let's have a look."

"Let me text Polly first, I don't want her coming back here until it's safe."

"Roseley will be the safest place for her. You look in The Book of Shadows for a spell and I'll ask Ethan to send a wolf for her."

Before I can move, he's back. "No spelling until I get back."

"OK."

I have to feel sorry for the poor sod. If he thinks I'm waiting around for him before doing any spellcasting, I'd say he's delusional.

When I find what I'm looking for, the spells getting cast.

At some point, a girl has to take responsibility for what's happening around her.

I flip back the cover and sit down at the table, searching through the spells. Pages turn, and the grandfather clock keeps ticking out time's steady beat. Jack will be back soon, and I've found nothing to help.

My thoughts drift to Polly as my fingers drum on the table. Polly's a romantic and will love the thought of a wolf protecting her. She's doomed to a life looking for Mr Darcy, with a six-pack. Not that Jane Austen would have known men had six-packs back in 1813.

I'm about halfway through the book and none of the spells have been any good. There is however a spell to quell frustration. Given how I'm feeling, it's a shame invoking irony isn't on the opposite page.

"Ah..." I snap the book closed, slamming my hands down on the green leather.

Magic tingles along my skin and I look down as the book rattles against the table, vibrating with energy and life.

"What the heck!"

Magic snaps through the air, swirling over the book. The leather cover flips open and pages flutter. Jumping back, I watch the paper quiver as a golden glow descends over the book. Light dims, and the pages lay still.

I lean forward to see where the book has stopped. On the left is a cloaking spell, and on the right a spell for concealing a scent.

I like the idea.

"You're brilliant book." It shimmers at my words.

I start to gather the ingredients as Jack mists in, his eyebrows arching in question at the herbs in my hands.

"What's brewing?"

The jars of ingredients clatter onto the granite. "Is Ethan sending a wolf for Polly?"

"Dylan Matthews' is on his way."

"Great, I'll text and let her know." I start patting myself down. No phone. "Phone… phone… phone. Where did I put it?"

"It's on the table."

"Thanks," I send a smile Jack's way, feeling more positive than I have for a while.

The old me is back.

My phone buzzes with Polly's response. It's fair to say she's super excited about being picked up by a werewolf.

Polly makes me smile.

Her romantic head is putting in as much overtime as she is. I hope Dylan won't disappoint Polly. I'd hate him to be old with a paunch and smelling of grease. Not that all old men smell of grease or have an oversized stomach.

When I turn my attention back to Jack, I find him with his head stuck in The Book of Shadows.

"What do you think? I'm going to merge the two spells together and personalise them."

"What are you wanting to accomplish, other than the obvious?" Jack asks tapping his chin.

"If we use a cloaking spell for werewolves and vampires, to cover their scent, when Aeden catches me and takes me to Aunt Dot they can rescue me without detection."

Verbalised, my plan sounds dumb. Still, as schemes go, it's easy to follow and is direct.

"How is Aeden going to get you?"

"Oh, yeah, sorry that bit stayed in my head. I'm bait, remember."

"Your idea sucks."

"No, The Seelie King and Keeper's plan sucks," I remind Jack.

"What are you going to do? Walk out the door and declare yourself available for capture?"

"Pretty much, though I was thinking more of *come take me I'm yours* it sounds better."

Jack frowns. "It sounds stupid."

There isn't room for error. OK, there's plenty of room for error, but it's the best I can come up with which allows for action, without MAMS becoming suspicious. Alston wants me to stop MAMS, and I can't do that stuck at Roseley. As Arthur says, I've procrastinated long enough.

"You with me?" I ask Jack.

"Do I have a choice?"

"There's always a choice, Jack."

"Hm…" Jack points at the spell. "Rather than doing individual charms for vampire and werewolf, you'd be better making a general one. By adding sandalwood, moss and ash, you will cover the scent of both, though getting them to accept the charm will prove difficult. Vampires hate magic outside of their own, and wolves have a natural mistrust of most things."

I shrug, no point in overthinking that part. Better to get the spell done first.

"To cover a ghost's residual energy, you will need a separate spell. Even though we aren't part of this world, we still leave a trace behind. A good sorceress will sense us."

"Right, let me get the ash, moss and sandalwood, then we'll do the ghost spell."

The sandalwood I have in the cupboard. Moss is a simple trip outside, and the ash I'll get from the log burner. Nothing too odious, and I race off to collect them.

When I return Jack is mulling over the spell.

I place the ingredients on the countertop with the others.

"OK, that's everything."

Reaching for Aunt Dot's big spell pan, I throw the ingredients in. While the mixture fuses together I reach for the wooden discs ready to soak them into the potion. The liquid turns from green to red, signalling its readiness for the charms.

"While the liquid absorbs into the wood, why don't we do the ghost spell?" Jack suggests.

It sounds good to me. "OK, so what do I need?"

"You'll need a bible."

Without asking why I run off to get Aunt Dot's bible.

"One bible coming up." I wave it above my head as I jog back into the kitchen.

"Open it on Luke 24:39 and swap it around so the saying is opposite to the actual meaning. Place a white candle between us and set a circle. Our hands need to hover above each other as you read the verse. Don't forget to put one of the unused wooden discs around your neck."

I pat the charm as it rests against my chest. "I'm ready."

My circle snaps into place, and I light the candles.

See not his hands, nor his feet,
He, himself, shall leave no trace,
No touch, nor energy felt,
For the spirit is not of flesh and bone,
I bid them not to see or feel his presence,
To those which the spirit calls its enemy,
As I mote it, let it be.

The flame extinguishes, and I drop the circle.

"Since we're casting spells, do you know of any which will stop Aeden absorbing power?"

Jack nods. "Good thinking. There is a spell we can use, but you won't find it in The Book of Shadows."

"Why? Is it a black or grey spell?" Some of my enthusiasm dwindles.

"Neither. You just won't find it in there."

Jack stares, gauging my reaction before continuing. "How much do you want to cast the spell?"

"If we stop him borrowing power, we reduce his strength, making him easier to kill, so yeah, a lot."

"Remember what you've said."

"You're making me nervous." I wipe my hands along my jumper removing the sweat.

Jack looks more serious than I've ever seen him. "You should be."

My teeth gnaw at my lips. "You're not selling this."

"I'm not trying to."

Hands on hips, I stare at Jack. "Stop playing with me and tell me what I need to do."

Jack inclines his head at the fridge. "You're going to have to use something you know Aeden has touched."

I stare at the fridge. "You mean the box don't you."

"No, I mean Dot's hand."

My mouth hangs open. "You have got to be kidding me."

"Am I laughing?"

"How do you know Aeden will have touched Aunt Dot's hand? Anyone of his freaks could have cut it off."

"Aeden enjoys getting his hands dirty."

"You mean he's a killer?"

Jack nods. "One of the worse."

"Crikey."

"The only reason Aeden joined MAMS was to protect himself and take up killing again. Despite what the Seelie King says, for Aeden it has nothing to do with the mixing of our species. He just enjoys killing things."

"I feel sick."

"You'll feel even worse when you make the spell."

I walk over to the fridge, somewhere deep inside me is the courage to open the door.

"Why didn't Alston tell me any of this?"

"No one likes to admit to their failures. As supernatural creatures, we think we're better than humans. We are after all supposed to be an intelligent species."

I stare at the fridge and tell myself it's just a box. With wooden limbs that don't want to move, I take out the container, placing it back on the table.

HUNTED

There are some things that I need time to prepare myself for, Aunt Dot's severed hand is one of them. The problem is, I don't have time.

"Err… I don't suppose you can do it?"

Jack looks shocked. "Ghosts can't touch the dead."

"Aren't you the lucky one." He doesn't comment

Gathering the remnants of my courage, I remove the lid. Aunt Dot's bloody hand sits on a bed of stained white silk. Dirt sits beneath her chipped fingernails, and blood congeals at the wrist. Bile fills my mouth and I have a hard job swallowing it down.

Near the sink is a pair of pink Marigolds. I walk over and slide the rubber gloves over my hands. With a deep inhalation, I grab Aunt Dot's hand, placing it on the waiting baking tray.

"What now?" I throw the gloves in the bin.

Jack stands on the outside of my circle.

"Light the red and the black candle, then scatter the sulphur around the hand."

Without a word, I light the candles, sprinkling the sulphur.

"Now repeat after me."

Where ghosts roam upon the plane of the dead,
I ask for the power to stop the thief,
From one touch, flesh on flesh,
Let the magic return to his victims,
And never allow him to take or borrow,
What nature didn't give him,
As I mote it, let it be.

The hand jumps and decaying fingers curl. Chipped nails beat against the metal tray and sulphur fills my nostrils, burning away nasal hair.

Flames flicker, and red smoke circles around the protection bubble. There's a flash of fire and I close my eyes against the light. When I open them, the hand has gone, leaving behind a pink liquid.

"Jack, where did Aunt Dot's hand go?"

Chapter Nineteen

Jack lips curl. The smile on his face should have been warning enough, but I'm too busy wondering how to explain Aunt Dot's missing hand to notice.

"What the heck, Jack, we've got to get it back. Julian and Nathaniel will go berserk."

"I'd say that's the least of your worries."

I can't peel my eyes off the vacant tray. My heart's beating against my chest and panic is making it hard to swallow.

The protection circle is still active, keeping Jack safe from any immediate action as his words penetrate my over-stimulated brain.

"What's that supposed to mean?"

"It means for the spell to work you're going to have to drink the liquid on the tray."

Jack's right the missing hand now holds no concern, neither do Nathaniel and Julian's reactions at finding it gone.

Horror and revulsion are the only emotions left.

"You're kidding, right?"

Jack shakes his head.

"Can't I put it in a vile and throw it at him, like they did in Charmed?"

"What's Charmed?"

I wave a hand at him. "Never mind."

"The spell transfers by touch. I can't see how putting it in a glass container and throwing it will work."

Suspicious, I stare at Jack. "And I suppose you didn't share this information with me before because…"

"No, because about it. You wouldn't have done the spell if I'd told you."

Inside, I'm gnawing at his dead bones like a rabid dog. That would wipe the smug look from his face.

"There are too many holes in your plan. It's flawed Jack. What happens if Aeden decides to fireball me into the next life, rather than strangle me, or something?"

"You listened when I said he likes to chop up his victims, didn't you? He's not about to miss the opportunity to send back pieces of you… limb by tiny… limb."

I pale at the thought. "Geez, don't colour it, will you."

"If I did that, this conversation will go on forever and the spell will have lost potency. Drink the liquid, Alice, before it's too late."

"Fine."

In the movies, they'd have taken the tray and thrown it down their necks in one. Me, I try to envision it as a strawberry milkshake, not what's left of Aunt Dot's hand. The imagery isn't working. Either I don't possess the imagination, or revulsion is too strong.

"In your own time." Jack prompts.

"Grrrr…" My growling earns me a chuckle from Jack.

I grab the tray, close my eyes, and tip the contents down my neck. The potion hits the back of my throat and I gag as it slides down. "I hate you; you know that."

Jack shrugs. "No worries, ghosts don't sleep so I won't lose any."

"I'd laugh, but you're not funny." My hand flies to my mouth. "I think I'm going to be sick."

"Take deep breaths." Jack encourages me.

My hands grip the work surface. "I know what I'd like to do."

"This was your idea, not mine."

For health reasons, I don't comment. In large gulps, I suck air in and out of my lungs, until the nausea passes.

The clock chimes and I'm conscious if I don't get the kitchen cleaned up fast, Julian's anger will fire at me like bullets from a machine gun.

Jack leans against the far wall, smirking as I race round the kitchen. I've just finished putting the last item away when the front door opens.

"Blimey, that was close," I sigh in relief

Jack points at the box.

"Shit."

There isn't time to hide it, so I shove it under the table and sit down, sliding The Book of Shadows to me, fingers strumming, head resting on my hand.

Emily saunters over, and I lift my head. There's a suspicious glint in her violet eyes, and her nostrils flare. The best defence I have is to ignore it and move her attention onto other matters. Jack waits for the fallout.

"Everything OK out there?" I ask her.

"It's all taken care of," Ethan says as he follows Emily into the kitchen.

"That's brilliant." Nervous energy makes my voice squeak.

Jack saunters over as Julian's voice echoes from the hall. "Who opened the box?"

I wince aware there is no point in lying. "We've been spelling."

Arthur tags behind Julian as they walk into the kitchen. "How did it go with Henry?" I ask.

"The box?" Julian's voice is like ice.

"Is everything OK. Where's Nathaniel?"

Julian ignores my question. "The box, Alice."

"I told you we've been spelling."

"Nathaniel told you to do nothing."

"It was just a few spells." I huff. "You're overreacting."

"And the box?"

I'm transported back to the Golden Fleece. Hands gripping the book, my anger rises. "In theory, if I don't use the spells, I've done nothing but prep-work."

Julian is relentless. "And the box?"

"One of the spells required Aunt Dot's hand."

"What type of magic did you do?" Emily frowns at Jack. "Well?"

"Why are you having a go at me?"

"Because you were supposed to watch her." Emily points in my direction.

I roll my eyes. "Blimey, it was a few spells."

"It's not the spells, it's what they represent." Ethan says.

I look at Ethan. "At some point, the strings on the puppet need severing. Isn't it better we're prepared? I used the hand to create a spell which will prevent Aeden absorbing magic. It's my protection against him."

Emily places a hand on Julian's arm trying to smooth away his anxiety. The swirl of emotions vibrating down our link tells me it's not working.

"Jack helped me adapt two spells, merging a cloaking and scent together means that vampire, werewolf or ghost, MAMS won't sense or see you. It adds to our defences, gives us the advantage Nathaniel is looking for. Aeden is coming for me, and none of us can change it, but we can ensure we're ready when he does. I'm no fighting machine, and though I've Aunt Dot's magic knowledge, I'm not a seasoned witch. Alston has made it clear. I'm bait, so let's give MAMS what they want... *me*."

The gnome's bell tinkles as he moves. "It's a stupid plan."

"Gee, thanks Grumpy, for a second there I thought you might like it, given it falls in line with the Seelie King... blah... blah... blah's plan."

"I don't like it," Julian says.

"It's too risky," Ethan agrees siding with Julian.

"You can't protect me forever. Times run out. Alston will force his will on us. This way, it's on our terms."

Julian turns to leave. "It's too risky, the answer's no."

"Hang on, this is my life, not yours."

Julian keeps walking.

Part of me wants to stamp my foot and scream at his back.

"Julian." I grab his arm.

There is more to his anger than my plan, something's happened.

"I assume it didn't go well with Henry." It's a wild guess.

Julian stops, his hand reaching for the door handle. "Henry and Anna weren't there."

"Where were they?"

"With MAMS."

It explains his uncompromising stance to my plan.

"Look, I know this isn't what you want, but it's time to let go."

"She's right, Julian." Ethan stands next to me. "With Anna and Henry gone, we have no way of knowing Aeden's next move."

Julian's shoulders sag. My plan will either work or it won't. Come tomorrow, I could be dead. What that means for me, who knows. I'm not sure I'll come back from the dead as a functioning vampire.

As luck runs, mine sucks. I'd end up a zombie of something just as hideous. On a positive note, I'd enjoy eating Aeden.

Julian lays his hands lightly on my shoulders.

"Are you sure about this, Alice?"

"No, but it's the only way."

"I'll tell the Seelie Kin..." I don't give Arthur time to finish.

"No, we keep this between ourselves. The fewer who know the better."

"I won't hear of it." Arthur's clog hits the floor.

"Then you will spend the rest of your time here locked up," Julian warns turning away from the study. "I'll speak with Nathaniel and let him know, in the meantime, let us look at these spells."

Before Julian moves, I throw my arms around his neck. The action takes him by surprise.

"Thank you." It's the first time he's listened to me. My happiness sends a cheerful buzz through our bond as his arms circle around me, holding me close.

"Be careful, Alice." He breathes into my neck.

"I will, I promise."

Jack is right about wolves not trusting and vampires hating any magic that isn't theirs. Julian stiffens as I place the charm over his neck.

"This one is for Nathaniel." I hand him the charm.

"I'll take it to him now, so he's prepared."

Emily holds out her hand, and I drop her charm into her palm.

"Look after him for me." She sends me an odd look but nods.

Ethan's eyes glow amber as I place the charm over his neck. "Thanks for sending Dylan to Polly."

I want to hug him, but things are messy between us.

"Where's mine?" Arthur asks.

"I didn't do you one." He looks stunned, as if I've slapped him.

Of late, I've known what it's like to feel like an outsider. The gnome is rude, outspoken and tramples over feelings like confetti, but he is loyal to his king.

"I didn't want you to feel obligated to come, and someone has to be there for the Seelie King. You're the best gnome for the job."

"Of course." His back straightens, as the armour around his ego snaps back in place. "I shall go back to my stump and start planning our attack."

"You do that, Arthur," I say.

Ethan steps out of the kitchen, following Julian and Emily. They all have a lot to do. It's not my fault that Aeden joined MAMS. But it is my fault if something happens to them, and I won't lose somebody else.

Aunt Dot's life hangs in the balance and I'm scared I'll never see her again. Or rather, the next time I see her she'll be lying in a coffin waiting for the earth to take her back.

Julian turns as he reaches the front door.

"Don't leave the house until we get back."

I nod.

The front door closes.

KATHLEEN HARRYMAN

"It's just you and me, Jack," I whisper.

Chapter Twenty

"Where are you going?" Jack strides in front of me as I pull on my boots and grab my coat.

"To give Aeden what he wants."

"That's not what we agreed."

The disbelief on his face is endearing. It's sweet how everyone expects me to adhere to their demands.

A few weeks of allowing them control over me, and being semi-compliant, and they think they are the master of my actions. They aren't. Underneath the confusion and trauma the independent freethinking me still lives. I had made my mind up when we opened the box and made our gruesome discovery that it was time for me to take back control. I might sound brave, I'm not, I'm regaining my sanity and stopping Mum's voice from haunting me.

"It was always part of the plan, Jack, I just never voiced it."

"Isn't that deception?"

I shrug. "Think of it as miscommunication."

He puts his hand on the door.

"That won't stop me."

The muscle along his jaw twitches. "Don't be stupid, this is suicidal."

"Thanks for the vote of confidence."

"I'm dead, Alice, don't you get it, I can't protect you."

"You don't have to save me, Jack. Just be ready to get the others."

"I don't like it. You're leaving yourself wide open."

"It has to stop, and now's as good a time as any." I swing the strap of my bag across my body.

A sigh escapes my lips. "Out of everyone Jack, I need you. You're harder to kill then the others."

"I still don't like it."

"Noted."

"You won't change your mind, will you?"

I shake my head. Resting my hand on the door handle, I turn to Jack. "If something goes wrong… you… know… if I don't make it back… would you make sure Jeremiah's OK. Keep him away from Arthur. He's taken a shine to the gnome and it's not reciprocated."

"Alice…"

"I know, but still it's nice to know Jeremiah will be OK."

Jack nods, disappearing into the charm around my neck.

My fingers touch the wooden disc beneath my coat. "Thanks." With the toe of my boot I move the crystal and the barrier around Roseley falls.

The temperature outside has dropped another few degree since Aeden left his gift, and a northeasterly wind howls over the drive.

Anna's thin form appears from between the old oak trees standing sentry at the end of the drive. There's no hooting of owls, or scurrying feet of a mouse, or fox, just the wind.

I stop in the middle of the drive as Anna's hips sway with confidence. Her eyes are like two black pits. Magic swirls around her.

It was stupid of me not to have realised how powerful she is.

"Why Anna, what a pleasant surprise." Some may see sarcasm as uncalled-for, I see it as the best defence mechanism available to me.

"I just bet it is. Well, rabbit, you're in the fox's lair now, and there's no escape."

"No, I'm serious, I was just thinking to myself, we should get together, have a drink. You know, let bygones be bygones, and all that crappy stuff."

Her foot hits my stomach, and air leaves my lungs.

"I take it that's a no."

She kicks out again.

This time I'm not giving her the satisfaction of sinking her boot into my flesh. In a flash, I grab her ankle and flip her weightless body through the air. A feral scream filters between her gritted teeth.

She should have used her magic.

"What's wrong Anna, you look stunned. Did you think the half-breed incapable of fighting back?"

"Bitch," she roars, charging at me.

Not giving her chance to twist a spell, my boot connects with her jaw. "Someone needs their mouth washing out."

"Will you stop playing with her. She hates you enough, don't make it worse." Jack's voice echoes in my head.

Anna can't know Jack's here, so ignoring him doesn't just suit me, it's essential.

"You know what I've been missing from my life... *fun*." I bend over Anna, resting my boot on her right arm. "Since friendship is out of the question, enemies it is."

Gravel flies from her left hand, and the sharp edges of the stones eat into my face.

"Alice!" Jack warns as hands grab my arms from behind, pinning them to my sides.

On instinct I slide my right foot back hooking it round the leg behind me. In one swift movement, we tumble to the ground. I'm already rolling away when a rock comes down. Anna swears as it misses me.

"Thanks for the rock," I shout at her as I send it crashing down onto the Redcap laying on the floor.

The thickset old man groans as his skinny fingers grab at the stone, talons sinking into the fibre of the boulder. Redcaps get their name from their caps which they soak with their victim's blood.

MAMS are like buses. As soon as I've taken one of them out another one appears.

"Get her!" Anna's scream brings more supernatural creatures running from the trees.

Two onto one isn't good odds. Three on one is even worse and five onto one will equal defeat.

"I didn't know this was a party. What about my plus one," I ask.

The vampire in me has been looking for this fight since Mum died and I let it have its release. My movements come in quick succession, as my legs kick out and my fists pound into flesh. Even as I retaliate to the violent actions of those trying to capture me, I'm aware that is why I'm out here. Despite my earlier words to Jack, I'm not about to tell them to take me, I'm all theirs.

"Enough!" Anna shouts, her hands moving as she threads a spell.

Her magic crawls over my skin and I'm unable to move. Fear never makes it to the surface. The spell Anna's cast will hurt, but it won't kill me.

She needs to deliver me to Aeden whole.

In sultry strides Anna saunters over to me, the victor, or so she thinks. Her hands clench at her sides and I know she's going to enjoy sinking them into my face. The spell she's cast has rendered me useless.

Given time, it'll wear off.

"I can't wait to see what colour you bleed."

If she wanted to know the colour of blood, she only had to ask. I'd have slit her throat and shown her.

Anna's foot sinks into my stomach, and I fall backwards. Hands dancing, she conjures another spell. Pain explodes in every molecule and I lose consciousness.

Part one of my plan is a success.

Part two is about surviving Aeden.

Chapter Twenty-One

Beneath me, the ground sways. It's like I'm on board a ship in the middle of a storm. This makes no sense. Water and fire don't mix, so why would a fire demon stick me on a boat, unless he was super crafty. That image doesn't fit the mental version I have of Aeden.

Anna's spell has left my skin itching and my head throbbing. In a couple of hours, the pain will subside as my vampire side heals the damage.

"Alice, you need to get up." Jack's voice sounds in my ear.

"Go away." I wave my hand, shooing him.

"Alice..."

I sigh at Jack's persistence. "OK… OK… I'm moving."

"No, you're not."

"Humph… well, I am now." I peel my body off the carpet.

The air is stale. Dampness rises from the floor, sticking to my clothes and hair, permeating my skin and sinking into my pores. There's a persistent dull ache in my side where I've laid on my bag.

"What are you doing?" Jack asks as I rummage inside my handbag.

"Looking for a mint. I swear I've got some in here somewhere."

"What?"

"A mint, there's a nasty taste in my mouth, like I've been sucking on damp carpet."

He opens his mouth, his eyes lingering on the stained wet carpeted floor.

"No, don't. Resist the urge to comment further, I don't want to know."

Out of habit, I offer him a mint. He stares at me for a while before shaking his head.

"Right, so, where are we?"

My high ponytail pulls at the tender skin along my temple where Anna's spell hit me. The tension subsides as I pull out the bobble and rub at my scalp.

"We're in a prefabricated building."

My eyes roam around the small room. Plastic sheeting hangs from the ceiling, reducing the floor space, and hiding the rest of the room from view.

"And the building is where?"

"Beats me." Jack leans in, his nose a millimetre from mine. "You look like shit."

"With compliments like that, do you ever wonder why your single?" I ask him.

"Can't say I've ever dwelled on the matter."

"You should."

"Thanks for the advice, but you're years too late."

I cock my head in thought. "Don't ghost's date?"

"I'm not having this conversation."

The ground is still moving, and while I consider mentioning this to Jack, the hostile jut of his jaw keeps my question from forming.

As I stand the swaying becomes more noticeable. Hands gripping onto the plastic, I steady myself. The make-shift curtain parts and I stare out at dark grey clouds over rooftops. Rain hits my face, and my breath leaves my body.

I have an irrational fear of heights. Without conscious thought my feet start back peddling. Eyes trained on how close the clouds are, my foot becomes tangled in the sheeting curling about the floor. Arms splaying around me, I tumble to the floor, grabbing whatever I can.

Jack peers down at me. "You OK."

"Peachy." I shove at the plastic.

The side of the building is missing, and I can see for miles. York minster looms before me. Houses and commercial properties splatter over the ground. The Roman walls wrap around York's city centre.

On a clash of thunder, lightning flashes across the sky, illuminating the pale stonework of York Minster. The building stands proud, almost daring the lightning to strike it, as it had in 1984.

York Minster started life as an Anglo-Saxon rush job, to baptise King of Deira and Bernicia, later known as Edwin of Northumbria, in 627. It has seen its share of change.

On hands and knees, I crawl a little closer to the opening. I stop two metres from the edge. A sense of being exposed and fragile falls over me as I stare down at the rooftops.

"How high are we?" I ask Jack.

"Haven't got a clue, fifty feet, maybe a hundred, or more."

My hands are shaking. Two foot is high for me. "There's a vast difference between fifty and a hundred."

"You want me to measure it for you? Either way, you fall, you die."

I so want to vomit. "Gee Jack, you know how to make a girl feel unsafe."

A rustling noise comes from the rear of the building, and whatever Jack is about to say dies. In long strides, he disappears from view.

Jack's sudden departure increases my anxiety.

The wind is picking up as the storm intensifies. Thunder clashes and I slide back away from the opening, throwing the plastic covering off my feet.

The swinging motion strengthens, and I feel seasick. My vertigo escalates and my legs shake with my fingers as my heart hammers. Hands gripping at the remaining curtain, I clamber to my feet.

"Jack." Silence can shout and it's screaming at me. "Jack." Still nothing.

He can't have gone far. The building doesn't appear that spacious. Unless he's left me to my own fate. My plan was crappy, I can't blame him if he did.

I grab the plastic curtain in front of me and yank it back. Anger is replacing, anxiety. "Jack!"

Light floods the room as lightning electrifies the sky behind me. Hands gripping at the plastic, a face appears beneath my fingers. Darkness falls and my fear is so consuming that I forget I'm not human. As my vampire lays dormant, I fumble about in the dark.

My screams bring Jack to my side in time for him to see me land headfirst on the floor. Lips sucking carpet, I try to untangle myself from the plastic.

Lightning strikes again and I point at the distorted face peering at us from within the folds of see-through sheeting.

"Is he dead?" I ask.

"That depends on how you view it."

"Eh? You are either dead or alive, there's no in-between."

"That would be a question best explained by Julian."

I crawl closer to the plastic. "He's a vampire?"

"No, he's a unicorn pretending to be a vampire."

I swing my head about the room, lifting my arms and peering under my legs in exaggerated movements.

"Ok, Arthur, what have you done with Jack!"

Hands on hips, Jack looks down his nose at me

"Arthur isn't here... Oh funny!"

"Well, you're as grumpy as Grumpy. So what's biting at you?"

Jack flops to the floor. "They've locked this place down tighter than ADX Florence in the US."

I lift my shoulders. "Never heard of it?"

"You're uneducated," Jack complains.

"I don't know why you're surprised. Arthur's been telling you that for a while."

Jack grunts at me. "ADX Florence is the most secure prison in the world. If any of the inmates see the sun, they are considered lucky."

"Oh..."

"This place is on lockdown. I've tried every square inch and nothing. At present, no one's getting in or out." Jack stomps up to the vamp wrapped in plastic. "And now we've a vampire to deal with. If he's not restrained what do you think he's going to want to do when he wakes up?"

I tell myself panicking won't help our situation. But my brain's working hard at urging me to flee and my heart's agreeing. With a deep inhalation, I suck air into my lungs, inflating and deflating them until I've a better grip on my swirling emotions. The inside of my lips are sticking to my teeth, and my shaking fingers rub at the vein in my neck.

"You're teasing him."

"Huh?" Jack points at my fingers. "Oh…"

Arms folding around my waist, I try to find a piece of my brain that's still working.

"It might not be that bad. We don't know if the vampire is dead… dead… or just dead." We both stare at the unconscious vamp. "How do we tell if he's dead… dead?"

Jack shrugs. "I haven't got a clue."

"Can't you sense him on the Ghost Plane?" I ask, pushing to my feet.

"Did you listen when I said no getting out or in!" He wafts his hands at me in frustration.

"Stop being Grumpy!"

"I'm *NOT* Grumpy!" Jack shouts.

"You sure sound like him to me."

"This was your bright idea and now we're trapped. I should never have let you talk me into it. What are Julian and Nathaniel going to say. On second thoughts, we both know what they will say." His constant pacing is driving me crazy.

"Then there's Alston, he will have my arse booted to purgatory and I'll spend eternity listening to demons prattle on about nothing. Then I will want to die for real. And there's Emily, she's still pissed I'm a warlock. She will be even madder when I'm dead for good."

"You're pacing."

"What." He stops and turns.

"You're pacing."

Lockdown was an element I hadn't seen coming, still, we aren't dead… yet.

With a sigh, I stand. "Maybe I didn't think through all the scenarios during my planning stage, but then who'd think they'd lock down a ghost. We aren't dead, and the vampire might be our best hope of escaping. Like you said, he's going to want to eat at some point, and with any luck ,we can convince him to eat them, not me."

Jack snorts.

"Don't be negative, at least I've come up with something." I walk over to the plastic. "Besides, he might even be dead... dead."

Brown eyes stare at me.

"Ah..." I leap back from the vampire colliding with the wall. There's a sharp pain in my side and a metal rod protrudes from my body. Blood leaks over my clothes and floor.

My heads spinning and I find it difficult to keep my eyes open. "Jack, I don't feel so good."

"Alice!" His skin loses colour, and he looks more ghost-like than I've ever seen him.

"Jack..."

"Don't panic. Um..." His head swivels, eyes roaming round the building. I want to tell him he's doing enough panicking for the both of us.

Jack points at the vampire. "He can make you better, you're going to have to bite him."

It takes a bit for Jack's words to sink in. "You want me to drink his blood."

"It's the only way." The fact Jack doesn't resort to some snarky comment tells me I'm in a bad way.

"Do you think he'll mind?"

"Who cares!"

The vampire's eyes lock on me, and I swear I saw his tongue sneak out. "I think he'd rather eat me."

"Don't look at him, it'll take the edge off when you drink his blood." Jack surveys the floor. "Use the nail near his feet to slice into his flesh."

"You're not selling this, you know that."

"I don't care. You're leaking blood faster than a river breaks its banks on a stormy night." Jack has a point.

Pain explodes as I slide myself off the metal rod. My hands slip as they become saturated in my own blood. There is a point when the sickness leaves along with the dizziness, and I'm so cold my teeth rattle.

The pain ebbs, and I know that is a bad sign. With nothing supporting me, I fall to the ground. Blood flows faster from the hole in my side. Fingers wrapping round the nail, I slither over to the vampire, my arms pulling me along the carpet. Jack is getting impatient at my side. His fingers dance against his hips as I fumble with the plastic, exposing the vamp's ankle. It takes a few attempts to get the nail deep enough into the vein for the blood to flow, but I manage it.

As I suck out the blood, I'm aware at how much I've changed over the last few weeks.

The vampire in me responds to the energy flowing from the vamp wrapped in plastic. The wound closes on his ankle and I flop to the floor, taking the plastic with me. Spread eagled across the carpet, my body heals.

When I wake the vampire is staring at me. Recognition is strong, and I know I've met him. It takes a while for my brain to listen to what my eyes are telling me.

"Henry?"

Thick metal chains infused with magic wrap around the chef's ample waist. A track of pink tears stain his cheeks.

"She did this." Henry sounds broken, and I get the impression by *she*, Henry's referring to Anna.

Henry blinks. "Why did she do it? I don't understand. In time I hoped she would be the Anna I first met."

I want to strangle the conniving little sorceress until life pours out of her.

"She betrayed you a long time ago, Henry," Jack hovers at my side, silent.

"But she hurt me." Henry's voice vibrates with shock.

Blood stains his torn jacket. The skin beneath has healed, leaving behind dried thick droplets of congealed blood.

"Come on, Henry, you're a fighter. Who else is going to feed the hungry diners at The Blood and Bone?" My rallying doesn't hit its mark.

"She's dying, you know, Julian is taking back the life he gave her." Henry sobs.

"Good." Jack's voice holds no emotion.

"My Anna has long forgotten why she lives. She's too consumed with hate to care. When they murdered her half-brother it changed her. His magic was weak, and he died. She blames it on his mixed birth, not the dangerous life he led."

Silence falls over us and I drop to the floor, watching the sun as it moves from behind the grey clouds brightening up the rooftops. I track the old Roman wall as the sun's rays bounce off the wet stone.

Centuries ago, the heads of thieves would sit on the spikes at the gates to York centre. A warning to all that tolerance towards looting and pillaging was unacceptable.

York is no wimp. It is a city built and fortified in strength. Though many of the Celtic beliefs from the British Tribes lay forgotten by the people living here, York has not.

The Romans may have founded the city in AD 71, but it never belonged to them.

Underneath the layers of earth, concrete and tarmac, the Roman roads still creep, used only by the spooks caught within a loop. Like most invaders, the Romans saw the natives as savages, barbarians to kill or enslave. They weren't the only ones looking to invade this beautiful place.

On the 1st of November 866, the Vikings arrived in their magnificent boats holding the city captive. As with any trespasser looking to hold York hostage, the city rose, adapting and unrelenting, free of ownership.

With the plastic sheeting removed, air circulates around the building. Despite Jack saying nothing can enter or leave, the wind carries the cries of the people who tried to tame York and make it theirs. Land can never be owned, for it has one mistress and Mother Nature refuses to share.

With each breath my resolve strengthens. Using York as my inspiration, I declare Aeden will not own me. He may think he has me trapped like a bird in a cage, but he's about to find out that pretty birds have claws.

Chapter Twenty-Two

A snap of electricity crackles along my skin, and dark magic fills the room. Anna teleports before us in a stream of bright lights. Jack slips away into the pendant hidden beneath my coat as she saunters over to me, hips swinging, her steps full of confidence and intention.

Stubbornness is one of my best assets, and it's the only thing going for me at the moment, so I remain crossed-legged on the floor. The pretence of nonchalance doesn't always pay off. However, I'm not prepared for Anna to see how scared I am.

"I see you've found some friends, Henry. Don't you just love reunions?" Bitterness makes Anna's voice shrill.

A light smile plays across my lips and I adjust my sitting position, so I don't have to crank my neck. Anna's eyes linger on the blood staining my clothes. I watch as they follow the trail back to the metal rod. She shrugs, dismissing the incident.

"What's wrong? Jealous because Henry has friends?" I ask her.

"Shut it, half-breed!"

"Sticks and stones, Anna. Name-calling won't break me."

Anna's left-hand lights up and a ball of magic appears. "Perhaps not, but this will."

"Maybe, but then I won't have to explain myself to Aeden. Harm me, or kill me, and I guarantee he'll do worse to you."

Smug, I cross my arms and smile at her. "Now, tell me how much you hate me? No one but Aeden gets to play with the half-breed, but you know that don't you Anna."

The magic ball disappears, and I get to my feet. Rage flows from her. Anna raises her hand to slap me across the face. Before her hand connects, I catch it.

Shock resonates in her eyes, and my grip tightens around her wrist. "Half-breeds are weak, are they, Anna? Then why haven't you been able to slap me?"

"But…" Anna stares at the blood.

"Oh, this." My hand swipes at my coat. "I'm all healed, thanks to Henry."

A shriek of madness escapes Anna's lips. There's a charge of vampire magic, and I recognise it as Julian's. No one may enter or leave, but magic can still get through if it lives within the person standing in the room. My fingers lock onto Anna's wrist and Julian's magic calls back the life Anna has borrowed.

Anna's hand decays and I let go, stepping away from her. She squeals in horror and my lips curl in repulsion.

Skin folds away, revealing muscle and bone. The stench of decomposition fills the room. I step further away, closer to the gaping hole in the wall. Rotting flesh drips to the floor in clumps. Henry watches his face etched in anguish as the woman he loves dies before him.

"What's happening to me?" Anna turns to Henry. "Make it stop!"

"Henry doesn't have the power, Anna. Julian is taking back what's his. You're dying." A series of emotions fall over Anna's face as my words sink in.

"He can't. I've sealed you in."

"Your spell hasn't just prevented us from leaving, it's sealed in the magic. I'm Julian's sister remember. Our magic is linked"

"But... but..." The decaying flesh spreads up Anna's arm, eating at the woman in front of me. It's a horrible way to die.

"Why?" Anna asks, her eyes unable to leave the decomposing flesh.

I raise my eyebrows in disbelief as Henry leans against his chains. "Don't you remember Anna, you gave your life to Julian, when you drank from me. You've betrayed him for the last time."

"No!" Anna's voice trembles with fear.

Panic and madness dance within Anna's muddy eyes as she comes at me. "Make it stop! You can do that, you're his sister. Make it stop."

Even if I could, I wouldn't. Anna may not deserve to die like this, but she deserves to die.

"You made your choice, Anna." Henry sounds hollow.

Betrayal, sadness, love and despair roll off him.

"She can make it stop!" Pieces of rotting flesh fall from her raised hand like confetti.

"No," I back away.

"You can and you will." Magic snaps out of control.

"No!" Henry shouts.

The vampire's energy levels are decreasing and I'm aware he needs to feed.

"If you don't make her stop this, I will." A dark glow radiates as Anna twists a spell between her bone hands. "I mean it, Henry!"

Like a budgie in a cage, I'm trapped with no place to hide.

"Anna!" She ignores Henry.

On instinct, I call my magic. All I can hope is my protection circle has enough power to stop whatever evil magic she's conjuring from penetrating.

"Alice, no. Get behind Henry." Jack's voice screams in my head.

I dive forward as Anna throws the spell. The magic tracks me as I hurtle through the air to Henry. She hasn't had time to assign a destination to the spell, and it eats at whatever it touches. In a squeal of pain, Henry's body jumps. The chains rattle and the spell creeps up the vampire consuming him.

"Henry!" There isn't a part of me that doesn't want to pulverise Anna into tiny pieces. "What have you done?"

Anna's eyes widen in disbelief. "I meant it for you."

Henry shakes his head as I reach out for him. "Don't touch me. I don't have a human soul to lose, you do."

Anna is fading fast. I need her to cancel the spell. "Whatever you've done, take it back."

"I can't, it's a soul catcher."

Jack's warning becomes clear. My protection circle is a product of my aura. Anna's spell would have absorbed it, removing my soul, until there was nothing left but a dangerous and monstrous shell. Julian and Nathaniel would have no choice but to end my life.

There would be no rising from the dead as a full vampire. Without a shred of humanity, I would be nothing more than an insatiable killer.

"Yes, you can!" I shout at Anna.

"No, the cost is too great."

"I don't care." The spell is now creeping up Henry's chest. "You cared for him once, Anna, don't let him become a monster. Please, you're dying there's nothing left here for you. Don't make Henry pay for loving you."

A vampire doesn't possess a human soul, but the magic still needs something to consume. Left with no other choice, it was eating away at Henry's essence.

Anna shakes her head, backing away. I grab her arm, propelling her towards Henry. If it's a soul the magic requires, a soul it will get.

Anna screams as she collides with the vampire.

The spell slips away from Henry, preferring Anna's soul above a vampire's humanity.

Tears fall, and Henry's body shakes with a mixture of grief and relief.

"*Shh…* Henry," I whisper.

While I want to tell him Anna isn't worth such over-whelming sadness or love, I keep quiet. The heart is irrational, and we love not by choice, but emotion.

Love is the epicentre of our soul, and worth it or not, it has to grieve. I long to take Henry in my arms and rock him until the pain quietens.

Until all fragments of magic leave the vampire, I'm left standing, watching his heart break.

"Anna!" Aeden bursts into the building in a cloud of flames.

Anna's body jerks for the last time as her soul ejects eaten away by her own spell.

Vacant black eyes stare at the fire demon as the last of her flesh bleeds away. The skeleton dances, digits twitching.

Too intent on Aeden, he doesn't notice Anna's dancing bones.

In a squelching leap, Anna thunders at the fire demon. I marvel at the fact she isn't dead. Maybe I've got that wrong and her ghost now inhabits her body, seeking revenge.

A shriek of wild laughter cuts through the room, like nails on a chalkboard.

Anna's bones circle around the demon's neck, her teeth sinking into his flesh as she rips at his skin. Together they stumble towards the opening. In stunned and grateful silence, I watch them fall out of the prefabricated building.

My vertigo doesn't want me poking my head out of the building, however I need to know they're not coming back. I can't trust my legs to get me there due to their uncontrollable wobbling, so I crawl along the floor. Anna never let's go as they tumble to the ground. The sound of her madness carries on the wind, causing a shiver to run through me.

Jack materialises at my side. "Now that has got to hurt."

"Do you think he's dead?" I back away from the opening.

"It's going to take more than a hundred-foot drop, with a bloodthirsty decaying girl, to kill Aeden."

"You know you can lie, don't you?" I point out resting my back against the adjoining wall.

Henry moans, his skin contains a grey tinge, and wild hunger burns within his eyes.

There isn't much time left, Henry's ability for rational process is decreasing as bloodlust takes him.

"We need to get Henry out of those chains." I tell Jack.

Henry shakes his head. "There's no time. Leave me."

I jump to my feet. "No!"

Tears spill as his jaws snap. "I can't keep the need to feed at bay much longer. Save yourself, Alice."

"No!" I yell at him, pulling at the chains.

"Henry's right, we need to leave now while the magic is down, and we can..."

"I said *NO!*" Turning, I pour out my frustration at Jack.

My jaw juts out as I cock my head at him.

"OK, have it your way." Jack stomps over circling around Henry. "How do you want to do this? There's no key, and the post he's strapped to is solid."

I bang my head against the post in frustration. Think... think... think... I command my brain. The action clears my thoughts enough to work out our next move.

"First, we get this building on the ground." I roll my head in Jack's direction. "Have you ever worked a crane before?"

"Getting the crane moving is going to take up a lot of my energy, I might not have enough left to get the others."

"I know."

"If your last idea stank, this one's worse."

"Yep, I get that too. But I'm not going without Henry."

"I just wanted to remind you, so when you want to call me Grumpy you can't."

"Lower the crane, Jack."

"Better hold on tight, it'll be a bumpy ride." I sink to the floor near Henry's feet as Jack disappears.

On the back of a loud squeaking noise comes a whirring motion, and the prefabricated building swings. A groaning sound erupts as the chains holding it to the crane snap against its flimsy body. My pale skin loses all colour and my stomach flips. Even when I was little, I never found theme parks and the contraptions they call rides, exciting. I like my thrills with my feet touching the ground.

Arms wrapping around Henry's legs, I cling, praying we make it to the ground in one piece.

Air flows and the plastic sheeting whips around the room. I try not to think about the particles of Anna's flesh which adhere to the sheeting and floor. However, trying not to think about Anna's rotting flesh makes me think about it. It is a confusing, sickening and traumatic episode I wish to forget.

The building hits the ground and my eyes snap shut, fingernails digging into Henry I wait for the building to decide if it is strong enough to absorb the impact.

"Despite my reservations, I've got to admit that was fun." With hostile eyes, I stare at Jack.

Henry looks in awful shape. I peel back the sleeve of my coat and present my arm. "Here, you need to drink before it's too late."

The vampire's head hits the post as he snaps his face away from my exposed wrist.

"He can't drink from you, Alice," Jack announces as I move position, thrusting my wrist under Henry's nose.

I turn my head in Jack's direction. "Eh?"

"You're Julian's sister."

"And?" It's obvious I'm not grasping the situation.

"He can't and won't drink from his master's children. It's forbidden."

"I'm not getting into shitty supernatural politics, now. Drink!" I shove my wrist back at Henry.

"Alice, no, you're not being fair, put down the wrist. Henry's using up his reserves trying not to bite you."

"Ah..." I stomp.

"A tantrum won't change anything." I stick my tongue out at Jack, removing my wrist.

"Fine." The word grinds from between my teeth.

Feet pounding against the carpet, I walk round Henry, taking in the chains and lock.

I look at Jack. "Do you think you have enough energy left to work the lock?"

"I'm a ghost, not a locksmith."

"It's a shame you never took crime up when you were alive. Haven't you heard of planning for the future?"

"Yeah, it's called a pension."

"How very human of you." I continue to walk round Henry. "If we can't pick the lock and we're not strong enough to break the chains, we need to find another solution."

I grab the lock and give it a yank. The lever springs open. In disbelief, I stare at it before I unravel the chains.

"Unbelievable." I smile at Jack.

"Err…" Henry's eyes bulge as his legs give way and he crumbles to the floor.

I run towards him, tucking my arms under his armpits and pull. Henry doesn't move. The vamp is heavy and sweat pours off me.

"Give me a hand." A look of horror falls over Jack's face.

I'm sure I haven't asked him to grab a pole and dance around it naked in public.

"He's dead, I can't touch him."

"Great." I look down at Henry. "How do you propose we get him out of here?"

"I don't remember. I was for leaving him."

I gaze at Henry's forlorn face. "Ignore Jack, I'm not leaving you, there's a solution, I've just got to think of one."

Time is disappearing fast along with our advantage.

My feet hit the carpet and I pace round the small space. "You know what I don't get." I say coming to a stop. "Why has no one wondered what a prefabricated building was doing a hundred-feet in the air?"

"That's magic, Alice." Jack says.

"Well then, magic boy, if you can't touch him, and I can't move him, we're going to shrink him." Henry quivers in fear at my suggestion.

Jack nods. "I like that." It's the first time the ghost agreed with me since we got here.

"Thought you might."

Eagerness oozes off Jack. "We need some of Henry's hair and a few skin cells and…."

"You won't make me drink it, will you?" I interrupt.

My comment surprises him. "No, why would I want you to do that."

I can still taste the pink potion he made me swallow. "Never mind, come on, I'll get the hair and skin cells while you get the other ingredients."

There's a nice little pile of varying horrible things waiting for me when I return from collecting my samples. I place Henry's skin cells and hair on top of them and call forth my protection circle. It snaps into place and together we say the spell.

> *What once was large*
> *Make small*
> *What once was heavy*
> *Make light*
> *Take the vampire and make him portable*
> *Like a doll that brings a smile to a child*
> *As I will it, mote it be.*

There is a moment of panic as I wonder if Henry is going to stop shrinking. "He's going to stop soon, isn't he?" I ask Jack.

His shoulders lift in a noncommittal response.

Moments later Henry lets out a sigh and the shrinking stops.

"Doesn't he look cute?" Henry's jaws snap at me. "In a man-eating crocodile kind of way."

"Just pick him up and put him somewhere safe, we need to get a move on."

"OK... OK... keep your pants on." I grumble at Jack.

Henry's teeth sink into my bag as it swings at my side.

"Is someone feeling *grumpy*?" The vampire responds to my question by kicking out his legs. "Come on, Henry, where's your sense of adventure? You'll be back in the kitchen before you know it."

I dig around my bag, pulling out a pair of woollen gloves. The vampire snaps and wiggles as I wrap one glove round him and sit him in the other, before placing him in my bag and zipping it closed.

"Ready?" Jack leans out the side of the building.

"As I'm going to be."

Together we step outside onto a building site. A sign on our right announces the development of two to four-bedroom luxury flats and houses. Under the building is Anna's black and red uniform from The Blood and Bone.

"Guess the wicked sorceress is dead." Jack sighs at my reference.

Rain hits my face like tiny needles. The wind drives the droplets of water into the ground, turning it into a quagmire. My boots slip in the mud and I trip over plastic piping, electrical wires, and spent barriers. All this restricts my plans for a quick getaway.

"Jack, why don't you get Julian while you can?" The ghost stops in front of me, turning to gaze over his shoulder.

"I'm not sure I have the energy left."

"Try."

He shakes his head. "I'm not leaving until I know you're safe. If Aeden comes for you, I need to know where he's taking you before I get Julian. Otherwise we could lose you for good."

"And what happens if Aeden seals the place again; we're back to square one." I shout above the wind.

"Try opening your connection with them?"

"I've tried, but I can't feel them." Worry hangs in my voice.

"It's residual magic from Anna's lockdown spell. As it targeted you it stands to reason the effect would be greater for you than me."

"Great," I huff. "Look, I know you don't want to, but I think it's best you get them."

"No, I'm not leaving until I know you're safe." He points at my bag. "Even little vampires have sharp teeth."

I lose my footing and my feet slide forward in the mud as I crash to the ground. Jack vanishes into the charm as a pair of burgundy trousers appear in front of me.

Aeden has arrived.

"Fancy meeting you here," I say using the only thing I have at my disposal — humour.

"Hm... fancy."

"You know I've been meaning to ask you, as your Alston's son and he's my grandad, does that make you my uncle? Or are you my cousin? But that doesn't work either, does it? Maybe we should go somewhere more crowded to discuss this phenomenon?"

Fingers too large to be human wrap around my waist, lifting me off the ground. I catch the smell of my capture's last meal as his breath sticks to my neck and left cheek. A mixture of rotting fish, garlic and stale cigarettes engulf me. From the amount of dirt under his nails, personal hygiene isn't an issue.

I swing my feet forward, using the extra force to kick back, hitting his knee cap. Spurred on by the grunt of pain, I raise my foot, kicking higher. The heel of my boot sinks into the soft tissue of his groin. There's a yelp of agony as his fingers let go and I fall to the ground. Rolling forward, I use my weight to take out Aeden. He crashes down and I spring up and run. The spell I'm carrying inside doesn't react. I need to be touching his skin and not clothes.

"Marcus! *Get her!*" Aeden's voice provides me with the motivation to speed up.

Feet sliding in different directions, I dash across the mud, not daring to look back. For a big guy, Marcus can move. His bare feet grip to the rubble, much better than the leather soles of my boots. A snarl comes from my right and Marcus flies at me. I hit the ground, Marcus on top. He laughs, delving his thick tongue in my ear and along the exposed side of my face. His bad breath lingers on my skin as his saliva stains it. I cringe.

"Marcus, stop that!" Aeden barks out the order. "You can eat her once I've finished."

There's a grumble of disappointment as Marcus lifts his weight off me.

Fists pound into my head, and I lose consciousness.

Chapter Twenty-Three

The continuous dripping of water penetrates my awareness, and I peel back my eyelids to find myself in a damp cellar. My head throbs and my teeth feel furry.

With reluctance, I push my upper body off the damp mattress. Water drips from the fractured pipe above my head, running down the side of my face and back. A florescent strip lights the immediate area around me, in a half-hearted attempt to illuminate the room.

"Good, you're awake." Jack stands near a heavy wooden door.

Not bothering to respond, I look round the room, my fingers patting my bag, feeling for Henry. The vampire responds by trying to impale my fingers onto his pointy teeth.

"Can you leave?"

Jack shakes his head. "Nope, this place is in lockdown."

"Is there any good news?" I'll take whatever I can.

"You're locked in a cellar, with decomposing bodies, there are bars on the window above your head, and Dot is dead. No, there isn't any good news."

"What?" A zillion questions fire through my brain. "Are you sure?"

"She's over in the corner. I'd say the sword sticking out of her chest killed her." Jack tilts his head towards the darkened corner.

We're both in a bad way, and I appreciate that on some level Jack needs me to concentrate on the fundamental of escaping. He's known Aunt Dot longer than me. I know he'll be hurting too. His flippancy is brutal, honest and raw.

I understand crying won't help my situation, but Aunt Dot is dead and though I've only just got to know her, the hole her death carves in my heart is real. Fingers shaking, I wipe away the tears, taking a laboured breath.

My head throbs worse than when I woke up, and my body hurts. Despite the uncomfortable lump in my stomach, it announces its need for food.

"Alice…"

"I know… I know… just give me a minute."

There's no scent of decaying flesh, just dampness.

A masking spell covers the stench preventing it from souring the air and the neighbours from becoming interested.

A pulse of power vibrates. Its dark earthy foul reek makes me gag. Bodies twitch and shoes scrape over concrete as fabric rustles and bones click.

"What's happening?" I ask, my unease growing

"Aeden must have a necromancer."

Aunt Dot moves away from the corner, her remaining hand grabs the sword pulling it from her chest. Blood darkens the blade. Logic is shouting at me, reminding me she's dead. But her body is moving. Eyes the same colour as Mum's stare at me, and I can't stop the small ray of hope forming in my heart.

"Aunt Dot?" The longing in my voice echoes round the room.

Her silver threaded hair falls over her face and shoulders in limp strands. Dirt and blood stain her clothes and skin. Motionless I watch her hobble towards me, sword pointing forward.

The other bodies stand in a mixture of groans and grinding bones, jaws snapping as lips smack. Lifeless eyes stare. Chaos erupts as they pull and push their way in my direction.

"Get your circle up." Jack shouts, shimmering at my side.

"What?"

"Get the bloody circle up, now!"

My aura snaps into place as the first body hits. It rebounds off the protective shield, stumbling to the ground and taking those close with it. An angry cry sounds and Aunt Dot leaps forward, bringing down the sword. In horror, I leap away.

"It's not Dot." Jack shouts as my circle wavers.

It looks like Aunt Dot, and despite the massive hole in her chest, I can't shake the feeling she should be alive.

"They are zombies," Jack says, explaining why the dead bodies are animated.

Zombies, it's an appropriate description of the creatures ripping at each other's flesh, in their haste to get to me. Aunt Dot raises the sword, and a head falls to the ground. The body keeps walking, arms outstretched.

"We need to find a way out." I nod at Jack. "Your circle's taking a battering and it's eating at your energy reserves. Given you've not eaten for a while, that's not good."

I look around the room. "The walls are solid stone and the doors locked. I can't see how we're going to escape."

"There has to be a way Alice, keep looking."

One of the larger zombies shoves its way through, throwing the others against the door.

"Look." I point at the far wall where a grate sits.

Jack follows the line of my hand. "Lower the circle and I'll go investigate."

"I can't. If a necromancer is controlling this lot, it's going to sense you and then you're going to try eating me like they are."

"*Bloody hell*, tell me again why I agreed to do this."

"I told you to get Julian."

"And how was I going to find you if I couldn't sense you?"

"Ah…" I scream.

"Not helping."

"Yeah, well, I feel better for venting."

The circle lights up as another zombie hits. Body parts are flying about the room and they keep on coming.

"How about a wind spell?"

Jack looks from me to the grate. "It could work, but it's going to be dangerous. How fast can you move?"

"Fast."

Jack doesn't seem convinced and his negativity is replacing my positive thoughts.

"Is there a way to stop them?" I ask.

"Kill the necromancer, you stop the zombie."

I pace round the confines of the circle. "How about burning them?"

"What? The necromancer."

"No, the Zombies."

The muscle in Jack's jaw pulses. "You use magic like that, you're going to taint your soul."

I rummage in my bag, careful not to touch Henry, whose jaws snap at my fingers like a crazed alligator. "Not magic, hairspray." I wave the can and a box of matches at Jack, smiling.

"What else have you got in there?" He looks at the contents in my hands.

I open my mouth as his hand comes up, silencing me. "It's a crazy idea."

"True, but it should buy us enough time to reach the grate." Jack doesn't look convinced. "As you said we can't stay here and wait for them to tear each other to shreds."

"Your plans suck." Jack announces.

"You got a better one?" He shakes his head. "Then let's burn them, burn them all down! *Ha… ha… ha.*"

"You do evil too well."

I take a bow. "Thank you."

We face the zombies. "OK, Jack, in the charm you go."

"I don't like this."

"Where's your faith?"

"If I had that, do you think I'd be dead?"

"I always thought it was poor decision making and reckless behaviour that killed you." Jack doesn't respond as he mists into the charm.

"Right then Henry, let's burn us some zombies." I say, patting my bag.

The match flares to life, and I press down on the aerosol can lowering my circle. Flames shoot forth, catching the sleeve of the nearest zombie. It stares at the fire, transfixed as it travels up its body. Despite the dampness of the cellar, the zombies are soon alight. Dancing around the room, they bat at the flames as they collide.

My finger presses down so hard on the plastic button the edges bite into my skin. Legs moving, I throw the empty can to the floor and run for the grate.

There isn't time to think as I dive at the grate and start prising it open. Bits of stone falls from the wall, covering my hands and clothes as I continue to pull. Feet braced against the wall to provide extra leverage, I'm aware of how vulnerable I am.

The metal gives and I dive inside the tunnel. Charred fingers grab my ankle, twisting I ram my free boot into the blackened flesh until bones snap and the fingers fall away. Reaching for the grate I snap it back in place. Hands poke through the holes at me and I sit back staring at them. One of those hands was Aunt Dot's.

My flesh twitches as something crawls over my skin. For the first time, I look round my surroundings. Bugs fill the disused priest hole, their tiny legs moving fast. They crawl over my skin and drip into my hair. In a frenzy of flailing arms, I scream, batting at them. There isn't room to stand and run, which means I'm going to have to crawl my way out of this hell.

The bugs are relentless as they scramble around looking for a place to hide from their intruder. My clothes seem to be appealing and I sense them crawling up my legs and down my back. Skin quivering from their invasion, I scramble down the narrow tunnel, desperate to get away.

Light bleeds from the dim light attached to the wall. The tunnel opens up and I jump to my feet, shaking my head, clawing at my hair and clothes. Jack appears in front of me and I scream.

"Will you stop doing that!"

Nails scratching at my flesh, I rid myself of the last of the clingers on. "I hate bugs, they crawl all over you like you're a free ride, nibbling away at your flesh."

With light comes relief from the critters as they favour the dark. Though I can still feel them running across my skin.

The tunnel splits in front of us. Neither one looks tempting.

"Which way?" I ask Jack.

"Your choice."

"Since all my decisions are bad ones, I'm surprised you're leaving it up to me."

Jack shrugs.

"You're setting me up, aren't you?"

Jack smiles.

The tunnel on the right is brighter, so I choose that one.

"Can the necromancer sense you here?"

"Animating that many zombies will have reduced his energy levels, so I should be safe."

"And what about getting Julian?"

"Still on lockdown."

"Lockdown, I hate that word."

"You hate a lot of things at the moment." There was no arguing with that comment.

****

The tunnel goes on forever, and I am thinking I should have chosen the other one. Jack is metres in front of me. If I'd been looking for companionship and conversation to pass the time, I'd feel neglected.

My boot catches on a piece of stone and I stumble forward, losing my balance. Frustrated, I sit on the floor with my back against the wall.

Henry pushes against the fabric of my bag. He's getting more agitated.

Jack is still wandering down the tunnel, failing to notice I'm no longer behind him. I'm going to have to get up soon and start walking, but I'm so tired.

A rustling noise comes from my right, and a rat appears. We spend awhile staring at each other. Its whiskers twitch and its tail flicks.

"Don't worry, I'm not stopping." Either the rat doesn't understand me, or it's unhappy with what it sees as an invasion in its home.

On back legs, it straightens. The rat doesn't look scared, but angry. Ears move in a way I've never seen a rat's move. Unease settles over me as I continue to stare at it.

"Go away!" My demand makes the rat scurry closer.

I'm not good with rodents. They creep me out. This has more to do with a gerbil I once had named Loki, after the Anglo-Saxon God of Cunning. Its teeth would sink into my fingers whenever the opportunity presented itself. Loki had a taste for blood and inflicting pain.

This rat is giving off the same vibes. Not daring to take my eyes off it, I wonder if Jack has realised, I'm missing.

There's a scratching noise, and another rat appears. Where there are two rats, there are more, and others soon arrive.

Bits of fur are missing from two of the rats, and their tails are much shorter. Gnawed off ears suggest this deformity occurred during battle or disagreement. They move to stand on either side of the original rat. My nerves are taking a hit and my heart thumps.

"Jack!" I shout, the sound of my voice carrying along the tunnel.

The first rat opens its mouth and lets out a horrible high-pitched squeal. It sounds demented. Angry and ready for battle. There is a scurrying of tiny feet echoing down the tunnel, and without encouragement, I jump to my feet and run.

"Jack!"

A sea of brown fur hurtles towards me and I'm thinking I've just made the top of today's menu. The tunnel's floor is uneven, and while I can move, my stumbling is proving no match for the supercharged and super hungry rats.

"Jack!"

Jack rushes past me and the rats squeal as he thunders into them, his form becoming brighter, almost blinding as he hits them. In a kaleidoscope of colour, he spins as the rats scurry away down the tunnel.

"What the hell was that?" I ask, my heart thundering in my chest.

"Demon seeker rats."

"Can nothing be simple?"

Jack ignores my question. "Come on, let's get moving before they come back."

He floats forward, and I follow, head down as I adjust my bag. The leather dances as Henry moves.

"Alice!"

My head snaps up as Jack shouts my name. "Wh…"

Thump, my forehead hits concrete. "Ow!"

"Watch your head, the ceiling lowers."

I fall to the floor, my legs splayed out in front of me. My head bangs against the hard floor and everything goes dark.

"You've got to stop passing out." Jack's voice carries into my unconsciousness.

Chapter Twenty-Four

I snuggle in deeper, aware that my pillow has lost its bounce, and my bed feels harder than usual.

To help my brain process the discomfort my bed is offering, I reason with it, explaining away the soreness my body exudes because of awkward sleeping positions.

A slight breeze caresses my skin and I make a mental note to close the window before going to bed. This additional factor doesn't persuade me to open my eyes.

Reality keeps snipping at my brain, but up to now, I've been able to refuse its demands.

"Alice." Jack's voice roars into my semi-conscious brain.

I'd like to say Jack had woken me from a wonderful dream. However, it appears my dream world is nothing but blackness.

"Alice." Jack's demands are becoming more insistent, and I wonder why people think it's acceptable to enter my personal domain without thought, care, or being invited.

"Hey, Sleeping Beauty, wake up, before the rats come back."

The mention of the demon seeker rats brings me back to the present. This reality is worse than the nothingness I have just left. It is an existence made up of pain, loss, and stupidity. My not so cunning plan to offer myself to Aeden isn't working the way I had hoped. Julian and Ethan aren't running to my rescue and the fire demon is enjoying life while I inhabit a damp dreary tunnel.

I lose my ability for coherent thinking as questions of no rational meaning crowd it.

Why call a fire demon Aeden? I scratch my head as the questions float round it.

"Why do people have stupid names? I mean, what's the point in them. If you have to tell someone how to pronounce your name... like Eoghan. What's all that about? You don't even pronounce the E for a start, so why is it there? And why not spell it as Owen, because that's how you pronounce it? Or you do in my world? And why call a fire demon Aeden?"

Jack is staring at me. "Wow... do you always wake up like this? It could be the reason you're still single."

"*Ha-ha-ha*... hilarious, Jack. Maybe we should set up a singles club for the unattachable and call it The Teflon Club."

Jack's eyebrows raise at my suggestion. "Or, and I like this idea better, we can get the hell out of here before the rats come back." He has a point.

"Fine, but why did Alston call his mad, irrational, psychotic son Aeden?"

"It means born of fire/the fiery one or little fiery one."

"Is he?" I ask.

"What?"

"Little?"

"How should I know, now get your arse moving!"

"Grr..." On unsteady legs, I stand.

"Watch your head," Jack smirks.

"Leave out the comedy quips, I'm not in the mood."

"Oh… so we're feeling grumpy, are we?"

"Jack…"

My warning doesn't stop his lips from twitching.

"Enjoy your moment, it won't last," I warn Jack.

The tunnel narrows as we travel down it. Dampness makes me sneeze as I keep my eyes trained on Jack's back. The ceiling lowers, forcing us to crawl.

My handbag no longer stirs and my concern for Henry's welfare increases.

The tunnel turns sharp right, and we hit a dead-end.

"Great." My back hits the wall, sending tiny pieces of concrete raining down on me.

Dusting off the masonry, I look up at the ceiling.

"Jack…" I point at the wooden hatch above our heads. "What do you think?"

"I don't like it."

"Why?" I ask bewildered.

He shrugs.

"I need more."

"It doesn't feel right."

"Well, I'm not going back." My chin juts out.

The tunnel echoes with the sound of squeaking and nails.

I scramble to my knees. "Rats!"

There's no time for Jack to poke his head through the door, to see what lays in wait. My fingers grip at the rusty latch and I tug. Metal groans and the hinges squeal.

Above our heads comes a rumbling.

"Down!" Jack screams.

I drop, flattening myself against the cold damp floor as the hatch swings open, crashing against the wall. The sound vibrates through the concrete construction, gaining a hollow sound as it travels. I grit my teeth as I wait for the door to stop swinging.

Dust mats my hair and I can no longer run my fingers through it. I long for a shower, just to feel clean and smell nice.

It feels like forever since I was clean, never mind smelling of something other than stale carpet, brick dust, and decaying flesh.

The opening reveals a small chamber, and I jump to my feet, squeezing through the narrow space. My legs fly about the air as I shuffle further into the room. For the first time since my body started developing curves, I'm grateful to be flat-chested. If my boobs had been bigger, I'm not sure I'd have gotten through the narrow opening.

The room contains no windows or furniture, and only one door. Perhaps we've entered a cupboard?

A rat jumps into the room and like a hurricane, it launches itself at me, mouth open, ready to sink its teeth into flesh.

"Ah…" I bounce back against the far wall, away from the frenzied creature.

"Get the rat." Jack shouts at me.

It must think Jack said, '*Eat Alice.*'

On hind legs, the rat leaps at me. It's squeaking war cries fill the room. Despite the hammering in my chest, I stand where I am waiting for the momentum of the rat's body weight and gravity to do their job. At the last second, I twist out of the way, grabbing its tail. The rat dangles between my fingers, twisting and snapping its teeth at me.

"Don't just stare at it." Jack shouts.

To show how petty I'm feeling, I swing the rat into Jack's face.

"Not funny, Alice!"

I smile at him. "What's wrong, Jack scared of a little old rat?" I let go of the tail, laughing. The rat tumbles into the tunnel. Not waiting to hear it hit the floor, I reach for the trapdoor and snap the latch back in place.

"Do you think it'll hold?" I ask as demon seeker rats hit the wood.

"Let's not wait to find out, I'll go see what's on the other side of the door. You stay here."

"What with the rats trying to break in?"

"Stay." The banging gets louder and I wait for Jack to disappear before I try the door handle.

A sense of relief and pleasure buzzes inside me as the handle turns and the door opens. As I let go, the door swings shut, and I trip over a rug that some careless person has left curled up.

"I told you to wait." Jack hisses as I sprawl over the floor.

The room is dry and clean. Nothing crawls along the floor but me, and I take an extra second to enjoy being in a habitable room.

"Sorry I didn't hear you," I say, breathing in the smell of cleanliness.

"No, you ignored me."

"Caught." I make no apology as I stick my thumb up at him.

Large, heavy furniture makes up the bedroom, reminding me of an old Hammer House of Horror set.

"Where do you think we are?" I whisper.

Jack saunters over to the half-open door. "There's only one way to find out."

"Hang…"

He disappears before I finish.

"Great!" My head connects with the floor as I beat out my frustration. I was going to ask if he could get Julian.

Jack's face appears through the door. "Stay, and I mean STAY!"

"Wait..."

He's gone again.

Ghosts are irritating things, and I would caution anyone looking to meet or wishing to contact one. I guarantee they will experience moments of high blood pressure.

Jack's demand not to leave the room feels like a challenge to do the opposite, rather than a requirement. However, as I'm the curious type, I have a nosy round first.

My vampire vision allows me to see without searching for a light. Given the secrecy, it's a handy gift to have.

There aren't any photos or even a book sitting on the bedside table. The bed is neat, and the contents of the drawers are sparse. Burgundy suits sit in the wardrobe and it's obvious the occupant wears nothing else. The suit colour also provides me with my first clue as to whose room I'm in.

I flop down on the chaise longue at the foot of the bed and stare into Aeden's wardrobe.

My fingers touch metal as they spread out behind me. I twist round to find a golden staff laying along the back of the seat. I pick it up and the orb flickers to life. It changes from blue to green and a face mists into view. His eyes lock onto mine, and while there are no features within the face, I know he is assessing me.

Old magic coats my skin. Light flashes and mist rises from the ground. I scream as a searing pain shoots up my forearm. A shape appears beneath my skin, crawling up my arm. Fingernails scratching, I try to stop the alien presence from penetrating further.

The mist disappears, and so does the staff beneath my skin. I blink, though my eyes can't see it, I know that it's there buried inside me.

"What the heck just happened?" My question floats round the empty room as my heart drums in my ears.

Jack rushes through the door. "We've got to go."

Reflex's responding to the thread of danger running through his voice, I leap off the chaise longue and aim for the door.

"Not that way!" Jack shouts.

I look at the door as he runs towards the room we've just come from. "I'm not going down that tunnel."

"You don't have a choice."

"Great." I run after Jack.

The bedroom door flies open and Jack dives into the charm as Marcus steps into the room. Seeing me the ogre smiles, his bulk blocking the light from the hall.

I'm never going to make it through the door in time. Jack curses in my head. He's not the only one wanting to scream.

"So this is where you've got to." Aeden moves from behind Marcus.

"Surprise!" I shout, lifting my arms above my head.

The fire demon thunders at me. Squealing I move out his way tripping over the rug. Marcus' arms grab at the space I vacated on my way to the floor. He grunts and stomps down. I roll to the side, gathering speed as I disappear under the bed and back out the other side.

"Stop her!" Aeden shouts at Marcus.

The open door into the hall is less than a metre away and I spring to my feet. The ogre's fist comes at me and I crouch down as it swings at my face. It ploughs into the wall, sinking into the plaster.

"Ha." Springing to my feet, I kick out. Bone crunches and Marcus yells as I take out his kneecap before running out the door.

The ogre recovers too quickly, his feet beating on the carpet as he grabs the hood of my coat. Fabric tears and like a freight train at full speed, I'm propelled back into the room, gathering momentum. I don't stop until I collide with a solid object.

The object is Aeden, and we hit the floor in a jumble of limbs.

I don't have time to rid the fire demon of his borrowed power. The need to touch him, flesh on flesh is causing some problems. Marcus stands looking at us, unsure of his next move, as he sees his boss sprawled across the floor. The ogre's indecision provides me with the opportunity for escape and I race out the door into the hall.

To my right is a staircase, my left several doors, not one of them a main door to the outside world and freedom. My feet dither in hesitation as I consider whether to run over to the doors or go for the stairs. The stairs win out. Aeden will expect me to head for the doors - *maybe*.

Marcus slams into me as I hit the first step. We lose our balance and sail along the tiled floor of the hall. I feel Jack leave the locket. He doesn't surface into the room. If he's looking for a way out, he'd better find one fast.

We come to a stop by a stone fireplace with the ogre straddling me. Marcus raises his body to get a better aim as his fist bears down at my head. I take advantage of his position, raising my knee and embedding it between his legs. His eyes bulge and he hollers, rolling around the floor, cupping himself.

Not waiting for him to recover, I grab the poker from the fireplace. The metal sits cold in my hand as I shove it into his heart. Blood spills out from the ogre's chest as my bag dances.

Henry rolls out as I turn my handbag upside down. The vampire's features are unrecognisable. He looks like a crazed monster; I guess that's what he is. Hungry Henry charges towards the blood, his little tongue hanging from his lips as he licks and sucks his way through the red river to Marcus.

Footsteps sound and Aeden walks across the floor with a smile on his lips. "I wonder how your magic will taste when I take it from you?"

Confidence spills from him and I'm looking forward to removing it.

"Why don't you come a little closer and find out." All I need is for Aeden to touch me, flesh on flesh and his powers will disintegrate.

It's my turn to smile as confusion replaces the fire demon's smug expression. "Well, what are you waiting for. Come here. Give me a hug."

I undo my coat, slipping it from my shoulders. It falls to the floor as I roll up my sleeves, opening my arms wide. "Scared of me?"

A buzz of power rolls off him. It's different from anything I've felt before, and yet it's also familiar. The energy is powerful and ancient. It wasn't there when he killed Mum. I don't think he's stolen the magic, more borrowed it. A green haze falls over him as the magic flows from him.

He throws back his head and laughs. "You're so stupid."

I shrug. "It won't stop me from killing you."

"You're no match for me, Vampwitch."

Power flies from his outstretched hands like lightning. I squeal, leaping out the way.

My foot hits the blood and I go down. Aeden's laugh bounces off the walls, and for the first time since discovering what I am, I let the vampire free from its leash.

On a wild scream, I lunge at Aeden. The demon moves, and I stumble past him, grabbing his hand. Contact is brief as his finger slide from mine, but it's enough. The spell slips from me into the fire demon.

Aeden raises his hands as I hit the staircase. This time lightning doesn't fall. It's more of an electric spark which fizzles without making contact.

The fire demon looks puzzled. "What did you do?"

"I gave back what wasn't yours."

Like a bulldozer, Aeden moves, face contorted in hate, breathing heavy, arms outstretched. Most people tower over me, so his size doesn't deter me, and I ready myself for impact. Feet light, fists waiting to connect with Aeden's flesh. My vampire howls in joy.

Kicking out my foot sinks into his stomach, winding him, and he drops to his knees. With a slight lift, I use all my body weight to punch my fist into his head. He grunts and his hand whips out grabbing my ankle tugging my legs from under me. I crash to the floor. As my body touches the tiled surface, I flip back onto my feet. Poised, Aeden waits for my next move.

He's an experienced fighter and in quick succession, our fists and legs clash as we strike and dance around the floor, the predator in me calling for blood.

I fall back as his hand sneaks through my defence, and I crash into the stairs. The fire demon takes advantage, running to the fireplace and plucking the poker from the ogre's chest. Like a javelin, it flies in front of him, whipping through the air. I drop to my knees and the poker sails past.

My energy levels are depleting, and I pull on the thread of power that links me, Julian, and Nathaniel. They stumble as I draw down hard, sucking at their magic. Relief consumes me. It's good to know our bond is back on track.

Victorious, Aeden runs for the poker. I'm channelling so much power my head feels light. Before he can reach the metal weapon, I'm on my feet and my foot is aiming for his head. He grunts and stumbles, falling back, his foot an inch from Henry.

The vampire doesn't flinch and keeps on sucking at Marcus' neck.

Aeden eyes cut to mine. He smiles as he reaches out for Henry. If he thinks I'm going to let him kill the little guy he's mistaken. It's time for the wee vampire to grow back to his normal size.

What once was small,
Make big,
What once was light,
Make heavy,
Restore the vampire,
Give him back his correct form,
As I will it, mote it be.

Magic fills the space, and Henry grows.

A blackhole appears swirling in front of me and I know I'm missing something.

Aeden's laugh is shrill. "I can still absorb magic."

Disappointment meets confusion as I try to work out what went wrong with the spell.

The hole is like a vacuum sucking at the slightest bit of magic it can sense. Henry's face folds in pain as it descends on him. Falling to the floor, I grab the poker. There's no way I'm letting the thieving demon have mine or Henry's magic and I throw the poker at the demon.

Stunned, Aeden rocks back on his feet as the poker slices through his heart.

The blackhole disappears and Henry goes back to sucking at the ogre's neck.

As Aeden collapses, the vampire leaves Marcus for fresh blood, his teeth latching onto the demon and he sucks in pleasurable moans of ecstasy.

Jack shimmers into view as the front door crashes open and Julian and Nathaniel run into the room. Ethan's wolf leaps, his enormous paws gliding to a stop at my feet. His nose nudging my arm his lips curl back at the unknown scent beneath my skin.

"What kept you?" Jack's eyes roll at my comment.

Nathaniel and Julian reach for me, their arms pulling me to them.

"That was bloody stupid," Julian says. "I've told you about going walkabout." His lips twitch at the corners. Relief pouring off him.

"I think you'll find I wasn't on my own, I took the best hunter I could find." Jack shakes his head, indifferent to my flattery.

"Let's get you back to Roseley." Nathaniel pulls me forward.

Jack looks at the wolf. "What's eating him?"

My hand rests lightly on the wolf's head. "He's just hungry, aren't you?"

Amber eyes linger on my arm. There is no mark, and the pain has gone. The wolf's being protective. I love him for it.

Fingers teasing his ears I drop a kiss on the wolf's head. "If you're a good boy, I might even let you have the last sausage, though I'm not making any promises you understand. I'm famished."

Julian walks over to Henry. The vampire's colour is returning, and the madness ebbing. "I'll take him back to The Blood and Bone."

Aeden stirs and I'm not surprised to find neither the poker nor Henry has killed him. At the base of the stairs, a set of five fire extinguishers lean against the wood. I'm not sure which one will kill him. At random I take the dry powder and walk over to the fire demon.

"How do you put out a fire? You extinguish it." I press down on the lever, dowsing the demon.

When the cylinder empties, I go back and get the foam.

Aeden withers in pain as I finish emptying the wet chemical extinguisher over him, and I go back for the next one.

When I reach for the last canister, I question if water is going to have any effect on the demon. From his lack of movement, I think he might be dead. However, I thought he was dead last time.

"What did you think I was going to do, set fire to you and let you recharge? I'm not that stupid for a Vampwitch." I tell Aeden's unmoving body.

Nathaniel takes the spent cylinder, prising my fingers off the metal. "He's dead."

I look down at the demon sprawled over the floor. "Good."

The need to kick Aeden's soulless carcass is strong. There's no satisfaction gained from his death. Mum is still dead and so is Aunt Dot, and countless others. It is also questionable how dead he is.

"He won't come back as a ghost, will he?"

Nathaniel shakes his head. "No."

I remain where I am. "How do you know? Jack is proof that the dead don't remain dead."

"Because he was only ever born to visit here once. Alston made sure of it."

I kick Aeden's lifeless form. "Good."

Nathaniel pulls me against his chest, kissing the top of my head. This time I don't pull away. Instead I take the comfort he offers.

It is time to accept my new life and Nathaniel. There's no way I'm going to turn out as bitter and twisted as Aeden. Maybe I have more cause than the demon to feel the pain of betrayal, and the envy of a more simplistic life.

Aeden was born into a world of magic, knowing who and what he was. And yet, he still wanted more, to such a degree he killed to get it. I know I'm nothing like him. Yes, I've killed, and I don't feel sorry for what I've done. But that doesn't make me a monster. Does it?

The wolf walks at my side as we step outside. Nathaniel's arm lingers across my shoulders as we walk over to where Julian stands holding Henry.

"Jack has gone back to Roseley to let Polly and Dylan know you're safe," Julian says, as my eyes wanders over the drive looking for Jack.

Nathaniel walks over to Julian. "Give me Henry, I'll drop him back on my way to inform Alston of his son's death."

Julian relinquishes his hold on the vampire, and Nathaniel makes his way over to the waiting SUV.

I grab Julian's arm as he walks away. "No, we burn down the house first."

He looks at me but doesn't question why I want it burning. On some level I understand that burning the house down won't eliminate the magic I felt while inside, nor will it remove it from inside me.

I know it's there. Its power buzzes under my flesh. It doesn't feel evil, just wrong. And yet comforting. These are conflicting emotions, and I need to work them out before I tell someone about the staff.

Julian reaches into his jacket, removing his mobile. I stand listening as he gives out the orders. Within minutes, a van rolls up and four vampires jump out. Ten minutes later flames dance inside the building. The heat is immense as windows crack and glass and flames burst free.

No one will ever play with Aunt Dot's body again. It can rest in silence with her soul. Tears fall as I stand watching the flames eat away at the property.

"What have I become?" I ask.

Julian rests his hand on my shoulder. "A survivor."

Chapter Twenty-Five

Sadness sits in the pit of my stomach, making it heavy and uncomfortable.

The closer we get to Roseley, the more significant the weight becomes. To lessen the pain that grief brings, I tell myself that some people lose everything, whereas I still have a lot to be grateful for.

My heart doesn't want to be logical. It wants a release from the torment.

The wolf stirs, sensing my growing unhappiness, and I catch Julian's gaze as he looks in the car mirror. There's been no time to grieve for Mum, and Aunt Dot's death just feels too much.

Killing Aeden does little to make me feel better.

It's funny because I'm not angry, I'm sad and lifeless and hollow. A world of nothing hovers waiting to take me. My body is heavy and my mind tired.

There is a need to sink deep into the upholstery, so deep no one can see or want anything from me. Even as I think this, I know it won't happen.

The fire demon is dead, but there is still a lot to do.

My first task is to organise two funerals.

Someone in the supernatural world will need to be creative in getting Aunt Dot's death through the human system, without producing a body.

Alston will have someone working at the registry office taking care of such meaningless tasks. Nonsensical perhaps to them, but important to me.

At some point, we all hate our lives, and the devastation it can inflict upon us. Today, for me, is one of those times.

Julian pulls onto the dirt track and Roseley looms before us. The lights are on in the kitchen and Polly stands at the window. I know the moment she sees Julian's car because she turns and disappears.

The front door bursts open, and Polly stands illuminated by the porch light, waiting for the car to stop. I climb out, the wolf at my heels. Polly opens her arms and I step into her embrace.

"Come on, I've got some food on the table for you." She pulls me inside and the front door clicks closed as we enter the hall.

Polly's an expert at understanding me. She doesn't ask how I feel or engage in conversation. Instead she takes control, guiding me where she wants me, without pressure or confinement.

I expected Roseley to feel different. But it doesn't. It feels the same. The hectic buzz of life zips along my skin, welcoming me home. Roseley is more than bricks and mortar. Thanks to the ley lines running beneath its foundations, it is alive. Strange how I have never noticed before.

Arthur stands by the staircase. His hat rotates through his fingers as his eyes lock on the floor a yard from my feet. "It's sad news."

Fae don't use words such as *sorry*, but I know that's what he means.

Arthur's thick white hair flops about his face, and tears stain his cheeks. He turns and walks towards the back door.

Such a confusing little man. I didn't think he liked any of us, however it seems he does — or did.

Polly pulls at my arm, guiding me through to the kitchen. "I know you won't want to eat, but I knew you'd be hungry, so I cooked."

The table is filled with food. Everything on it is high in fat, protein and carbohydrates. If a doctor other than Ethan saw Polly's spread, they'd have a fit, screaming warnings of heart disease.

I sit down, my stomach growling. She's right, I don't feel like eating, but I've passed the stage of hunger and moved on to starving.

Mouth-watering, I sink my teeth into a large slice of pizza, biting through the layers of meat and cheese. Fat dribbles down my chin, as my taste buds dance in happiness and my stomach groans in anticipation.

There is a lot of criticism around my relationship with the wolf and our sharing of food. Given this, I take a bowl of sausages and place it at his paws. To hell with them. Me and the wolf, we understand each other.

Dylan stands near Polly as she places the kettle onto the Aga's hotplate. From beneath lowered lashes, he watches his alpha take the food I offered. He remains silent as the wolf at my side eats. There is no disapproval, only acceptance, and I wonder why Jack believes our sharing of food is a big deal.

There is no stopping my hunger, and after polishing off the pizza, fries and the mini pies, I reach for the steak, wrapping it between two thick slices of bread. The remaining steak I drop into waiting jaws, earning me a tail wag.

I take the chocolate cake and divide it into two. It isn't until the wolf and I have cleared the table I realise no one else has eaten.

Polly grabs the singing kettle, and Dylan walks over to his alpha. The wolf moves and I lean down, wrapping my arms around his neck and breathing in his scent. His enormous pink tongue licks my arm and I watch him leave with Dylan.

Julian pulls out the chair next to me as Polly places the steaming cup in front of me. Her arms fold over her chest as she checks out Dylan's lean form.

"Alston will need to speak with you. For now, though, get some rest."

The thought of seeing Alston isn't a pleasing one. In fact, I'd rather stick my head in an ice bucket. There isn't much I can say that Nathaniel won't have already said. Dead is dead and knowing the circumstances of his son's demise won't make the fire demon less so.

"What's going to happen?"

My question is all-encompassing and refers to me, Roseley, and everything else my life entails.

Julian's fingers touch my hand. "Roseley is yours. As for everything else, nothing changes. We remain as we are, here at Roseley." I nod, accepting what he says without judgement or argument.

Today isn't the day for decisions or actions, other than dragging myself upstairs.

"Right." How one word can cover everything I'm feeling, I don't know, but it's all I've got.

My fingers play with the mug as my eyes skim over the kitchen. Polly isn't the tidiest of cooks. Part of me thinks *leave it, it'll be there tomorrow.* But Aunt Dot wouldn't leave the kitchen in this state, and neither will I, so before I leave for a deep clean, the kitchen will get its first.

Polly takes the plates off me. "I'll sort it, you get yourself upstairs. I'm sure Julian won't mind helping me."

In stunned silence, I try to imagine Julian doing dishes. No matter how hard I try, I'm not seeing it.

Polly waves me out of the kitchen and turns to Julian. "Pass me the pots off the table, and I'll load the dishwasher." My jaw hangs open as Julian complies to her demands.

I think having brothers at a young age assists her in getting what she wants from the male species. Whereas they have always baffled me. Their antics leading to misunderstanding and frustration on my part.

"Here, take this with you." Polly hands me a bin bag. Her meaning is obvious.

My clothes have reached the end of their life.

"Leave it outside your door and Julian will collect it." My brother frowns but doesn't argue.

One day I will learn how she does it. "Thanks Pol."

Someone has been adding steps to the staircase, I'm sure of it. My tired body agrees with this assessment, even if it is an impossibility. When I reach the landing, I'm ready to drop, however, I will muster the energy required to make it to the bathroom for a shower.

I open the bedroom door, revealing a very snug cat sprawled over the bed. He twists his body, looking at me from upside down, and blinks. While it is obvious, he's not missed me, it's good to see him.

"Don't bother moving," I say as Jeremiah continues to stare, with no intention of movement, other than to flex a paw.

There are lessons we can learn from cats. For example- how to treat your owner with contempt, their home as a hotel and snub them when they want a cuddle. Exercise your feline right to the best spot in the house, refusing to share. As a cat owner, I will love him regardless. It is a messed-up world.

I step into the shower pledging never to take being clean for granted again. It takes vigorous scrubbing before I feel sanitised.

Water droplets fall from my hair as I dry my soap scented flesh. Wrapping my hair in the towel, I apply liberal coatings of creams, deodorant and perfumed body lotion to my glistening skin.

There is something about being clean that revitalises a person. Cleanliness cascades over me, providing a sense of luxury and gratification. No matter how brief the feeling, it is there, and I revel in it.

When I walk back into the bedroom, Jeremiah has adopted his normal position of hogging all the bed. Most pet owners at some point, will debate how something so tiny can take up so much room.

Jeremiah opens his eyes and stares at me as I throw back the duvet. If he is aware of my expectation for him to move, he shows little action in acknowledging it. Tired, I'm not prepared to grip onto the edge of the bed, so I slide my right leg across the expanse of the mattress. Protected by the thickness of the duvet, I'm ready for any attack formation Jeremiah wishes to use. The cat pounces on the offending mountain that has appeared beneath him, claws sinking in, teeth biting at the fabric.

There is no peace for my furry friend as I slide the rest of my body into his vacated spot and soak up the warmth his body has left. I smile, while Jeremiah looks on in disgust.

It doesn't take long for my eyelids to droop. Tiredness can be a blessing and a curse. It allows me to sleep without thought, leaving behind my sadness and guilt. The ghosts of

Mum and Aunt Dot hover within the shadows, but don't, for tonight, interrupt my sleep.

****

The bedroom door opens, and I wait to see who's decided not to allow Sleeping Beauty to slumber. Sunlight bleeds through the half-closed curtains, making me aware it's late in the day.

My intruder doesn't appear. The soft tread of shoes on carpet suggests they are small in stature. Even though both are taller than my invader, I'm hoping it's the wolf or Ethan for obvious reasons.

If it's the wolf I get to snuggle longer, if it's Ethan, do I take the fact he's in my bedroom as a romantic sign?

The ringing of a bell destroys that idea, and yes, it's fair to say, I'm now grumpier than Grumpy.

Given the gnome's angst against everything and anyone, I need to exercise caution. No point in receiving a tirade of abuse and lengthening his stay further, when I can avoid it. So I ensure my groan is internal.

"I've brought you a drink." Arthur places the mug on the bedside table.

Not what I'm expecting. It seems the gnome can produce the odd surprise.

Uninvited Arthur jumps onto the bed.

Jeremiah swishes his tail but makes no move towards him. The little man is old news, and no longer causes a spike in the cat's curiosity.

I grab the mug and breathe in the sweet smell of camomile and honey.

"Alston is on his way." My eyebrows raise at the lack of title awarded to my grandfather.

The gnome removes his hat and begins threading it through his fingers. I remain silent, wondering what he wants, that is so difficult to say.

"When would you like me to move out?"

His question takes me by surprise. "Why would I want you to move out?"

"Dot is dead, Roseley is yours."

"I still don't see the relevance."

Arthur stares at me.

I've never noticed how green his eyes are before. They're every shade of green imaginable.

"Then I can stay?"

"The stump's yours, I'm not about to throw you out of it."

"Mine!" He looks surprised.

"It's a tree stump Arthur. Unless you know different, I can't see the problem with you living in it. In fact, think of it as my gift to you."

Arthur's eyes widen in surprise. "You would do this? For me?"

The conversation though confusing is insightful. It makes me wonder what hardships the gnome has endured in Faerieland. Whether he wishes to admit it, the time he's spent here has had a dramatic impact on him.

"Yes, I would."

The hat goes back on his head, and I see the blossoming of a smile.

On the tinkling of bells the gnome jumps off the bed. "I will let Alston know you have chosen for me to remain here."

That wasn't how the conversation went, but Arthur is out the door before I can comment.

"Well, what do you think of that?" I ask Jeremiah.

The cat's head rests on his paws, and he closes his eyes.

As the contents of my mug disappear, I become conscious I need to make a move.

I want Alston gone so I can get on with arranging Mum and Aunt Dot's funeral. A lump form's in my stomach and tears sting my eyes. Throwing the duvet back, I walk into the bathroom and turn on the shower, appreciating the feeling of being clean. It will take a while before showering gets old.

My tears mingle with the water cascading over my face. It makes me feel like I'm not giving into grief but allowing my emotions an opportunity to express themselves. I turn off the faucet, gathering myself together enough to ebb the flow of tears. It does little to lighten the weight that settles within my stomach, not to mention the pain stabbing at my heart.

Polly meets me on the landing, and she threads her arm through mine. "You look and smell better than last night."

"Good morning to you too." She laughs.

"So, what you up to today?"

Polly's face lights up. "I'm in work this morning and then meeting Dylan for lunch."

"Look at the two of you."

"I know. We really hit it off last night."

"Dim the wattage you're blinding me." Polly nudges me as we walk into the kitchen.

Ethan is at the Aga frying up some eggs. "How many?"

My heart skips, and the skin along my jaw pinches.

Polly pulls on my arm. "And he can cook." She mouths.

I refrain from commenting.

There would never be just the two of us in any relationship I had with Ethan. That doesn't bother me as I know the wolf has accepted me and we have a harmonious balance that requires no words. With Ethan, it's different. I know he likes me. There is a thread of chemistry and excitement between us. It still doesn't mean he wants to take things further, and uncertainty is a killer.

I never wanted a relationship with Ethan. Now I want it more than anything, and I'm scared to find out if he feels the same. As Confucius once said: *Life is really simple, but we insist on making it complicated.*

"A dozen for me, please," I say pulling out a chair and grabbing the juice.

"What about you Polly?" Ethan asks reaching for another box of eggs.

"As much as I'd love to indulge, I'd better stick to cereal. Humans have a tendency to put weight on when we overeat."

Sausages land on the table with my eggs. Yellow yolks run as I cut into the eggs. Polly stares as I shovel the food into my mouth.

"I still can't get over how much you can eat. You've always had an aggressive appetite. However, it's increased even more since... well, you know..."

"It's the vampire in me, plus I'm using my witch ability more, which is affecting my need for food."

"You are the envy of all humans."

Ethan laughs at Polly.

"It's OK for you to laugh, you don't know what it's like choking down a lettuce leaf when all you want is cake and steak. It's a tough life for us humans."

The slamming of a car door signals the end of breakfast.

"Blimey he's eager isn't he." I try not to sound disgruntled at Alston's arrival.

"In that case, I'm out of here." Polly picks up her empty bowl. "It's not like I'm deserting you, it's just…"

"I get it, don't worry."

Ethan takes her bowl. "Dylan will drop you at work."

Polly turns around, her smile bigger than a banana. "Best morning ever!"

"Sure you wouldn't rather stay and chat to Grandpa Walton?" I ask her.

"I'm more into the athletic type, thanks. Best get ready." Polly sighs walking out of the kitchen and heading for the stairs.

"You're already for work, remember," I shout at Polly.

She turns flashing me a smile. "Now I need to get ready for my lift."

"There's a difference?"

"That statement alone tells you why Polly's having fun and Alice isn't." She makes a fair point.

Resting my head on my hand I stare at the table. "I suppose we should get this over and done with."

"It's not about getting it over with, it's about growth and acceptance."

I cringe as Julian walks into the kitchen. "My toenails grow, and I accept they need cutting, but I don't relish cutting them." The vampire blinks at me.

I wave a hand at him. "Never mind."

Footsteps echo from the hall, and Nathaniel and Alston's voices mingle in a low mumble.

Jack floats in as Polly closes the front door. I envy her freedom.

"This is where you're all hiding."

"I wouldn't say hiding." Jack looks at me, unconvinced.

Julian's hand cups my elbow. "It's time."

Together we vacate the safety of the kitchen and enter the living room.

Alston sits in his usual spot near the fire, the large sofa all to himself. We stop next to Nathaniel and like an over-packed suitcase we all sit on the same sofa opposite the Seelie King.

The door opens, and Arthur walks in. He hesitates as he looks at Alston, his head dipping in a mark of respect. It seems he's full of surprises today, as he comes to a crossed legged position at my feet. I try not to flinch, so I don't upset him.

Alston's eyes linger on the little man. His scrutiny makes me nervous and I scratch my arm, giving my mind something else to focus on.

"I've given Arthur the tree stump in the back garden." It's unclear why I need to clarify the gnome's actions.

There's the briefest of silence as we wait for The Seelie Kings reaction. Those who need to ingest oxygen take a lung full while we can.

"You are a lucky gnome, Arthur," Alston says.

The gnome bows his head, his cheeks glowing. "I am."

Who would think giving someone a tree stump could mean so much?

"I'm... well... you know... about Aeden," I say.

Alston stares at me. "Are you?"

"No, after what he did to Mum and Aunt Dot and countless others, he got what he deserves. I am, however, sad for the pain his death causes."

My arm itches like hell. It's like I've touched something I shouldn't have, and now I'm suffering from an allergic reaction.

"What's wrong with your arm?" Alston asks as the skin beneath my nails turns red.

"Oh… nothing…. just nervous energy, I guess." I move it behind me.

Alston tips his head to the side and I try not to squirm. "There's something different about you."

"It's called relief."

The king shakes his head. "No, it's magic."

A soft gold light emerges from the king. It slithers over to me, hissing louder the closer it gets.

I look at the others for a sign they can see it, but they don't react. No one seems concerned about the magic but me.

"What are you doing?" I ask, pushing my back into the sofa, tucking my legs into my chest.

"You see it?" Alston looks shocked.

"Of course I can bloody see it, I'm not blind." Arthur's back stiffens against my legs, but he doesn't comment about being respectful to the Seelie King.

The magic stops. "Look at me, Alice, and tell me what you see."

I'm fed up with his games.

Julian and Nathaniel's unease grows, and when I look at Ethan, his eyes are a golden orange.

With reluctance, my head swings back to the king.

"Huh…" My jaw hangs near my chest.

Alston is like a golden buddha. His hair folds around him in soft glistening waves. The sofa he's sitting on is tiny compared to his size. I would call him a giant, yet the title would not describe the size of the creature in front of me.

Heat runs along my arm. There's a pulsating sensation beneath my flesh. Julian and Nathaniel jerk as they feel its presence through our bond.

"How?" Nathaniel asks.

"What have you done, Alice?" Alston's accusation fills the room and my anger flares.

"Nothing." I need to get away from the pressure consuming the room.

As I stand, a bright light shoots from me and green smog falls. The song of a heron echoes around us. When the smog clears, the staff sits within my right hand. We are all surprised by its appearance.

Jack, if possible, pales. "You said it was under control."

"It is." Alston snaps.

"What's under control?" I ask.

"You're not going back Jack. I gave you my word. It still stands." Alston's remark doesn't remove the agitation coming off the ghost.

Nathaniel leans in close, his lips almost touching my ear. "The coven had Jack murdered for his alliance with Le Sang. Ankou took his soul and held him captive. We rescued him."

Ankou is the Fairy Lord of Death, and that's about all I know. This information is as insightful as Nathaniel's, maybe less so.

"How did you get the staff?" The calmness in Alston's voice is as unreal as the persona he presents to the world.

The Seelie King and Keeper's true self is beautiful and frightening. His magic is powerful, but it is not as great as the magic contained within the staff. This power is older than Alston. I recognise it and feel it. It is part of me, as I am part of it, yet I don't understand why or how, I just know.

"The staff was in Aeden's room. I didn't steal it or anything, it just disappeared under my skin."

"Why didn't you tell me?" Jack is now pacing behind the sofa. "This is bad."

There is a cutting response waiting to come out, however I swallow it down. "We were busy fighting Aeden and Marcus."

"You could have said something after."

"I forgot."

Jack stops pacing. "No, you didn't forget, you didn't want us to know."

It's hard to look incensed when I'm holding the object causing the rift. Why it chose now to reappear is both bewildering and annoying.

"Ok… you got me. I didn't tell you because I was unsure how you'd react. Besides, it's not like I got a choice in the matter. One minute it's laying on the seat, the next it's worming it' way under my skin."

"If you'd told me, I would have been better prepared." It's a fair point.

Nathaniel's voice cuts into our exchange. "If The Heron has woken, we need to work together to stop him."

"Yes, it appears we have more pressing matters, now." Alston is back to looking like John Boy Walton.

The staff shimmers and disappears from sight, though I still feel its presence beneath my flesh.

"I don't know why it does that, just so you're all in the loop." No one responds.

There's no winning with this lot, they want you to tell them stuff and when you do, they're not interested.

"So who is this Heron?" I ask, as no one is filling me in.

Arthur moves back against my legs as I sit down on the sofa, flanked once more by Ethan, Julian and Nathaniel. Jack remains standing by the unlit log burner.

The gnome looks up at me, a worried expression on his face. "The Heron's correct name is Manannán mac Lir. He is responsible for the separation between the Mortal Realm and that of Faerieland. Now he's awake, he will look to reclaim the mortal world."

"So why do I have his staff?"

"The staff's magic has always been unpredictable." I scratch my arm at Nathaniel's words.

His fingers touch my arm. "It isn't an innate object it is a living entity."

"That's creepy."

"For whatever reason, it has formed a connection. One we will use to capture The Heron." Alston's fingers drum on his knee in thought.

His coolness rattles me. "I cannot believe you're thinking of using me again."

"It's the only way. The Heron isn't stable, we need him back in Faerieland where he belongs."

"You mean contained." Everyone looks at me. "Why did I say that?"

"It's the staff." Jack is back to pacing again.

"Great, now I feel like a ventriloquist dummy." Arthur coughs, it's got to kill him not to say something.

"If this Heron chap separated the realms, why does he want to un-separate them?"

"It's complicated, Alice," Julian says.

I sigh. "It always is."

"Fine," I grind out, throwing my hands in the air. "Use the link it's not like I get a choice in the matter, but not before I've laid Aunt Dot and Mum to rest. You owe them and me that."

Alston nods. "Agreed. Though if the connection strengthens, you must tell me."

Chapter Twenty-Six

From my vantage point on the roof of the concrete office block, I watch the humans dash about like ants. Never still always busy. Busy destroying what I have given them.

They are a plague, infecting and devouring with no thought of what they are doing. Showing little in the way of understanding or care for the realm they inhabit. How can they? They are incapable of such feelings.

I take a deep breath, inhaling the poisons they emit into the atmosphere. Their putrid odour fills my nostrils and burns my lungs.

Free to live a life they have chosen. To feel the sun upon their skin, and to breathe the air they pollute. They are freer than I. This knowledge is exasperating, niggling away at me until any empathy I have for them disintegrates.

I hate them. There is no other way to describe it. Meaningless lives filled with petty fights and squabbles.

Here, I am forced to hide my true self, taking on a form I loathe to blend into their realm. I twist my hand in front of me as I stretch out my arms. My skin glistens in the winter sunlight. As I stare, the lines on my palm disappear, and the white flesh changes to a soft pearlescent green. Heart thumping with guilt at my indulgence I glance over my shoulder, making sure I am still unobserved and alone.

No one is here, it's just me. Concealment from the other fae is paramount, should they learn I no longer slumber, my plans to reunite Faerieland with the Mortal Realm will crumble. And magic will remain stilted.

Below, humans scatter, as the first few plump raindrops announce the oncoming downpour. Anger festers within my stomach and my lips curl in distaste. The need to end their existence so strong, it is as if they have plunged a knife deep within my chest.

What good have humans ever done? None.

They are nothing but brilliant talkers, speaking of saving their planet, but doing nothing about it. With pockets full of metal, paper and plastic they count their fortune, believing it tips the scales of power their way. It is an illusion. Magic holds the sway of power. It is the essence of control.

I have the power to sweep through their minds, holding them prisoner and making them do my bidding.

Fae can sense magic, it is how we rule over the lesser magical beings, forcing them to accept our dominance. I am not ready for them to discover me. So I shall withhold my magic and let it drip like small droplets of water upon a hot surface. Evaporating too soon to leave a trace.

There are places in the Mortal Realm which can't sustain life or magic. Coated in death by human hand, the land is barren. Still, they build their weapons, fighting amongst themselves for a scrap of earth they will never own. You cannot own the land. It belongs to Mother Nature. Since turning their backs on their ancient beliefs and cultures, few understand the power of nature.

When my time comes to wipe away my wrongs, mortals will see how forceful Mother Nature is, as she takes back control and exercises her right to speak. No human shall outwit nature. She is as savage as she is beautiful.

HUNTED

In Faerieland the trees speak, and the vines creep along the ground and walls, snaring those who dare to forget the power of nature. The delicate fragrance of flowers assail our senses, sweet, intoxicating and alive. Never do we take Mother for granted, she is the reason we live, providing the magic which saturates our world.

A smile spreads over my lips. Killing them isn't enough for me anymore. I want them to suffer. Like I have suffered since I woke from slumber. Some of my anger of course is over my own stupidity.

Jealousy eats at a being, consuming them until it is in control.

It is the reason I threw down my green cloak severing Faerieland from the Mortal Realm, until the fae became tales of mythology.

The blame over my current predicament lays at the delicate feet of my wife Fand and her lover Cuchulainn, the hero son of Lugh. Cuchulainn took Fand from me, defiling our love and marriage. My revenge, however bitter, was not to hand over the Mortal Realm to humans; but to leave Cuchulainn stranded here, while Fand lives out her time alone deep within the fairy hills.

Cut off from Faerieland Cuchulainn would wither and die. There is not enough magic here to sustain him, unless he has harnessed the magic of Faerieland through a portal, he should be dead. I do like the sound of that. Dead.

How curious.

It seems my hatred for Cuchulainn has remained undiluted during my slumber.

Perhaps I have lived too long, seen too much, and tasted too much sorrow and pain. Whatever the reason, my heart has grown cold.

I have allowed humans to infect me until they have killed my compassion.

Manannán mac Lir – son of the sea shall rise once more, for he is a warrior and a king. Ruler of the Otherworld — Emain Ablach, Land of Promise.

The mist of invisibility cloaks the whereabouts of my home and the sidh who dwell there. Despite my slumber, my magic remains strong.

When I first met Aeden the fire demon, he was a desperate soul looking for a quick solution. I gave him the power to take what he wanted, keeping those I needed busy and out of my way. Of course, all magic is fickle, and while Aeden's demise was unfortunate, it is the loss of my staff I feel the most. It has forged an association with a creature I have yet to determine. I look forward to meeting it, soon.

The time is coming for me to walk once more upon this pitiful realm as Manannán mac Lir.

A bubble of laughter escapes, my mood brightening as madness takes me. I stretch my arms higher, leaping off the office block. Gravity pulls at my limbs. In a flash of magic, I transform from man to heron, soaring into the clouds.

Green-gold eyes shine within the distance. I see her watching. She is unaware how deep our connection has become. Her heartbeat increases, and I turn, swooping down at her as she sleeps.

The cry of a heron echoes through the sky as I soar closer.

****

I know I'm asleep, but the attack is real. The Heron is close, so close I feel the beat of its wings. My mouth opens and I scream.

"Alice! Alice, wake-up!" Hands grip my arms, shaking me until my teeth rattle.

The smell of wolf engulfs me, and my eyes snap open.

"It's getting worse, isn't it?" I ask, wiping a trembling hand over my face.

"I'm afraid so." Ethan holds me against his chest, as his wolf comes forward offering comfort.

Tears sting my eyes. I'm so tired and angry as I lay in bed, sweat trickling down my face and between my breasts. Since the staff invaded my body, Manannán mac Lir — The Heron, trespasses through my unconscious mind. It seems so long since I've slept without hearing his vengeful voice. His intentions are to kill and destroy.

The two realms he separated can never reform. It would end human life. I have many emotional affiliations with humans, above all stands Polly. There is no way I'm going to let The Heron inflict his revenge. However, at present, I am not privy to how he intends to bring the two realms together. This lack of knowledge is as frustrating as it is unhelpful.

"Another nightmare?" Julian stands in the doorway.

Ethan's arms fall away, and the wolf recedes.

Arthur runs into the room. The cup and saucer he's carrying clattering together. "I've brought you some camomile tea. I thought it would help."

Since Aunt Dot's death and giving him the tree stump, Arthur is less grumpy. This new attitude is making me skittish. I can't help but wait for him to remember how much he dislikes me.

Julian's wording my dreams as *nightmares* isn't correct, they aren't bad dreams. They are visions into Manannán mac Lir's thoughts and desires. Even now the tickle of the ocean breeze rests on my skin and the cry of the heron sears across my mind. Manannán mac Lir's actions today confirm he is aware of my presence, and the connection the staff has forged between us.

Why the staff has done this, I don't know. I have put this question to it several times, as it seems to enjoy springing up around the house of its own accord. While the staff's actions are perplexing, the strangest action of all is everyone's acceptance of its presence. I have overheard Polly talking to it as she eats her breakfast. Perhaps our connection is as simple as it wanting to receive recognition and company.

I don't want to utter the next words, but I need help from someone who understands these things. "Julian, can you contact Alston, it's time."

Julian's relief strums down our bond as he leaves.

Arthur sits on the bed. "It's for the best. The Seelie King and Keeper will know what…"

"I'll get breakfast going, come on Arthur, you can help." Ethan interrupts before the little man can say anymore.

"Gnomes don't eat human crap and I'm comfortable here."

"Help or not, you're coming with me."

Arthur's eyes narrow, but he doesn't argue. Instead, his clogs make a loud thud on the carpet as he jumps off the bed.

"Very well." Arthur grumbles, stomping out the door with Ethan. "Wolves are such tetchy creatures."

Arthur hasn't mentioned Martin since he arrived. He must know by Martin's death that his life span is reduced in the Mortal Realm. Perhaps it's none of my concern, other than I'm responsible for him, given he's living at Roseley.

I wonder if he can pop back to Faerieland for a lifespan recharge. While I may not always like the gnome, I don't want him dead, or old before his time.

The aroma of food drifts into the bedroom, interrupting my thoughts and causing Jeremiah to jump off the bed and investigate further.

It is also my incentive to get myself out of bed, washed and dressed.

Tomorrow is Aunt Dot and Mum's memorial service. Julian and Nathaniel have arranged the guest list, and for the Wiccan Priestess and Priest to conduct the service. While I wanted to be the one making all the arrangements, it soon became clear there was, and still are, parts of Mum and Aunt Dot's life I don't understand. My plans of organising the memorial service is soon downgraded to arranging flowers.

****

Emily paces in front of the Aga, her brows nip together and her lips purse.

What gets my instant attention are the shoes on her feet. The heels are around twenty inches (I may exaggerate a little, but they're very high). Straps twist around her feet, offering little in the way of support or security. I'm not sure how her feet remain in them, or how she can strut around the kitchen like she's wearing loafers. But they do, and she does.

"What's up?" Emily turns at the sound of my voice.

"Staff issues. I hate all the politics."

"Don't we all," Polly comments as she bites down on her toast.

Julian and Nathaniel own several wine bars scattered across England. Their latest venture is a converted church up on St Saviourgate in the heart of York's city centre. My lips twitch at the thought of demons walking around a church.

"So what's up with the staff?" I poke my head in the fridge, perusing the contents for something refreshing to drink.

"The barman took a bite out of the new barmaid."

"Ouch…" I grab a carton of orange juice, closing the fridge door.

"Yeah, it's the bloody paperwork that goes with it I hate."

"Bad choice of words, Emily," Ethan says as he flips over the bacon.

"It would be bloody too, if I had my way. Why couldn't he have bitten off site?"

"Your sympathy for the girl is amazing." Emily frowns at me.

Polly puts down the toast she's munching on. "Blimey… it use to be roaming hands in my day. Things have changed a lot."

"You were a barmaid for about an hour, Pol." I pull out a chair, sitting next to her as Ethan passes me a clean glass.

"Sixty minutes can feel like forever."

Emily resumes her pacing. "I wish it was roaming hands, we could have cut them off."

"You're kidding, right?" Polly asks.

Emily shrugs. "They'd grow back."

"Won't it be difficult for him to pull a pint with no hands?" I point out.

"True, but it's more fun than paperwork."

Ethan places a loaded plate of food in front of me. My stomach groans in thanks.

He laughs. "Tuck in before it gets cold."

I pick up my knife and fork, the barman's hands forgotten. "You know I can get use to this."

Polly nudges me. "Oh, I bet you could."

My cheeks warm.

"Other than Emily and Julian, what's everyone else up to?" I ask.

"I'm out with Dylan." Polly beams. "He's err... going to check out my car..."

"It's new Pol, won't the garage be better looking at it if there's a problem." She kicks me.

"I'm sure it's nothing, but Dylan offered."

"It is just the car he's looking at, isn't it?" She kicks me again, a sweet smile on her face.

"If you want to go for a run around two, I should be back by then." Ethan leans against the Aga, throwing the tea-towel he used to deliver my plate over his shoulder.

"That sounds great." I refuse to acknowledge Polly, who's grinning like an idiot.

"And I'm out of here," Emily says as Jack mists in.

"What did I do?" The ghost looks puzzled.

"Julian, you ready yet?" Emily's voice echoes down the hall.

"You don't have to do anything, being here is enough," I say.

Jack rolls his eyes. "You'd think she'd have gotten over what happened by now."

I wasn't sure Emily would ever get over Jack's betrayal.

"So, to what do we owe the pleasure of your company?" I ask.

"Nathaniel asked me to tell you Alston will be here at four."

I watch Ethan as he strides around the kitchen, putting things away and clearing the surfaces, his jeans moulding to his bum.

"Hm… why's Alston coming?"

"He misses you."

"Huh?" I look at Jack.

Jack spreads his arms. "How the hell should I know? I'm just delivering the message."

"Eh? Oh sorry, my mind was on other things, he's coming to sort out my Heron issue." Ethan is still parading round the kitchen, taking up most of my concentration.

Polly laughs. "As entertaining as this exchange is, I've my own entertainment to grab. I mean car to sort out." She squeezes my shoulder. "Good luck with Tinkerbell."

"Thanks."

"Whose Tinkerbell?" Jack asks.

A smile tugs at my lips. "Alston…"

"Oh… I was slow, wasn't I?"

"A bit."

Julian pops his head round the kitchen door. "Do you want me back for four?"

"That'd be nice. I could do with the moral support."

"What were you thinking about?" Jack looks at me with interest.

"Where I put my running trainers."

Polly's plate clatters in the sink. "Of course you were." Her eyes slide in Ethan's direction.

I refuse to comment.

"I'd best get off if we're going running." Ethan walks out the door, oblivious to how I feel about him.

Jack raises his eyebrows at me.

"Don't say a word," I warn.

"I wasn't going to."

"Of course you weren't."

Polly is still tittering to herself as she follows Ethan out of the kitchen.

"I'll catch you later. Hope you find your trainers." Jack mists out.

A soft snort escapes my lips. "Yeah, so do I."

The sound of voices drifts into the kitchen as Julian and Emily leave. Polly soon follows them with Ethan.

It's amazing how quickly silence becomes oppressive. I walk out of the kitchen searching for something to occupy me until Ethan gets back.

I look down at my jeans. Perhaps I should change into my gym things and do a bit of yoga.

It's a thought.

Chapter Twenty-Seven

A slight breeze teases my hair as I sit in the lotus position on the orangery floor. The open windows carry the smell of rain. With a big intake of oxygen, my stomach inflates in full yogi breathing technique.

Earth and moss fill my senses.

"Sorry, I'm late. You still want to go for that run," Ethan asks.

It's half two, which doesn't give us much time for our run, as I want to get washed and changed before my meeting with Alston. However, I'm still going running with Ethan.

"It doesn't matter, we'll make the run shorter."

Ethan holds out his hand and I place mine in them, as he hoists me to my feet. He's already in his running shorts.

"Race you," I shout, leaping towards the patio doors.

The wolf in Ethan growls, and he jumps forward, his trainers an inch away from mine. The cold air slams into me and goosebumps form. I keep running, not looking back, knowing Ethan is gaining ground.

Our bodies find a rhythm as we run through the woods, jumping over fallen branches. Sweat trickles down my back and my breath catches in my throat. We increase our pace, trainers pounding over the ground. With Ethan in human form, his speed is slower than in his wolf form. He's still fast, forcing me to lengthen my stride.

Ahead of us a tree sprawls over the ground. I jump over my legs stretching out. Free-falling down. I find myself at the bottom of a shallow pit. Ethan stands at the edge, laughing as I pick leaves out of my hair. He offers me his hand. I smile fingers clasping round his, I pull hard, catching him off balance. Losing stability Ethan lands next to me in the pit. Dirt falls over us. Using Ethan's body as a lever I jump out of the hole, turning I look down at him.

"Come on, Joe Slow!" I shout, running off.

The wolf roars as Ethan leaps forward, firing after me like a cannonball.

Branches tug at our clothes as we run. I can hear Ethan's breathing as he chases me. His hands grip my waist, and we sail through the air, his weight catapulting us forward. We hit the ground and I roll back to my feet. Bits of leaves, moss, and twigs stick to my clothes and hair.

"You should have said you want to play dirty." His cherry brown eyes are alive with the burnt amber of his wolf.

They are both up for the play. "Dirty," I yell at him. "I haven't even started."

My hands reach for the branch above my head and I swing my body up onto it. Like a squirrel, I jump from branch to tree. The wolf bares his teeth as Ethan leaps up to catch my ankle. His body mass too heavy for the branches. I laugh at him.

"What's keeping you?" I ask as my feet land on the ground.

Ethan roars as he stampedes his way through the trees. I will my legs to move faster, as the wolf closes the gap. Together we break clear of the woods and hit the grass, leading us back to Roseley. The house looms in front of us. There's no way I'm losing this race. The problem is, neither is Ethan.

"Ah…" I scream hitting the ground.

My fingers grab at the grass, fingernails biting into the earth as Ethan catches my ankle and hauls me to him, flipping me onto my back. Breath catching in my throat, I stare at Ethan as he hovers over me. He's magnificent and victorious in his capture. I let Ethan have his moment, before springing to my feet, grabbing hold of him and covering his face and arms in mud. Without thinking, I close my hands over his cheeks and kiss his nose.

Fingers sneaking up his chest, I smear mud over him, before pushing his body away and legging it to the house. There's a howl behind me, and my smile grows bigger.

My trainers hit the concrete slabs. Eight meters away, the doors into the orangery stand open and inviting. The battle is almost over, and it appears the winner is me.

Ethan's arms circle my waist, and we go down, losing our footing. My breathing is erratic as he hovers on top of me, grabbing my arms and pinning them to the concrete.

"I think you will find I'm no Joe Slow."

His face is so close to mine. Lips hover above my mouth, and I want to tell him he can be anything he likes so long as he kisses me.

The wolf and Ethan are as one, both alive and present as their eyes feast on me. My heart pounds hard against my ribcage, and my tongue slips out, licking at my dry lips. As my lips part, Ethan dips his head closer.

We freeze as tyres crunch over the gravel drive. I want to scream not now, but Ethan has already moved off, grabbing my hand and pulling me to my feet.

"Bloody Seelie blah… blah…" I curse.

Ethan smiles, looping his arm about my shoulders and pressing me to his side as he steers me to the open doors.

We kick off our trainers as we walk inside.

"You go get cleaned up, I'll stall him."

His arm falls off my shoulders, and I stomp upstairs in frustration.

"You look dirty," Arthurs says, as I walk past him.

"Not half as dirty as I wanted to be."

He looks at me, a puzzled expression falling across his face. I don't enlighten him further.

****

A large pearlescent box sits in the middle of the bed. Suspicious, I walk from the bathroom teasing my damp hair with a towel. The staff flashes, and I think it's winking at me. I stare at both objects with caution and curiosity.

"Is this your doing?" I ask the staff.

It doesn't respond.

I'm not a lover of surprises, they never end well, or that's my experience. But inquisitiveness is encouraging me, so I walk over and take the lid off.

"Well, I didn't expect that." A dress isn't on my radar of expectations.

The fabric is the smoothest silk I have ever felt. It slips through my fingers in a wash of blues and greens, like the sea rolling in the moonlight. No… it couldn't?

"Did Manannán mac Lir's leave this?" I point at the dress.

The white orb on top of the staff blinks. *Does that mean yes or no?*

It's the first time the staff has acknowledged that I've spoken. Either that or the sun shining through the window has provided me with the impression it has responded.

It is a mystifying world I live in.

With delicate fingers, I remove the dress, holding it against my body. The fabric falls to the floor in soft waves. In the box, under the dress, is an ornate belt and my fingers run over it as I place the dress onto the bed. Upon the breastplate is the face of the sea god.

"What do you think it means?" This time the staff doesn't respond in any form.

There's a knock at the door and Arthur walks in before I can mutter the word *'enter.'*

The gnome's eyes widen as he looks at the dress.

"Oh, dear…" He turns running from the room.

I grab the dress, and staff and run after him. "What do you mean… *oh dear…*"

For a little person, he's blessed with the speed of light. The open door into the living room gives away his location and I make my way there.

Alston sits waiting for my arrival. Julian, Nathaniel and Ethan, who has showered and changed, sit on the opposite sofa. Arthur stands in the middle of the floor, gesturing at me.

The staff has disappeared, leaving me wondering why I bothered to pick it up.

I hold the dress up, gaining everyone's attention. "This arrived while I was in the shower."

Arthur sits where he is and stares at the dress, a mixture of emotions falling over his face. I'm not sure if his positioning in the centre of the room is an attempt at being neutral or if he's tired from his sprint downstairs. The silence is over-powering.

"OK, someone's got to speak soon." My audience remains silent.

Unable to get them talking, I walk over to the log burner and open the door. Heat from the fire stings my face.

Arthur grabs my hand. "What are you doing?"

"I didn't think the dress was important given the lack of response, so I thought I'd burn it."

Alston jumps to his feet as I move the dress closer to the flames. "Don't!"

I close the door. "Thought that might get your attention."

"You play a dangerous game." Arthur sighs, sitting down and crossing his legs.

The king walks closer, his hands hovering near the dress before turning away. "The dress is not as important as the meaning behind it."

"And the meaning?" I ask.

Silence consumes the room once more. Alston sits down, placing his hands on his knees, staring at the dress. Impatience like a storm rages inside me, but I refrain from letting it out. Instead I wait.

"The staff is integrating you into The Heron's world. Think of it as an initiation. One you cannot refuse. It appears it has selected your costume for the memorial service."

"I can't wear this, it's not appropriate."

"You don't have a choice, if you don't wear it, I'm not sure what the staff will do. There is a reason it has presented it to you. That reason may never become clear. But you will wear it."

I know what I want to do with the dress, and wearing it is low on my list of options.

"Fae magic is not always direct, nor is it clear. The dress signifies acceptance from a magic older than me. Think of it as an endorsement at the highest level. The dress is owned by Una, the High Queen of Daoine Sidhe. She has heard the staff's request and granted her blessing. Worn by a non-full-bloodied fae, says many things."

I stare at the dress. "Does it need washing?"

Alston doesn't comment.

"Fine, I'll wear the dress. But just so everyone is clear, I'm not happy about it. It feels wrong."

Alston nods. "Noted."

The ocean air circles round the room and the call of a heron's cry beats down on us. My heart pounds and blood gushes through my system as my body jerks.

I look around the room through the eyes of Manannán mac Lir. My fingers wrap around the staff as it blinks into view.

Words fall from my lips, but the voice isn't mine. "Hello old friend."

Alston's magic pulses. "It has been a long time, Heron."

"Do you feel the confinement?" My head tilts as I wait for an answer.

"Confinement?" Alston says. "No, you mean, suppression."

"Ah..." I nod. "Yes, I believe I do."

"The world has changed whilst you slumbered. We are no longer free to rule or play within the Mortal Realm. Though our magic has reduced, and mortals have lost their belief in the old ways, we can survive here."

"They destroy."

"We all destroy things?"

My head shakes. "It is not the same."

Alston nods. "No, it is different."

Green mist rises, dividing the space between me and Alston. The smell of the ocean becomes stronger. From behind me, the wolf growls. A laugh escapes my lips as my feet leave the ground. Suspended a metre from the floor, I begin to spin and Manannán mac Lir leaves my body. Mist conceals us and I'm not sure I'm still in the living room at Roseley or if The Heron has transported me into a different realm

Within the mist, he stands. "I see you have something that belongs to me."

At first, I'm not sure if he is referring to the staff or the dress.

The staff glows. "It's not that I have it as it doesn't wish to leave." I reply.

"Hm…" The Heron looks at me with open curiosity. "That is a curious thought…"

The mist whips and I spin wildly. From the edges of the midst voices scream, merging until I can't tell who it is that's shouting, or understand what they are saying.

Manannán mac Lir vanishes, his words drifting through the mist. "Until we meet on the battlefield."

Light pours in blinding me, and the staff disappears as the mist clears. I fall to the ground. Ethan grabs me and I'm pressed against his chest. The howl of the wolf fills the room.

Arthur stands transfixed in fear, the dress at his feet. Julian and Nathaniel stand behind Ethan, they don't come closer.

My hands shake as I touch Ethan's face. "It's OK, I'm fine. No damage done."

Ethan blinks and the amber leaves his eyes, though the wolf's presence still strums close to the surface.

"Protect her." Ethan's voice is gruff, half human, half wolf as he calls on Alston to do something.

The Seelie King steps forward, placing his right hand against my chest. Magic filters beneath my flesh, ripping at my insides. It sizzles through my body, snapping at Ethan. But he refuses to let go, pressing me tighter to him.

"Let her go Ethan before the magic binds...."

"No!" He snaps, shaking his head and cutting off whatever the king is about to say.

The magic pushes on, invading each molecule of my body. Something inside me responds to its call, and I cry out as pain blasts through to my nerve endings. I can feel the structure of my DNA reconstructing itself. Like a caterpillar turns into a butterfly, my skin becomes a chrysalis, protecting me while I change.

The wolf howls and my fingers grip Ethan's t-shirt as I hold on to him, using him to ground me. To stop me changing into someone, or something unrecognisable.

Alston hovers above us, his face a beautiful glow of gold. I can't contain the magic, and it leaks from me into Ethan. I can feel the bond between us deepening, forging us together.

I want the man and the wolf, not one or the other, and our magic responds to my request.

Jack mists in as the pain relinquishes its hold. "You've woken the fae in her."

Alston steps away, retreating to the sofa. "I did what I had to do."

Nathaniel holds out his arms, but Ethan refuses to let me go. He turns and looks at Jack before walking over to the sofa. "Manannán mac Lir was here, there was no other choice. The change will protect her from The Heron."

"If Manannán mac Lir has made his presence known, it means he's ready to carry out his plans," Jack says, joining Nathaniel and Julian as they move to the sofa.

Ethan cradles me at his side and a snuggle deeper into him.

"Why does The Heron hate humans so much?" I ask.

"Concern has been growing amongst the fae regarding our human involvement. When Manannán mac Lir punished his wife over her affair with Cuchulainn, he did so, knowing our worlds required separating. Fand's affair drove him into throwing down his cloak, an act we had been encouraging him to do for some time. The Mortal Realm was drawing too much magic from Faerieland, it required stopping. Humans once worshipped us as Gods. When they turned their backs on us and forgot the old ways, some like Manannán mac Lir saw this as an insult. If the worlds are reunited humanity must die for Faerieland to keep its power."

The Seelie King looks lost in thought. "Manannán mac Lir is Lugh's foster father. The young God of Light left his son Cuchulainn in The Heron's care. Because of this Cuchulainn's disloyalty cut deep. It is hard to forgive those close to you."

What drives a person to do what they do is hard to understand. All I know is it's been a tiring few month, and I want some peace. I'm fed up with fighting my way through one problem to uncover another. Yes, there are people to save, but for now there is little I can do about it. First, I say goodbye to Mum and Aunt Dot. Then I face Manannán mac Lir.

I push myself off the sofa and walk over to the dress, picking it off the floor. "I'd best hang this up otherwise it'll get creased."

Jack points at the dress. "Where did that come from?"

"It was a gift from the staff for Mum and Aunt Dot's memorial service." I say putting my hand up. "Whatever your feelings are about the dress, they're about as irrelevant as mine."

"You'll look great in it," Jack says.

I raise a questioning brow at his unnatural use of diplomacy.

The fabric shimmers in my hand. "I'm not sure what shoes I'm going to wear with it."

"Shoes?" Arthur is aghast at the thought. "You're not supposed to wear shoes with it. The dress resembles the sea. It is freedom, one with nature. You do not put a barrier between the two."

I sigh. "No shoes then, best get my toenails painted."

"Is this your way of saying you want to be alone?" Arthur asks unsure.

"You're getting very astute. I'm impressed."

"Do you want me to bring you up a camomile tea? I would bring you some biscuits, but someone has failed to go shopping."

Hm…. maybe I was too fast in using the word *astute*. "No, I'm good."

I stop at the door. "Who ate all the biscuits?"

The gnome's cheeks redden. "Ur… I'm not sure."

"I'll add them to the order, it's due tomorrow." Closing the door, I walk up to my bedroom.

The dress hangs off the wardrobe and I sit on the bed staring at it, aware that my toenails aren't getting painted.

Chapter Twenty-Eight

Roseley is awash with colour, despite the ever-popular requirement within the Mortal Realm to wear black. It's easy to spot the humans amongst the guests in their sombre black tones and disapproving stares.

A Welsh lake fairy known as the Gwragedd Annwn saunters across the room, her gown trailing over the floor. There is a lot of flesh on display within the shimmering near translucent watery cloth. Her hair cascades down her body in spun golden curls, teasing and tantalising. It isn't just the men that are staring and eating each curve with their eyes, women also ogle the beautiful creature. Whispers of outrage fall from jealous lips while in secret they wish their bodies carried such perfection.

My own outfit has also caused a stir. While my choice of attire seems peculiar to some, others view it with open hostility and unquenchable envy. The staff's gift is causing friction within a portion of fae well-wishers.

"The service was beautiful." A man I've never met takes my hand, clasping it between his thick palms.

He's unaware I can feel the thin thread of magic used to hide his true form. Some Fae use glamour out of vanity. On this occasion, the requirement for glamour is essential, given the man gripping my hand is an ogre.

Even for a human, he is tall, and his bottom canines protrude from his lips. There are several small children roaming round, and the ogre has shown restraint by not eating them. The saliva dripping from the side of his mouth is the only sign he'd rather have chewed on them, than the leg of lamb he'd eaten earlier.

I slide my hand from his. "I'm glad you liked it."

The normal response of *thank you* remains unsaid. Never thank the fae, you'll end up in their debt, and that's a place you don't want to be.

"I'll miss her. She was a fine witch, and friend."

Fae can't lie. This will not stop them from bending the truth or manipulating people. I take the compliment offered, inclining my head.

"Such a sad loss." The ogre's lips smack together.

Polly walks over unaware ogres are temperamental creatures, and best practices for a long life dictate not to interrupt them.

As always, Polly is a walking kaleidoscope of colour. The neon accessories do more than brighten the black dress, which I know she loathes, but felt it was appropriate to wear.

"Not to seem rude, but I just need to borrow, Alice."

With that, I'm dragged away from the ogre as his eyes bulge, and his skin reddens. Anger radiates from him.

Alston steps forward, diverting the ogre's attention. The supernatural creature's anger doesn't disperse, but it is now under control.

Polly stops at the entrance of the orangery where a group of fae gather. She points to where the staff is enjoying the attention. The orb is a mixture of glowing green and white light.

"I think you might have a problem."

"The little minx," I sigh, walking over and grabbing it.

"We talked about this," I tell it. Not that I think it cares or is listening. "No appearing today… people talking… too many humans… are you remembering any of it?"

The staff continues to glow as a wave of magic vibrates through its length into my hand.

My eyes narrow. "You're laughing at me, aren't you?" It flickers. "Great even the objects in this house think I'm hilarious."

Fae gasp, like strings being plucked on a harp. The staff brightens further.

"Come on, you've caused enough of a scene here," I tell it as I walk out of the room.

Ethan places a hand on my back, amber eyes challenging the fae as they follow. The crowd of fae fall back as a low growl rumbles from his throat.

Arthur stands in the corner near the stairs. He's been there ever since the memorial service ended and everyone started milling. His feet dance from side to side in an aggravated manner. Curious, I walk over to him, leaving Ethan's side.

"You OK, Arthur?"

"Fine." He sounds anything but *fine*.

Behind me, someone sniggers and the tips of Arthur's ears turn red. A glance over my shoulder reveals a group of gnomes pointing and laughing at Arthur. Their rudeness shocks me, never mind their lack of respect. Whatever their problem, this isn't the time or place for such lack of manners.

I turn and stride over, pointing the staff at them. "What's so funny?"

The gnome in the middle of the bunch closes his lips, bringing his fingers to his mouth making a zipping motion. My eyebrows raise as he nudges the gnome on his right, and the bell on his hat rings with laughter.

I bang the staff on the wooden floor and the gnome stops tittering with his friend and for the first time looks at me.

"Today is about celebrating the life of Dot and Sophie. Whatever your problem with Arthur, you do not bring it here today, or ever. He is part of our family now." Raising the staff, I point it at the door. "You're no longer welcome, now leave."

Alston's magic tingles the air as a veil falls, concealing us from the humans in the room. The staff glows deep green, and an ocean breeze fills the air around us and the front door opens. A gust of wind pushes the gnomes outside in a heap of gasps and fear. Julian and Nathaniel step forward with Ethan.

"I won't have rudeness, not today." Is my only explanation.

Since Arthur arrived at Roseley, he has been uncivil and obnoxious. Fast becoming the most unpleasant creature I have met. Given time, he will be so again, when the shine of the tree stump wears off. Yet, he is family now and having lost two members of my family, I will not allow criticism to fall on those remaining. The staff is of the same opinion as the door closes behind our unwelcomed guests.

Alston's magic drops and the room buzzes to life with the chatter of our guests. Fae look at me with interest. Polly loops her arm through mine.

"Let's get something to drink. I reckon we could both do with more than juice and coffee."

"What about…" I stammer as Polly pulls me to the kitchen, undeterred about our guests and protocol.

A bottle of wine sits on the table and I lean back against the chair, my fingers playing along the rim of the wineglass. Julian and Nathaniel sit opposite me, Ethan to my right and Polly on my left. Jack stands by the large patio doors and Arthur sits next to Polly, his hands resting on his stomach.

"Do you think we should go back in…" I ask, inclining my head where our guests mingle.

Julian shakes his head. "Alston is seeing to them."

The staff has done its normal disappearing act as we entered the kitchen. It's had its fun for the day and gone to wherever it goes when not around causing mischief.

"How will The Heron reunite the realms?" I ask, pondering the coming battle.

"To reunite the realms he will lift the cloak he threw down, which acts as a shield between the worlds. The Heron will be wherever the cloak is."

I look at Nathaniel. "It's a stupid question, but does Alston know where the cloak location might be?"

"No."

"I didn't think so. It would have been too easy."

Jack walks away from the glass doors. "Alston's plan to use Fand is risky given their history."

"Fand. You mean the wife that did the dirty on The Heron, blimey why not ask Cuchulainn to come along as well I'm sure that won't send Manannán mac Lir over the edge." I say, flippancy dripping from my voice.

Nathaniel, Julian, Jack and Ethan exchange looks.

"You have got to be kidding me. Manannán mac Lir is hurt, dysfunctional and angry, and Alston's arranging for the two fae that betrayed him to… well, I'm not sure what he expects them to do, other than wind up the unstable and powerful fae."

"The Seelie King and Keeper knows what he's doing." Arthur leaps to his king's defence.

I send the gnome a sharp look. "That's easy for you and The Seelie King to say, you aren't human."

"As the only human in the room, I agree with Alice. Did anyone not think…" Polly pauses. "No, I don't suppose anyone did."

"It's not just humans, Pol, if Manannán mac Lir merges the realms, a vampire's favourite food diminishes to zero. Drinking bunny blood doesn't provide the level of magic human blood does. Vamps have as much interest in stopping Manannán mac Lir as humans. Plus vamp's can't enter Faerieland."

"How come?" Polly looks at me intrigued.

"They eat the fae," Jack says sitting down next to Arthur.

"What? Don't vampires have better control than to go around eating people."

"It's not control they lack. Fae blood is addictive. It's why Emily and Henry aren't here. Julian and Nathaniel carry immunity through the bond we share, and my fae heritage. Otherwise it would be like The Las Vegas Massacre in 2017, with no guns, just teeth."

"Shit…"

"Uh-huh." I nod at Polly.

"Betrayal is part of life in Faerieland," Arthur says.

"It might be part of life, but Manannán mac Lir didn't throw down his cloak and separate the realms because he was having a bad day. He did it because Fand's affair hurt him beyond reason." I remind the gnome.

"You're right." Ethan agrees. "However, The Heron isn't at full power, which is why he's not lifted the cloak. Seeing Fand and Cuchulainn might just give us the advantage to stop him before he's at full strength."

"Or make him madder," Polly points out.

"True, but betrayal is a potent emotion, and needs answers from the betrayer before they inflict vengeance. It doesn't matter if you're fae, human or supernatural you want to know why." Ethan says.

I'm conscious of how little I know about Ethan. At one point he was human, but someone took that away from him in one bite, infecting him with the Lycanthropy virus. Was it accidental, or on purpose? Given what Ethan's said, I'm thinking it was personal.

Fingers curling round my wineglass, I take a gulp, hating the thought of Ethan being anything with anyone but me. I try not to think about Lucy as it highlights how messy the whole situation is between us. If there is a situation.

Alston appears at the kitchen door. "Your guests are leaving."

"Right." I stand up, my hands smoothing away the wrinkles from my dress.

"Are you still OK if I go out with Dylan?" Polly asks.

"Yes, have a wild time, Pol."

She hugs me as I walk into the hall. I hate this part. People shaking your hand, telling you how sorry they are, and going out for pizza and a pint afterwards, talking about the future.

It takes forever before they all leave, and I can close the door and replace the crystals. I'm too relieved that they've gone to bother about the amount of cleaning now required.

Like a robot, I walk into the orangery and start stacking the empty plates.

Ethan places his hands on my shoulders. "We'll see to it. You go sit down in the living room and I'll send Arthur in with a cuppa."

"Go on." Julian encourages me.

Too tired to argue, I walk into the living room, my head spinning with questions, theories and a mixture of emotions. The memorial service was a chance for me to say goodbye. But the wound remains open and my pain still relevant in this time and place rather than sitting within the past.

Jack stands by the window watching darkness take hold as night falls. He looks lost in thought as I flop onto the sofa.

"A penny for them," I say, tucking my legs under me.

"They aren't worth that much."

"I'll be the judge of that."

He walks over and sits down. "You'd think being dead I'd come to terms with death, but I haven't, it's the reason I'm still here. If The Heron merges the realms, I'm not sure I'll survive the imbalance it causes."

"Still not ready to die?"

"More not ready to give up."

"On what?"

"A lot of things, most of all Emily."

I stare at Jack for a long while, thinking things through. "Have you thought that Emily's resistance in resolving your issues isn't about what you did, as much as losing you forever?"

"What?" Jack looks confused.

"I know she cares about you, even if she refuses to acknowledge it. The fact she gets angry whenever she sees you is a defensive reaction. If she forgives you, what then? Do you remain as you are, or look to move on?"

Jack's shoulders lift. "I don't know."

"And that's the problem, isn't it? If she allows your relationship to return to what it was, pre-betrayal, there's nothing to keep you here."

"I hadn't thought about it like that."

"I don't suppose Emily has either. It's better to stay mad then risk realising why your angry and having to do something about it."

Jack smiles at me. "When did you become so perceptive?"

"Don't worry, it's an off day."

The living room door opens and Arthur walks in carrying a mug of tea. I seem to live off the stuff at the moment. While I don't think I look that stressed out, the gnome either thinks I do, or he's repaying me in camomile tea for the tree stump.

The gnome sets the mug down on the hearth and sits on the floor.

"There's plenty of sofa space, you don't have to sit on the floor."

"I like the floor." The little man says.

"I'll see how much progress is being made in the kitchen." Jack stands, leaving me alone with Arthur.

The gnome looks as if he's made from terracotta clay. His eyes stare at me unblinking, his body motionless. Discomfort spreads over me, and I'm unsure of what to do. It seems a strange place to go into hibernation. Afraid to speak in case I wake or scare him I sit in silence.

The clock in the hall makes its presence known. Tick… tock… tick… tock, the sound echoes through the wooden door until it increases in volume and intensity.

My tea is getting cold, the tension becomes too much, and I crack under the pressure the gnome's silence is inflicting. "Arthur."

He blinks but doesn't move. "Arthur," I say louder.

A ripple runs over the gnome's body as he shakes himself out from his transfixed state. "I was thinking."

While I want to ask what is on his mind, I don't. Instead I pick up my tea, sipping at the cooling liquid. Voices rumble from the hall along with the sound of pots clanging.

"What you did with the other gnomes, it meant something," Arthurs says.

Taken by surprise, I stare at him, uncertain how to proceed, aware my actions were a big deal to the gnome.

"Like I said, you are family."

"Family?" He looks at me, puzzled.

"Yes. I've lost a lot these past few months. Everyone here living at Roseley is my family. They are special to me. We may not always get on, families don't, but as long as we're there for each other, it's all that matters."

Various emotions fall across the gnome's face.

Arthur nods. "I like that."

"Good."

The living room door swings open and everyone pours into the room, signalling the end of our conversation.

Chapter Twenty-Nine

I walk along the sand, my bare feet trailing in the water. The salty breeze coats my hair and skin, as it teases the frown from my face. It feels good to shake away the stench of human from my flesh and be me, without glamour or the need to hide. Fingers extending, I reach out and touch the invisible shield that prevents any creature from noticing me. Even the most powerful of fae cannot detect me. My magic has returned.

The short meeting with Alston, as he's known at the moment, was interesting. However, more intriguing was the girl in which the staff has forged an alliance. Contentment and pleasure run through the staff over the union I share with the girl. Why her? She seems simple and very ordinary. Her fae magic sits unused and wasted, her image forgettable. But then Fand was beautiful and her betrayal painful.

The staff's trickery is of little consequence. My transformation is almost complete and come tomorrow I should, at last be strong enough to lift the cloak.

There are enough humans within Faerieland, thanks to the changelings, to sustain our growth in numbers. The fact we need humans to breed from is somewhat worrying. Once the realms merge, we can enhance our breeding project allowing humans to breed together ready for breeding with fae. It is unfortunate that we need the changelings to sustain our own reproduction. Full-fledged fae are rare. For whatever the reason, producing our own children remains difficult and we have not achieved a full-bloodied fae for several centuries. The humans in Faerieland will not perish like those in the Mortal Realm. Faerieland is the greater of the realms. Its magic will shield the humans as it has slowed down their rapid aging process.

Meeting Fand is unavoidable once I enter Faerieland. I tell myself I have long gotten over the natural requirement for answers concerning her betrayal. I know deep in my heart that is not so. Love amongst the fae is as common as giving birth to a pure blood and I had loved Fand. Perhaps I still do, which is why the pain will not stop sinking its teeth into my heart.

Gull's cry from high in the sky and I nod my head, agreeing with them. I shall deal with Fand later. For now I turn my thoughts back to the creature living inside me where our bond whispers. She is an oddity. There is much sorrow within her. It is a shame she will be dead soon.

Death is a part of us all. Ankou still rides his cart, stopping to collect the souls of those who have ceased living. He is a dark creature made of bone, draped within black cloth. Upon his head is a wide-brimmed hat, and in his hand, he claps a scythe. Onyx horses pull his cart as he makes his journey from place to place.

Ankou is a creature without a soul or humour. When I merge the realms, perhaps then his thirst for souls will quieten as he feeds on the humans within the Mortal Realm. It will be a bounteous meal for one who is used to the soft trickle of souls.

The girl is stirring. I feel her heart increase its beat as she invades my thoughts. Having someone trespass their way through your mind as she does is a violation. It forces me to be careful, to ensure my true plans remain hidden. She seeks me without conscious awareness.

I need to divert them and now is the time to act on it.

HUNTED

Her eyes snap open, and I smile.
Do have fun little one…

****

I look about the room with unseeing eyes, aware that everyone is staring at me. The sea wind blows around me and I smile.

"Do have fun little one…"

The words though spoken from my mouth aren't mine, and neither are the eyes that look around the room.

Manannán mac Lir's magic seeps from me. Julian moves away from me as fae magic bites into his skin. The wolf stirs within Ethan, neither man nor wolf welcoming The Heron's invasion.

"Alice?" Julian says, his voice cutting through the thin veil of mist.

A low rumble of a growl emits from Ethan's lips. The smell of moss and earth threads its way through the scent of the ocean, banishing it from me. Though Ethan sits next to me, I see his wolf as we enter Manannán mac Lir s plane together. The wolf's ears twitch and his lips roll back, revealing sharp teeth. He pushes himself to his feet and walks over to me. It is interesting that man and beast can separate, protecting me on all planes. As one tends to my body the other tends to my soul. My hands reach out for the wolf and he leans into my palms, sitting at my side. This is where we both belong. Together. A howl rings out, chasing away the last of the ocean breeze.

"What is it?" Alston asks.

I blink, and the room snaps into place as my brain makes the leap from multiple planes. Amber lights Ethan's eyes, as his wolf's spirit returns to him.

Manannán mac Lir shares my confusion about our connection. The object that has united us remains silent on the subject.

Salt sits on my skin and Ethan's hand tightens its grip on my arm, grounding me. I place my free hand on top of his. "It's OK, I'm back."

"What did you see?" The king demands.

My shoulders move. "I can't make sense of it."

Restless, I get up from the sofa and pace. The dress brushes against my bare feet. It's been a long day, and it looks like it's getting longer.

"The Heron plans to lift the cloak tomorrow, but there's more to it. He seems smug."

"Smug?" Alston says.

I can see his point. Fae, have a tendency towards smugness, Manannán mac Lir's attitude will appear natural to the king. Upmanship, egotistical, self-righteousness — fae have a natural predisposition towards these attitudes.

"There is something else happening, it's more than just the cloak. The Heron's power is growing, and he's shielding so it all gets muddled in my head. I know he's lifting the cloak tomorrow, and I think he's looking at a way to keep us busy."

The clock strikes twelve, signalling tomorrow has arrived. "Better make that today."

Nathaniel steps forward, hands resting on my shoulders, stopping me from pacing. "Did you see where the cloak was?"

I shake my head. "No, he's being guarded with his thoughts."

Alston stands. "I had best get back to Faerieland and arrange for Fand and Cuchulainn to help us. Nathaniel."

My father's hands drop from my shoulders. "Of course."

Nathaniel turns to leave with Alston, stopping at the door, he looks at the others in the room. "Look after her."

Arthur leaps to his feet. "Gnomes are magnificent fighters."

I refrain from commenting.

Jack walks to my side as Julian and Ethan nod.

For the first time, Nathaniel opens the bonds so I can sense his anguish. He thinks he's deserting me, again. I know that isn't the case, and I hope my silent message reaches him. Over the last few months, I have grown up. Nathaniel may always invoke some conflict within me, but I have tasted the pain he carries at leaving Mum long before I was born. While I find it hard to understand, I can at least acknowledge its presence.

The door closes behind the master vampire and king, and the room turns colder even though flames lick at the sides of the log burner.

"What now? Do you want me to see if I can track Manannán mac Lir?" Jack asks.

I rub my arms, trying to remove the coldness. "No, we will know soon enough what he plans."

The gnome walks over to the door. "I'll go put the kettle on."

Not waiting to see if anyone wants a drink, Arthur leaves the room, his clogs banging against the wooden floor.

"Is there a reason why he's obsessed with making tea?" I ask.

"It gives him the opportunity to dip his hands in the biscuit tin." Jack replies.

"Ah... that makes more sense. Though I am getting waterlogged."

"Don't tell him, he'll start complaining, and we can do without one of his lectures," Jack groans.

I play with a lock of my hair. "He's been a lot nicer since I gave him the tree stump, he might take it better than you think."

"Arthur's opinions may have altered, but he's still the same gnome he's always been." Jack says unconvinced.

"I'd take the tea." Julian says agreeing with Jack.

"You're not the one getting drenched in it." I complain. "Being a vampire is paying off for you."

"True, but we will suffer when he complains about your lack of gratefulness."

"Fair point. But I don't see why he can't eat biscuits without making tea."

Ethan smiles. "And admit he enjoys eating human food?"

I flop down on the sofa, nestling between Julian and Ethan. "OK... I'll drink the tea, although this will be my tenth... or eleventh... it might even be the thirteenth cup today."

The conversation stops as the tinkling of cups float towards us. I nudge Ethan. "Brace yourself, you're in this with me."

"That's what you get for being alive." Ghosts think they're funny.

Biscuit crumbs litter Arthur's beard as he enters the living room.

I lean forward and accept the offered mug. "Brilliant, just what I wanted, Arthur."

The gnome beams as he thrusts a mug at Ethan.

"It's a shame other aren't as grateful."

I nod at the gnome. "I know."

Ethan coughs into his cup and I try not to laugh.

As I blow at the tea, I try working through what I've learnt from Manannán mac Lir. The cloak's location remains a mystery, however one thing I know is he's still reeling from his wife's affair. Ethan was right about Fand and Cuchulainn's presence being required. There is a lot of suppressed pain within The Heron over his wife's fling.

The crunching of tyres on the gravel drive grabs everyone's attention. I wave a hand at them, unconcerned, my mind still mulling over my latest encounter with The Heron. "It's Polly coming home."

Jack walks over to the window, walking through the glass to investigate further. "Unless Dylan drives a van and Polly has changed sex, I'd say we've got visitors." He says walking back into the living room.

Julian steps forward. "Anyone we know?"

"No, it looks like a delivery man."

"It's bit a late for dropping off parcels," I say, recalling a similar situation with Aeden.

Nathaniel is in Faerieland, and Polly's in the safe hands of Dylan. That limits the number of body parts of those I love being delivered to zero. We stand and wait for the doorbell to sound. When it does, I still jump.

"Do you want me to get it?" Arthur asks.

Ethan pushes himself off the sofa. "I'll come with you."

The van's door slams shut, and the engine rumbles as it makes its way back up the drive. Even though my curiosity is demanding I investigate, I stay where I am.

Arthur walks in shaking the box. "It's very light, I don't think there's much inside."

"Let's hope it's not fragile," I say as he drops it in the middle of the floor.

Jack looks at the nondescript brown box, hands on his hips. "There's no trace of magic on it, maybe it's not from Manannán mac Lir."

I can smell the ocean on the box. "It's from The Heron."

"Do you want me to look inside?" Jack asks.

"No, whatever is inside isn't lethal. He doesn't want to kill us." I set down my mug and walk over to the box. Ethan hovers next to me as I open it. My eyebrows raise in surprise as I remove a small length of thirty-two-millimetre diameter yellow pipe.

Julian plucks it from my fingertips inspecting it. "What is it?"

I take back the pipe. "It's polyethylene pipe. Given its colour, I'd say it's used to transport gas. Yellow for gas, blue for water, red for electric cables and green for telecommunications."

"You got all that from a bit of yellow pipe?" Arthur asks.

I smile at the gnome. For once, I'm ahead in the information steaks. "The gas infrastructure is extensive, with most of it running below ground. It's all over the world." My fingers play with the pipe as I think about Manannán mac Lir. Why the pipe? What is he trying to tell us? When the idea forms, I almost wish it hadn't.

The Heron's words ring round my head. *"I need to divert them and now is the time to act on it."*

"Bloody hell… it's the gas infrastructure, that's the distraction. It's got to be." Everyone looks at me.

"Manannán mac Lir wants a *diversion* and what better way to get it than to use the gas infrastructure."

Jack stares at the pipe. "It's a clever idea if he can pull it off."

I shrug. "I'm no expert in gas, but if you want to cause a diversion that will kill humans, gas is a good place to start."

"How?" Julian asks.

The pipe sitting in the palm of my hand looks innocent. But multiply its length and add a volatile substance to it, and it no longer looks so innocent.

"I'm thinking." Teeth munching at my lip ideas rattle round my head.

Jack looks at the pipe. "Is there a note or anything inside the pipe?"

I look inside the tube, shaking my head. "We're out of luck on the note idea."

Arthur sits on the floor by the box. "That's not helpful."

I recognise, I'm being testy over my own failure to think up a plausible strategy on how to kill people using the gas infrastructure. However, I cannot stop the sarcasm that falls from my lips.

"We're not living in some Batman movie where the bad guy leaves a riddle behind so we can save the day. This pipe is the only clue we're going to get."

"Whose Batman?"

Shocked, I question how the gnome has not heard of Batman? Perhaps because he's a gnome?

"Never mind," I say.

"How will The Heron use the infrastructure?" Ethan asks.

I hold the pipe up. "Did you know natural gas doesn't smell? They inject an odorant into it." Everyone stares at me. "I had a temping job a few years back working for a gas transporter."

Julian plucks the pipe from my hand. "Could someone put something else into the gas network other than odorant?"

"What, like a bomb!? We have gas here. What about my stump?"

"Calm down Arthur, your stump's safe. The gas pressure is too high to add a bomb into it. It would end up shooting into the sky. Think of it like a pressure cooker."

Jack paces. "Then why send us a bit of plastic pipe?"

"Who knows what goes on in that unstable mind of his," I say. "There is a reason The Heron's sent us the pipe. We just need to work it out."

"What about the odorant injection site, is there anything that can be added there to make the gas more volatile?"

I frown at Julian. "Not that I can think of…. hang on. What about oxygen?" Everyone looks at me. "Oxygen causes gas to become unstable, and it's easy to add as it's not a solid compound. Oxygen will also travel through the filters in place to capture any dirt particles from entering the network. It's a long shot. There are warning systems attached to the gas treatment unit monitoring fluctuations in pressures."

Jack stops pacing. "It sounds complicated."

I look at Jack. "True, and why go to such lengths? Not only that, but how will he get near the injection site, never mind know what to do?"

"Manannán mac Lir can control primitive minds… it doesn't take a lot of magic," The gnome says plonking his bottom on the floor.

I stare at Arthur. "I'd start clearing out your stump."

Jack scratches his head. "The guy's delivering the pipe were wearing some kind of florescent boiler suit. What you're saying makes sense."

"It sounds stupid." The gnome crosses his arms over his chest. "Manannán mac Lir is a powerful creature. All he has to do is lift his cloak."

"And what about him being insane?" I ask Arthur.

The gnome huffs at me.

"It's about control," Julian states.

Arthur has turned a strange shade of white as he contemplates the demise of his stump.

"Manannán mac Lir doesn't need minions to make the gas pipes go boom, magic can do it for him. He's toying with you. You need to go to that place you mentioned, that's where he wants you, and save my stump."

"But what if I'm wrong?"

"You need to stop thinking like a human and use magic." Arthur grumbles.

I frown. "But I don't have the magic required to locate The Heron."

The gnome jumps about the place in irritation, the bell on his hat ringing. "Not your magic, stupid!"

It takes a lot of effort not to whip the hat off the gnome's head and throw it on the fire.

"You use the staff," Arthur shouts at me.

I swear the hat is a goner.

"Alice…" Julian warns, feeling my growing anger and frustration.

"I know… I know…"

The staff is fickle, its appearance unpredictable. I haven't seen it since the episode with the gnomes earlier. It could be anywhere.

"Anyone got any ideas how to get the staff to appear?" They look at me with blank expressions. "Yep, that's what I thought. So what do we do now?"

Julian walks over to the sofa and sits down. "We wait."

"Wait," Arthur yells.

"Calm done, Arthur. It's obvious The Heron wants an audience, and the staff wants to play," Julian says unconcerned.

"I hold you responsible should anything happen to my stump."

Julian raises a brow.

"You know Arthur, a cup of camomile would go down a treat right now," Jack smiles at me.

I want to punch the ghost into silence.

Arthur springs to his feet. "I'll make it."

"I haven't drunk the last one yet and neither has Ethan."

Arthur runs out of the room. "It's cold, I'll make another one."

"Or you could just eat the sodding biscuits and stop making tea every five minutes," I grumble after him; aware he won't be able to hear me.

"Where's the nearest odorant site to here?" Ethan asks. "If The Heron wants a diversion, using the gas network to create one is a good plan. He knows we can't let him use it to kill. It will also need to be close by. We can investigate while we wait for the staff to appear."

"Hold the tea, Arthur," I yell. "There's a site at Towton. It's near here."

"It's a starting point and it'll prevent us from drowning in tea," Ethan says.

Julian stands. "Jack, go let Alston and Nathaniel know where we're going."

Arthur stands by the kitchen door. "Where are you going? I thought you were waiting for the staff to appear."

"We're off to the odorant site at Towton. Are you coming?" I call over my shoulder.

There is a lot of grumbling, but as the front door slams shut Arthur is sitting in the back of Julian's car.

Chapter Thirty

"No heroics, Alice." Julian warns as he parks the car near the gates of the odorant site and climbs out.

A padlock sits on the inside its lock clicked into place. In the distance, cocooned within the fenced-off area, a trail of torch lights flicker. Boots echo on concrete and the soft whisper of voices cut through the morning darkness. Mist crawls, rising upwards, covering the ground.

Violence threads through the air, coming up from the earth. The savagery and brutality from the Battle of Towton vibrates around us.

On the 29th of March 1461, the largest and bloodiest battle on English soil started here at Towton. When King Henry VI (the Lancastrian King) surrendered his right of succession to the English throne, passing it to Richard, Duke of York it created a backlash of violence.

With King Henry's wife, Queen Margaret, unable to accept the arrangement made by her husband and see her son deprived of his birthright, England found itself with two kings. On Palm Sunday, in the middle of a snowstorm, the armies met. Between fifty and sixty-five thousand soldiers confronted each other. Twenty-eight thousand men lost their lives in the battle. Towton became the definitive victory for the House of York.

Blood soaks the soil. Embedded so deep it stains the earth centuries later. Trapped within the grotesque and bloodiest of deaths, solders re-enact their last seconds, they cry and die in a continuous loop.

"The cloak's here," I say feeling the soft strum of energy vibrating from it.

"You sure?"

I nod at Julian.

It's magic throbs, like the land itself. The beat of hooves thump over the ground; the ghosts of the past feeding the cloak. I'm not sure why I can feel its presence, but I do. Manannán mac Lir can't conceal it from me, not at this distance.

Jack shimmers into view. "They're on their way."

"Good, we're going to need them." Julian's words resonate through our bond.

Nathaniel answers by throwing his magic into me, aware he might be too late.

"Ready?" Ethan asks.

The skin pinches at the corner of my eyes. "As I'm going to be."

I grab hold of the wire fencing, pushing myself over the six-foot metal barrier. The dress fans out around me as my bare feet hit the ground. Ethan and Julian at my side. Jack floats through, his image taking on a translucent glow.

Arthur's chubby fingers poke through the holes in the wire fencing as he moves his body up. He's like Spiderman, but without the grace. An oath comes from him as he rips his trousers on the fence. The hat on his head bobs and the tiny bell tinkles into the night. I had considered telling him to leave the hat at Roseley but thought better of it.

The gnome's breathing is erratic as he lands on the ground, disappearing into the mist at my feet.

"Here." I lift him onto my shoulders. "You can be our lookout."

His head dips, and his bell rings, accepting the task without argument. Julian shakes his head, aware it's not a lookout we need, but at least the little man won't get lost within the smog.

Arthur's fingers grip my hair as we make our way to where Manannán mac Lir stands waiting for us.

Vivid green eyes shine with malice as we approach. The Heron's cape whips around him and in his hand is the staff.

"So that's where you've got to," I mutter beneath my breath.

Above our heads is the cry of a heron. Golems stand like a wall in front of Manannán mac Lir. Made from clay, Golems were first created to protect the Jewish people. Now they stand ready to fight, kill and destroy as Manannan mac Lir, commands. Gas pipes weave before them, separating us.

A laugh rings out, setting my teeth on edge as Aeden walks forward.

"Aren't you supposed to be dead?" Anger burns, warming my skin at the fire demon's resurrection.

Ethan's hand grips my arm as Arthur's nails dig into my scalp.

The Heron inclines his head at the conceited fire demon who's too busy basking in his egotistical self to notice. "Your mistake is seeing me as a deity, not as I am — a master magician. If you knew me, you would have known my pigs give eternal life."

Manannán mac Lir stares at Aeden, sensing his narcissistic flaws. "What I give I can withdraw."

Anna's decaying body springs into my head. The demon deserves every horrible way possible to die.

Nathaniel had reassured me that Aeden would never return. Either my mind is playing evil tricks on me, or Alston isn't as clever as he thinks he is. So long as the next time I kill the demon he remains dead, I can live with the minor setback.

Without warning, Aeden rushes at me and the battle begins. Arthur jumps from my shoulders, launching himself at the fire demon. Ethan and Julian step forward, creating a barrier in front of me as the Golems charge at us.

Stubby legs lock around Aeden's neck, as the gnome rains down his fists on the Aeden's head. Hands clawing at Arthur's legs, Aeden tries to dislodge the gnome. Arthur's not about to give up and locks his legs tighter around the demon, maintaining his advantage.

Golems fly at us, one after the other. Fists and legs strike in quick succession as Ethan and Julian fight to keep them from penetrating their barrier. Earth billows around us as the Golems fall.

Behind me, footsteps sound and I turn to see two Golems heading my way. One of them pulls a gun from his pocket and opens fire.

Arthur sails past me, limbs dangling at his side. I don't have time to think about the gun. I leap into the air, grabbing hold of the gnome. Hugging him to my chest, I try to cushion the little man as we hit the ground. There's a loud bang and a bullet slices through the air. It misses us, hitting the concrete.

"You OK?" I ask Arthur as I jump to my feet.

Manannán mac Lir walks towards the line of trees away from the fighting, his diversion now in place, he's free to lift the cloak without interference. The gas infrastructure was an illusion. His plan worked. We've fallen for the silent threat. I cursed my own stupidity. Arthur was right, we've been thinking like humans, not as a manipulative and conceited master magician.

Bullets whiz through the air and Golems fall as the blast tears through their clay bodies crumbling to dust. They show no care towards who or what they hit. The chamber keeps releasing the bullets, keeping the Golems happy.

Julian and Ethan are still throwing the army of Golem's around, dodging bullets and clay fists. More replace those who have returned to their natural form.

We're lucky Manannán mac Lir hasn't had time to stabilise the Golems. The magic is easy to destroy. Had the magic been stronger we wouldn't have stood a chance against the golems and the clay would keep its new form no matter how it landed or whether bullets rammed into its clay flesh. As a diversion, they are an invincible foe.

"I'm going after him," I shout, pointing at The Heron's disappearing form.

"Alice, No." Julian screams at me.

A body lands on the ground at his feet, the crumbling clay making the ground uneven. Another Golem launches itself at Julian, and he goes down as he loses his footing. Ethan charges at them as Arthur runs over to help.

The gnome looks up. "Go."

I nod and run after The Heron.

"Alice." Julian screams.

I don't look back. If Manannán mac Lir lifts the cloak, the end is already here.

"I'll go with her," Jack calls out.

Green mist follows me as I enter the woods. Tree branches pull at my unbound hair and the sea breeze cools my skin. I come to a stop at the clearing. Manannán mac Lir stands in the middle of the grass within a fairy circle. He flexes his fingers touching the grass. At his touch, it turns into cloth, revealing his cloak.

"Don't…" I take a step, my hand outstretched, my heart going mad against my ribs.

"Don't get too close." Jack stands at my side.

The sky darkens and the earth beneath my feet moves. The thin veil between the realms begins to fall. Faerieland shimmers into view, masked behind a screen where the realms sit beside each other unconnected.

"Lifting the cloak won't make your problems go away," I say.

The Heron turns, and the staff falls to the floor. Bright light shoots out from the orb on the staff and I raise my arm, protecting my eyes against the brightness of the light. Jack's screams fade as the light increases.

When I remove my arm, I'm standing in a room made of nothing but light. Manannán mac Lir stands next to me, and Jack has gone.

"What's going on?" My voice echoes into the nothingness.

Manannán mac Lir shakes his head, his long white hair falling about his shoulders. The staff has gone, and it appears we're alone.

"Where are we?"

"We are where we shouldn't be." The fae's response adds to my confusion.

Footsteps sound, and a figure emerges. The dark shape comes into focus and a small boy stands in front of us. He looks around five years old, but his eyes are of someone a thousand times older.

"Do you want a cherry lip?" In the boy's hand sits a white crumbled bag.

I shake my head and the boys shrugs.

"Of all the things I've tasted, these are the best. It's the name *Cherry Lips*. It's an odd name for a sweet. They stick to your teeth too." He opens his mouth, pointing at the lips sticking to his teeth.

"I like to see how many I can fit into my mouth. The last count was eighty, but I think if I put some along my gums, I'll be able to fit another twenty in."

The boys tilts his head. "A hundred little red gummy sweets in the shape of lips. Think of all the words that could fall from those lips."

I remain quiet at Manannán mac Lir side.

"He knows who I am, but you've not got a clue, have you?"

"No," I reply.

The boy laughs. "That's funny."

He holds out his hand. "Let's sit down. No one comes here anymore."

Taking his hand I'm led to a set of red sofas which appear. Manannán mac Lir walks next to me.

A silver teapot appears in the boy's hand. "If I can't interest you in sweeties, perhaps who'd like a cup of tea?"

The boy smiles. "You've had enough tea, haven't you?"

He laughs at his own joke, and the teapot disappears.

"You're hilarious, and I do like spending time with you."

The boy puts his hand to the side of his mouth, concealing his lips from the fae at my side. "He doesn't like you."

"Yes, I know."

"It's not your fault. He's so bad-tempered these days." The boy removes his hand and smiles over at the fae.

"You need to learn to like her, she's funny."

The Heron stares, not reacting, and the boy turns his attention back to me. "I don't want him to lift the cloak. But he won't listen to me. It's not in his nature to listen to anyone anymore."

The boy leans forward, his voice a whisper. "I've got a secret. Would you like to hear it?"

"I'm not sure," I say.

Laughter fills the room.

"Oh, you are funny. Isn't she funny?"

Manannán Mac Lir remains silent.

"You see what I mean about conversation." I nod in agreement.

"Since sweets and tea are out, how about a biscuit?" The boy asks.

"I'm not hungry at the moment."

"You're always eating." He makes a fair point.

"I'm too worried about my friends and family, it's putting me off food."

The boy points at Manannán mac Lir. "You've put her off her food."

"She was interfering." The fae responds.

Annoyed, I turn to face Manannán mac Lir. "No, I was trying to save humans."

"Interfering."

The boy watches our exchange.

"Do you think you'd fancy a biscuit if you saw how they are getting on?" He tilts his head. "Perhaps not."

I jump to my feet. Something is wrong. I have to get back.

Manannán mac Lir grabs my hand and pulls me back on the sofa. "Sit."

The boy pouts. "You can't leave. I've got something to tell you."

Apart from the sofas, the area is empty. There's no floor, ceiling, walls or door. No escape. It seems I have no choice but to stay.

"I'm not allowed to have visitors. But he," the boy points at Manannán mac Lir, "lifted the cloak enough for you to gain entry. But that's not why you're here."

The boy looks over his shoulder, there's nothing to see but bright white light. "They're coming."

I look but can't see anything.

"Do you want to know my secret? It's very good. I'm going to tell you why I've linked you together." The boy puts his hand back over his lips and points at the fae. "He doesn't even know why."

My mouth drops open.

"Oh, I think you've just caught up." The boy looks pleased.

"You're the staff?"

"I knew you'd get it." The staff bounces on the sofa, clapping his hands.

"As you have a tendency towards names, you can call me Seberg. It means Sea-glorious."

He turns to Manannán mac Lir. "See, you were wrong."

The fae stares in front of him.

"He never talks. Why doesn't he talk to me? He talks to you." A small finger points in my direction. "I'm not angry about it, I know he needs me, but it's not very nice. Do you think it's nice?"

Before I can respond a biscuit appears in Seberg's hand. "Can we have a tea party? Not now, I've got to tell you my secret, but later." The biscuit disappears.

"Your connected, because you're already connected." The staff blinks, waiting for my reaction.

"Huh?" I look at the fae at my side, he looks as confused as me.

"He's your father." The staff announces.

"I have a dad, his name's Nathaniel."

Seberg waves his tiny hand at me. "No, not your dad, your father."

"You've lost me, aren't they the same thing?"

"Oh no, they're very different."

I look at Manannán mac Lir. "Do you know what he's on about?"

The fae shakes his head.

"Your magic. He's the father of your magic, not the Seelie King. That's why the fire demon is useless. The Seelie King is nothing but a pompous arse."

I won't argue with that. "So he's not my grandfather?"

"Yes, he is." The staff sits back. "You don't understand."

I point at the fae next to me. "But he's been asleep for… well… forever."

"Your great… great… great… great…" The staff counts in his head, fingers following an invisible line. "Well, let's say there has been a lot of great aunts. And one of them was the daughter of Manannán mac Lir. The magic has been dormant, waiting for a host so it can grow. You're the host."

"I feel invaded," I mutter under my breath.

Seberg frowns. "Here." Tiny fingers clasp mine and Manannán mac Lir's.

Magic burns along my skin. The sofa disappears, and we're suspended in the air by a multitude of lights. Pain explodes within my chest and I cry out as light spills from my body, connecting with the magic spear protruding from Manannán mac Lir. As our magic merges the pain subsides leaving me breathless.

"See, you are one and the same. Your magic connects you. I just helped reunite it." A smile lights Seberg's lips.

The light around us flickers and the boy fades.

"Don't forget about the tea party." Seberg calls before disappearing.

Chapter Thirty-One

I hold on tight to the sea God's hand as we float through the nothingness. Cries from the battle surround us as we tumble. The sound of gunfire cuts through the blackness. It's hard to say how fast we are travelling through the dimensions as we free fall.

Manannán mac Lir's arms bring me in close to his chest. I taste his fear and confusion over what the staff has told us. It echoes my own.

Our legs collapse as we hit the ground.

"Heron!" Cuchulainn's voice carries from the trees.

Manannán mac Lir stirs at my side within the fairy circle. I feel him go still as rage and hatred boils inside.

"Just so you know, this wasn't my idea," I say.

Cuchulainn bursts through the trees followed by Jack, Alston and Nathaniel.

"Look what you have done to me!" Cuchulainn shouts, golden curls flying about his shoulders as his hand beats against his bare chest.

His fur boots hit the ground, and the ghost solidifies. "I am dead."

Julian and Ethan race forward, Golems snipping at their heels, to their left Fand walks clear of the opening. She is like a beautiful, treacherous god. Black-blue hair cascades down her back like a waterfall. Her skin shimmers as she walks towards her husband. Liquid blue eyes plead with him to stop.

Cuchulainn's eyes widen as he looks at Fand. Desire sparkles within his eyes and he walks over to her. Fand's hips sway, taunting him as she walks past. The Heron's wife is a player. It's a shame he never noticed. It would have saved him a lot of pain.

Beautiful fae have a tendency to only be beautiful on the outside. Inside, they are warped and sadistic.

"Fand." Cuchulainn whispers her name.

My fingers seek Manannán mac Lir's. Through his anger are desire and love. Fand is a hypnotic creature.

"You have slept a long time, my husband." Fand's voice is soft.

My fingernails dig into The Heron's hand, grounding him, getting him to stay focused.

"Why does he remember? The potion I gave Cuchulainn and his wife Emmer should have wiped away their memory."

Angry at Fand's dismissal of him, Cuchulainn snatches at her arm, his fingers float through her flesh.

"Death has a way of bringing back memories. Your potion no longer has any hold over me."

The warrior paces behind Fand. "While you slumbered, I became old. My skin wrinkled and decayed, and my hair lost its lustre. No one wanted to know an old warrior who had long past his right to live."

Seberg appears between our entwined hands.

Manannán mac Lir squares back his shoulders. "You tasted what was not yours to sample and have paid the price.

Your anger does not sit with me, it is yours to own. Làeg, your charioteer has been waiting for you. Leave this world and learn from what you have done."

Light shoots out from the staff and the turning of wheels sound. Cuchulainn's head drops. "I don't want to leave."

Fand turns to look at her ex-lover. "There is nothing left for you here."

A dapple-grey horse appears, pulling a golden chariot. It stops by Cuchulainn, snorting, and hooves beating at the ground.

Làeg pulls hard on the reins. "It is time for us to ride the clouds, my lord."

Cuchulainn steps into the chariot, coming to stand next to the charioteer, accepting his fate.

"One day, Manannán mac Lir, we shall meet again, I hope when that day comes you will not be ready." Raising his sword, Cuchulainn lets out a battle cry.

The horse responds and Làeg raises the whip. The chariot gains speed as it hits the trees and disappears. Cuchulainn's cries join the soldiers who died fighting for their king's and country.

Manannán mac Lir turns to Fand. She winces. "I find I no longer like you."

"My husband…"

"Do not call me that. Go and never seek me out. You are no longer welcome to share my home."

Fand looks confused. She has relied on her beauty for so long she thinks she can wiggle her hips and bat her eyes lashes and creep her way back into Manannán mac Lir graces.

"But… but… where will I go?"

My fingernails sink further into The Heron's flesh as he wavers. There is a torrent of emotions thumping through his body and mind as his heart breaks a little more.

"That is up to you." His voice cracks.

Manannán mac Lir's magic is stabilising, and so is his mind. Our hands remain locked together as he draws on my strength of will to send away the beautiful creature he loves and hates.

We both understand pain, loss and betrayal, and the treachery that people around us commit. And we both hate Fand. Even though I have no reason to, I do.

Alston takes Fand's hand. "I will see she gets back to Faerieland."

"No, she belongs to the Unseelie." The Heron stops Alston.

Fand gasps. "You don't have the power to cast me out of the Seelie Court."

"The Queen of Air and Darkness does."

She looks at the man at my side. "But… how?"

"The black diamond." Seeing Fand's confusion Manannán mac Lir explains. "I was the one that placed the black diamond in the mine, which the dwarves found and presented to the queen, while her sister Titania went swimming. Each of the ten-facets within the black diamond opened the door, allowing her true self to emerge. The Queen of Air and Darkness lost her physical form when she embraced her true destiny. In accepting my gift, the queen owes me a great favour."

Fand falls to her knees in a cry of pain. Her beautiful features turning hideous, she spreads her hands before her, staring at the blackened skin.

"The queen has heard my request and has accepted it. Your own transformation has begun."

Hands shaking, Fand screams. Her luscious body convulses, and her skin darkens as her hair turns white. From the sky an obsidian hand stretches, its fingers wrapping round the withering creature and sucking her into the night.

Fand's screams die as she disappears. The wind increases, whipping at our clothes. One by one the Golems crumble, and the mist recedes.

"I still think humans should die, but I know you love your friend. For now, I shall leave the cloak. But you owe me a favour."

Our fingers part and his arms spread out. The Heron soars into the sky, its cry echoing upon the coming dawn.

Seberg disappears, and I sigh, walking over to Ethan and Julian. "Let's go home."

Arthur stands at the line of trees. "I'll put the kettle on."

Ethan laughs as I groan.

Gunfire sounds and Ethan hits the ground, blood pouring from his chest.

"Ethan!" I fall to my knees, clutching him to me.

Blood covers my hand, leaking through my fingers.

"Watch out." Arthur shouts.

Aeden laughs, pointing the gun at me. "Say goodnight."

His finger squeezes the trigger as Julian and Nathaniel lunge at him. Alston stands frozen in place as he watches his son. The gun goes off and blood drips from Nathaniel's shoulder.

"Do something." I scream at the king, but he stands unmoving.

The Heron swoops down and Aeden falls, his eyes locked open in a lifeless stare, as his body turns to ash.

Julian and Nathaniel move back, running over to where I sit cradling Ethan. Jack stands at my side as Arthur sits next to me.

"Help him. Make him better." Tears roll down my cheeks as I look at Julian and Nathaniel.

"Alice, we can't he's a werewolf."

"What do you mean you can't. You've got to help him." I'm sobbing and I don't care, I just want Ethan better.

Jack bends down so our faces are level. "Alice, their blood can't heal him."

My fingers touch Ethan's face. "He can't die. I won't let him."

Jack raises his hand. Magic pulses. Ethan screams and the bullet flies out from his chest.

Arthur catches it. "It's not silver."

Ethan's fingers reach for mine as he changes form. The wolf lies next to me, his amber eyes full of pain.

"The change will help him heal," Julian says as he bends and cradles the wolf in his arms.

I walk with them, my fingers resting in the wolf's fur. Nathaniel kicks the gates open and I crawl into the boot of Julian's SUV, laying down next to the wolf, draping an arm over his body.

"You're going to be alright." I kiss the side of the wolf's face.

"Alice..." Whatever Nathaniel is about to say dies as Julian shakes his head at him.

"He won't hurt me," I say, laying my head back down.

Arthur jumps in the front of the SUV. "I'm not sitting in the back, he'll eat me."

HUNTED

Julian climbs in and starts the engine.

"Jack, go let Connor know," Nathaniel says as he closes the rear door.

Jack nods and disappears.

"Who's Connor?" I ask.

Nathaniel turns in his seat. "Connor is Ethan's Beta. As an Alpha, Ethan is the major link in the pack. He's vulnerable, and the pack knows it. If a wolf was to challenge their Alpha, now would be the perfect moment. We need Conor to minimise the chaos."

Dust flies up as the SUV shoots forward. Towton isn't far from Roseley and with the speed, Julian is driving it takes less than twenty minutes. As the car sails down the gravel drive, several cars are already waiting for us.

Nathaniel curses under his breath at the large number of wolves lining the drive.

Ethan's wolf stirs as Julian draws the SUV to a stop. Shaking out his coat the wolf pushes himself to his feet in readiness for the boot to open. Lips rolling back, the wolf leaps from the car. Though I can sense his pain, now is not the time to show weakness. I want Ethan inside where I can care and keep him safe, but even that will have to wait.

The wolf's large paws send the tiny stones flying as he walks to the wolves gathered outside Roseley. Their eyes lower as he approaches. Lifting his head, the wolf howls. Silence falls, and the wolf walks away. A man step's forward.

I stop breathing as he begins to transform into his wolf. The man's eyes lock onto Ethan's challenging him. Bones click, skin stretches, and grey fur covers the man. Amber eyes watch as the grey wolf pants.

On hind legs, the grey wolf leaps at Ethan. Julian's fingers wrap around my arm, preventing me from going to Ethan's aid.

Nathaniel comes to stand next to me. "Don't interfere."

Fur flies, and blood ferments the air as the wound in Ethan's chest reopens. The grey wolf lunges forward, catching Ethan's injured side. Off balance, he goes down and I cover my mouth to stop from screaming. A howl of victory comes from the grey wolf.

His eyes lock onto me. I swear he's smiling. The grey wolf leaps and Ethan jumps, ramming his body into the wolf. The animal goes down and Ethan leaps on top of him, his teeth sinking into his neck and tearing at his flesh. The wolf beneath Ethan whimpers.

With a swift motion, Ethan snaps its neck. No one moves. Ethan looks at his pack, a low growl of warning falling from his lips. I walk over, my fingers brushing his fur, and together we walk into Roseley.

"Someone get that body removed."

"That's Connor," Jack says materialising at my side.

For the first time, the house is silent. Our footsteps echo against the floor. When we get to Ethan's room, the wolf collapses and I wash down his fur, cleaning his wound.

Chest rising and falling in rapid succession, the wolf rests. Tears fill my eyes, dropping onto his fur. The wolf's licks my arm.

"Sleep," I urge him as I slide the duvet off the bed, tucking it around him.

"It's going to be OK." I don't know if I say this for my benefit or his.

Maybe I say it for both of us.

Chapter Thirty-Two

"Wow, this looks fantastic." Polly says as she walks into the kitchen.

It's a week since Aeden shot Ethan and the grey wolf challenged him. It feels like an eternity. Ethan has healed and though neither of us has been able to verbalise how we feel about each other, I'm too happy Ethan's alive to care. For now, anyway.

A pink flowery cloth covers the table and I've dug out Aunt Dot's best china. Arthur is on tea making duty again and stands on his stool by the Aga, waiting for the kettle to boil.

"Good timing, you can help me get the food out," I tell Polly.

"Why do I feel like I've walked into the Mad Hatter's tea party?" Polly says grabbing hold of the plate of sandwiches I thrust at her.

The sun streams through the patio doors, catching hold of the bright bunting I've hung around it.

I smile. "It's strange you should say that."

Ethan walks in, his nose twitching. "Something smells good."

His hair is damp from this morning's run. While I'd left to wash and change the wolf had gone in search of a snack.

"No eating anything until everyone has arrived," I warn him.

Arthur grabs the singing kettle and starts filling the teapot. "I don't know why you're waiting for the vampires they don't eat."

"He has a point," Polly says, eyeing up the food.

"You're just saying that because you're hungry, Pol."

Polly raises the cake she's holding to her nose. "It's still a valid point."

I take the cake, placing it on the table.

The front door clicks open and Julian and Nathaniel walk into the kitchen.

"Now can we eat?" Polly asks.

"Hang on one more thing."

"OK, Seberg, its ready when you are." I call.

A bright light flashes and the staff appears at the table on the far chair.

"Take your places, we're going to have a tea party," I tell them.

The orb on the staff flashes and the tinkling of laugher fills the room.

Note from the Author

Thank you for reading Hunted.

Each story is born from an idea and requires constant nourishment from the author. Writing is a remarkable gift. To tell a tale and take a reader to new places and capture their imagination — in the same way the story had captured the author. It brings author and reader together.

Please take the time to leave a book review. It's the most amazing gift you can give me. It keeps me dreaming and creating new stories for you.

About Kathleen Harryman

Kathleen Harryman is a story-teller and poet living in the historically rich city of York, North Yorkshire, England, with her husband, children and dog.

Kathleen was first published in 2015, a romantic suspenseful thriller entitled *The Other Side of the Looking Glass.* Since then, Kathleen has developed a unique writing style which readers have enjoyed, and she became a multi-genre author of suspense, psychological thrillers, poetry and historical romance.

FOR MORE INFORMATION ABOUT KATHLEEN HARRYMAN VISIT:

Website:
www.kathleenharryman.com

Twitter:
https://twitter.com/KathleenHarrym1

Amazon:
http://author.to/KH-AUTHOR-PAGE

Goodreads:
www.goodreads.com/httpstcoyo1g8QEBAq

Facebook:
https://www.facebook.com/WriterK

All-Author:
https://allauthor.com/author/kathleenharryman

BookBub:
https://www.bookbub.com/profile/kathleen-harryman

The Independent Author Network:
https://www.independentauthornetwork.com/kathleen-harryman.html

Printed in Great Britain
by Amazon